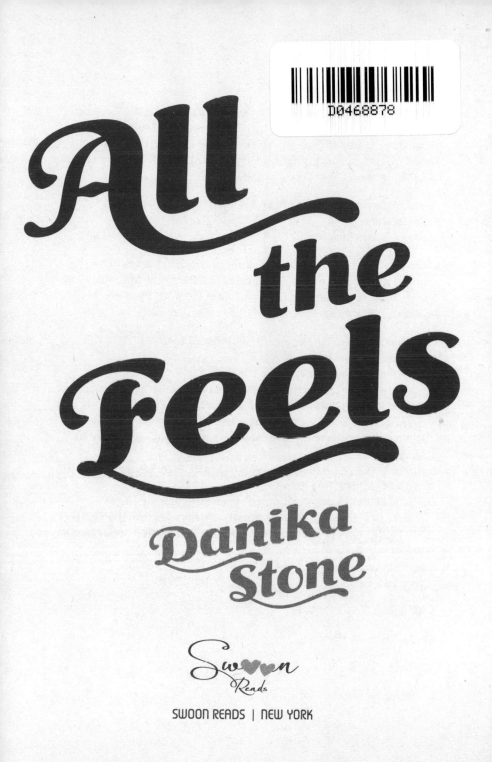

All the Feels

Danika Stone

Swoon Reads

SWOON READS | NEW YORK

A SWOON READS BOOK

An Imprint of Feiwel and Friends

Library of Congress Cataloging-in-Publication Data
Names: Stone, Danika.
Title: All the feels / Danika Stone.
Description: First edition. | New York : Swoon Reads, 2016. | Summary: "When uber-fan Liv's favorite sci fi movie character is killed off, she and her best friend Xander, an aspiring actor and Steampunk enthusiast, launch a campaign to bring him back from the dead"—Provided by publisher.
Identifiers: LCCN 2015026919 | ISBN 9781250084095 (paperback) | ISBN 9781250084101 (ebook)
Subjects: | CYAC: Love—Fiction. | Friendship—Fiction. | Fans (Persons)—Fiction. | Motion pictures—Fiction. | BISAC: JUVENILE FICTION / Love & Romance. | JUVENILE FICTION / Social Issues / Friendship.
Classification: LCC PZ7.1.S754 Al 2016 | DDC [Fic]—dc23
LC record available at http://lccn.loc.gov/2015026919

Book design by Liz Dresner

First Edition—2016

10 9 8 7 6 5 4 3 2 1

swoonreads.com

For @CoulsonLives,
who showed me how to raise the dead

If the dream is a translation of waking life,
waking life is also a translation of the dream.

—RENÉ MAGRITTE

Part One

BOULDER, COLORADO

1

"MY PRECIOUS!"
(*THE LORD OF THE RINGS*)

The star freighter's hangar lay destroyed in the aftermath of the massacre. Overhead fluorescents flickered on and off, yellow safety lights humming in darkened corners. Blood marred the corrugated panels of the launch floor, and fingerprints marked the last moments of the flight crew. The dead were piled in heaps . . . but the room was far from empty.

The hangar echoed with macabre slurping. Alien creatures hunched spiderlike as they fed on the bodies of the dead and dying. Across the deck, interstellar transports were tumbled like children's toys, some untouched, others burning. Electricity buzzed and snapped from exposed wires. Only one escape pod remained intact. Its door hung agape, a forgotten oxygen pack and the remains of what could have been a young man alongside it.

"Dragnat all anyway," a voice grumbled.

From the far corner of the room, a rugged man with sweat-slicked blond hair limped into view, a little girl wearing an oversize freighter captain's jacket a step behind him. Both carried blasters—the jumped-up weapon of the Rebellion—though the child's dragged along the floor, too heavy for her thin arms. The man's broad shoulders were hunched in anger, his expression determined despite the bloody slice across one cheekbone and the bullet wound spreading blood below his right knee. He glanced both ways.

Faint beeping filled the air, the time remaining flashing on panels around the room.

1:32 . . . 1:31 . . . 1:30 . . . 1:29 . . .

The child stared up at him with wide eyes. "Spartan?"

He gazed longingly at the escape pod. Perhaps forty feet separated the craft from the mismatched pair, but there were at least twice that many feeders blocking their path. "The bugs are still at it. Gonna be a hell of a fight to get through." The aliens were engrossed in their gorging, but any movement would spark another attack. He knew this from experience.

A small hand tugged at his jacket. "Can we go back and hide?"

He crouched beside the girl, brushing a tangled curl behind her ear. Pain tightened his features, but he forced it away with a confident smile. "Countdown's already on. We've gotta go, darlin'."

The girl nodded. "Is there another way out?" she asked, her eyes drifting to the grisly tableau beyond his shoulder.

"Not this time."

The little girl lifted her blaster. The oversize weapon wobbled in her hands. "You run," she said, nodding to the teeming deck. "I'll cover you."

The man let out a choking laugh and stood. He ruffled her

hair. "Next time. All right?" He reached for her gun. "I'll take both blasters. You run to the pod."

The girl let him take her weapon but didn't move. "But if you—"

Spartan cleared his throat. "Get in the pod and blast out of here the second the door's latched. I'll follow you in the next pod." He winked. "Easy as pie."

The child twisted around, searching for the second escape shuttle she couldn't see. Spartan touched her chin, forcing her to look up at him. "When you're free of the ship, punch in the codes for Terra and—"

An ear-shattering alarm blared through every speaker in the freighter, and the child threw her arms around Spartan's legs. *"Warning,"* a woman's electronic voice announced. *"Self-destruct protocol in thirty seconds. All personnel in escape pods launch immediately. Twenty-nine... Twenty-eight... Twenty-seven..."*

The alarm unsettled the aliens from their meal. The bugs rose on spindly legs, exoskeletons clattering as they scuttled nervously away from the corpses. The clicking of mandibles reached the man and child, still poised in the doorway. It was a warning, the last one they'd get.

"You ready, darlin'?" Spartan asked. His attention was on the bugs, moving in. A blaster would slow them—not stop them—and he knew it.

"Fifteen... Fourteen... Thirteen..."

The nearest bug crouched, its compound legs compressing as it prepared to leap.

"G'bye, Spartan," the girl whispered. "I'll wait for—"

The lights abruptly switched to red, flashing alongside a deafening beacon. *"Ten..."* Another flash. *"Nine..."* Flash.

5

The bug hissed.

"*Run!*" Spartan bellowed.

The girl sprinted across the metal deck, her shoes sliding on patches of blood. The roar of weaponry echoed off panels and girders. The nearest bug flew backward, shot midjump. The girl dashed past. Drawn by the sounds of the attack, the other aliens charged. Light flared from the barrels of both blasters. The closest bugs fell, their crustacean exo-skins torn open, but for every one that stopped moving, two more replaced it. The feeders clambered over the dead and the bodies of one another, focused entirely on the single remaining human who dared attack them.

"*Seven . . . Six . . .*"

Alone and unseen, the child climbed into the pod, slamming her small fist against the door release, and buckling herself into the chair. The only time she looked up was when the sound of the blasters stopped.

"*Five . . . Four . . .*"

Tears on her cheeks, she hit the release button and was launched backward from the grip of the dying ship.

"*Three . . . Two . . .*"

For a moment, everything hung, unchanged, against the black sheet of night. The ship rippled. With a shudder, fire spewed across the hull in a chain reaction. In a flash, a recoil implosion drew the ship's metal sheathing inward like crumpled tissue. After that, there was only silence.

A solitary escape pod, containing the last remaining member of the once-proud Star Freighter Elysium, crossed the darkness of space, en route to Terra.

The aisle lighting came on with a faint buzz, and the spray of stars on-screen faded from reality into two dimensions. A young woman in the front row watched, heart in throat, as the credits rolled. Music swelled in a trumpet blare as the *Starveil* theme surged. Tears filled her eyes. The first and largest name hovered on-screen for an interminable moment: *Tom Grander in his final role as Matt Spartan.*

"No!" she cried.

The movie theater was oddly quiet. A few people stumbled drunkenly down the aisles, their faces racked with horror. A woman at the back blew her nose with a honk, and someone else cleared his throat. The final credits rolled to a stop, music fading, and those remaining stared at the screen, hopeful.

There was no postcredit clip as there'd been with the previous four films.

The main lights rose, revealing a luminous young woman, with tears streaming down her face, and her companion, a dark-haired man, like a photograph from another century. He had one ankle crossing his knee, a pair of docskin gloves clutched in one hand, and a pocket watch dangling from his lapel.

The brightness had released the audience, and the exodus from the theater began in earnest. A middle-aged woman did an awkward two-step as she exited in front of the pair. Subdued chatter followed the dwindling crowd, whispers rather than hoots.

"Liv, are you okay?" the young man asked.

Liv shook her head, her long hair falling forward to hide her face. "No," she croaked. Xander would never understand what this felt like: watching your favorite character die. He wasn't a *Starveil* fan like she was.

The strangely dressed young man glared at the faded

7

screen, eyes hooded in subtle dismay. "That ending was . . . not quite what I'd expected."

"He's not dead," Liv said. "He can't be."

Xander ran his hands down his velvet lapels, signet ring twinkling. "But if the girl got in the last pod," he mused, "and the countdown was on four, then by the time—"

Liv spun on him. "He's not dead!" she shouted. "They'd never kill Spartan!"

He opened his mouth, then closed it again. After a moment, he lifted his pocket watch and peered down at the crystal surface. It was nearly 3:00 a.m., the midnight showing of the newest *Starveil* movie finished. Across the continental United States, countless other fans were emerging shell-shocked from theaters. Liv knew they should go, but she was rooted to her seat. If she left with Xander, then it was over. It was real.

Spartan can't be dead!

Xander dropped the watch back into his pocket. He sat up, pulling on his gloves.

"We should go," he said gently.

"I can't. Not yet."

A vacuum started. Xander stood, flipping the long tails of his jacket behind him and stretching. "Liv," he sighed. "I get that you're upset. But they're starting to clean the—"

"No!"

A long, uneasy silence followed her outburst. The final patrons filed out the doors. Besides the cleaning crew, Xander and Liv were the only ones left. She knew he was waiting for her, but her long fall of brown hair blocked him from view. She felt the first rush of panicked sobbing about to start, and she forced it down.

Not dead, her mind screamed. *Spartan can't be dead!*

His hand brushed her shoulder. "You wait here," Xander said. "I'll go get the car."

She nodded. Xander squeezed her shoulder before he sprinted up the aisle.

No! No! NO! This can't be happening.

Liv's hands began to shake, the tremors spreading to her arms and legs. *I don't believe it! MRM would NEVER kill off the main character. This is WRONG!* She could feel the words bubbling in her throat, rage tipping the balance of her pain. Xander reached the door and glanced back one last time. *This isn't real! I can't handle this! THIS ABSOLUTELY CANNOT BE HAPPENING!*

He stepped through.

Liv waited until the theater door closed before she surged to her feet. The nearby attendant—a pimply teen sweeping popcorn—looked up with cow-eyed interest.

"This is wrong!" Liv shouted at the screen. "You can't do this to people! Spartan deserved a better ending! It's not FAIR!"

The boy's sweeping stopped.

"Spartan wasn't supposed to die! He had a mission—I believed in that! . . . I believed in HIM!" Tears choked her words. "Spartan always makes it through, no matter WHAT! He's the hero of the story! He's the reason the resistance exists! He's . . . He's . . ."

"Miss?" the boy asked. "Are you okay?"

She turned on him, hands rising. "No! I'm not okay!" she screamed. "I'm ANYTHING but okay!" Liv took a sobbing breath. "Spartan's DEAD, don't you see? H-how is that supposed to be okay?!"

The attendant stared at her. "Miss, I—"

"WHAT?!"

The boy's eyes darted to the other attendant, staring open-mouthed at Liv's display. "Miss, I think you should probably leave the theater."

Liv took a few defiant steps forward. "Fine!" She kicked the empty popcorn bag out of her way and stomped up the aisle. The second attendant swung the door for her and jumped out of her way as she passed.

"Thanks!" the attendant called. "Come again!"

～

@LivOutLoud: Spartan can't be dead. I don't believe it. I need brain bleach. Something to UNSEE the last ten minutes of that film. *ugly crying*

@StarVeilBrian1981: @LivOutLoud You got into an early showing too?

@LivOutLoud: @StarVeilBrian1981 Yes-but I wish I hadn't! DON'T GO BRIAN.

@StarVeilBrian1981: @LivOutLoud Too late. Furious with MRM! How could he do this to us?

@LivOutLoud: @StarVeilBrian1981 How? He hates the fans. No question about it.

@StarVeilBrian1981: @LivOutLoud So done with this franchise. We deserved a better ending.

@LivOutLoud: @StarVeilBrian1981 Agreed. I couldn't leave the theater. My heart is broken. :(#RIPSpartan

@JoesWoes: @LivOutLoud @StarVeilBrian1981 Liv? Brian? Just logged on. How was Starveil 5? Tell me ALL the smutty details! MUST KNOW! :D #Spartan

@StarVeilBrian1981: @JoesWoes OMG OMG OMG DON'T SEE THE MOVIE, JOE!!!!!!!! STICK WITH FIC!!!!!!!!!!!! You can't unsee this. :(#Spartan #AllTheFeels

@JoesWoes: @StarVeilBrian1981 @LivOutLoud What happened?!?!? Tell me!

@LivOutLoud: @JoesWoes Search the #Spartan tag. Or don't . . . Ugh.

@JoesWoes: @LivOutLoud Searching now.

@JoesWoes: @LivOutLoud This just-NO. It's a hoax. Some troll having fun!

@LivOutLoud: @JoesWoes This is not a hoax, Joe. It's real. I SAW THE MOVIE. MRM deserves a slow, painful death.

@JoesWoes: @StarVeilBrian1981 @LivOutLoud AAAAAAAHHHHHHHHHHHHHHHH!!!!! WHAT?!?!?!?!?!?!?!?!

@LivOutLoud: @JoesWoes *gentle hugs* Sorry, bb.

@JoesWoes: @StarVeilBrian1981 @LivOutLoud I can't believe that's real. TELL ME THAT'S METAPHORIC DEATH, NOT LITERAL.

@LivOutLoud: @JoesWoes The credits said "Tom Grander in his FINAL role as Matt Spartan." This is NOT a metaphor. It's real. Spartan's dead.

@JoesWoes: @LivOutLoud No! It can't be! *clings* This is AWFUL!

@StarVeilBrian1981: @JoesWoes @LivOutLoud

@LivOutLoud: @StarVeilBrian1981 If I wasn't crying, Brian, I'd laugh. Your Photoshop skills are amazing. That's EXACTLY how it is!

@LivOutLoud: @JoesWoes *hugs* Sorry, hon. But you should see it prepared. (Bring tissues.) Tom Grander is phenomenal, but . . . Ouch!

@JoesWoes: @LivOutLoud MRM killed our unicorn! I will NEVER get over this.

@StarVeilBrian1981: @JoesWoes @LivOutLoud Look at this one. RT: @Veilmeister

@JoesWoes: @StarVeilBrian1981 @Veilmeister It's good, but it doesn't make me feel any better. *sobs*

@LivOutLoud: @JoesWoes @StarVeilBrian1981 Me neither. :(((((I'm heading off to read some fic and cry.

@JoesWoes: @LivOutLoud AU fic, I hope. :(

@LivOutLoud: @JoesWoes AU forever. :(*sighs* This can't be real.

Liv stared at the empty kitchen table, considering her options. She and her mother had a large stash of plastic cutlery, but tonight she reached for the metal ones. Two glass tumblers followed the forks onto the table. Salt and pepper shakers finished the look. The effect was immediate: real, not pretend. On a whim, Liv considered using cloth napkins rather than paper towels, but she had no idea where to look. Liv couldn't remember the last time they'd eaten anything but takeout. Dad had been the one who cooked.

She moved from one spot to the other, arranging the settings while she replayed the last ten minutes of *Starveil Five*. She sat in the same position at the dinner table she'd sat at all her life. Her mother, Katherine, always took the place next to Liv, facing the empty spot that no one ever took, not even her mother's boyfriend, Gary, when he stayed for dinner. The chair and untouched place mat were like the artificial flowers in Grandma Fortin's house: sterile, scentless. But year after year, the dusty arrangement stayed.

Liv stepped past the empty chair, her memory full of the other nights in her childhood when her dad had sat there. *It was a Thursday*, Liv thought. *I was setting the table—same as now—and he was already gone.*

She pressed her lids closed, breathing slowly until the tightness in her chest faded.

I didn't know he was dead.

Hands quaking, Liv pulled down two plates and closed the cupboard doors. Her mother would be home with dinner soon. She'd be bringing something precooked and easy to serve. Takeout wasn't a question in the Walden household. It was a fact. Another thing that had changed that long-ago Thursday.

If she'd been feeling ambitious, Liv might have picked up groceries and persuaded Xander to teach her another of his "soon to be famous" recipes. With three little brothers and a mom who worked nights, he had taught himself how to cook. As Xander always said, "it was that or starve," but Liv had been proctoring in the audio lab all afternoon—adjusting audio levels for amateur musical performances—and by the time she made it back, she was wiped. Besides, Liv reasoned, whenever Xander cooked, he talked. . . . And tonight she wasn't in the mood to hear about his latest cosplay ideas, or—worse yet—his last date with Arden, his bubbly girlfriend. The duo made a striking couple. (Liv could see that as much as anyone.) Arden was light and laughter to Xander's brooding looks, but Liv wasn't in the mood to hear about their evident happiness.

She was grieving.

Liv flopped onto the couch and pulled out her phone to scroll through the latest postings on the various Spartan web-sites. Almost a week after the Christmas Eve release, there were spoilers everywhere. The entire *Starveil* fandom was in an uproar over Spartan's death. Liv's throat grew thick and painful, and she searched until she found a fix-it AU, posted just today. She was halfway through reading it when she heard the garage door open. Katherine swirled through the doorway, coat flapping like the sails of a ship.

"Dinner's on!" she called, dropping a moisture-soaked bag onto the floor of the entrance.

Liv popped her head around the corner, snatching up the bag before it could soak through. "Smells good."

"Hope it tastes as good," Katherine said. "Missed lunch because of the presentation. I'm starving."

Liv peeked inside the paper bag as she headed to the kitchen. She groaned.

"Mom, you know I hate fried chicken."

Her mother gave a long-suffering sigh. "I had a coupon, Liv. Two can dine for—"

"I know, I know. It's just greasy and gross and—"

Katherine set her laptop bag on the floor next to the table. "I thought you said it smelled good."

"I did."

"Then what's the problem?"

Liv slumped in her chair. "It's the *thought* of it I don't like, Mom, not the smell."

"Then pretend it's something else."

Liv lifted the corner of the first lid. "Not working."

"Oh, Liv. Just work with me. All right?"

Liv put spoons into the paper tubs and took an extra helping of coleslaw. (You could survive on coleslaw, couldn't you?) Her mother nudged the chicken toward her, and Liv took the smallest piece in the tub.

"How was your day?" her mother asked.

Liv made a production out of picking off the chicken skin and dabbing the meat with a paper towel. The action gave her time to collect her thoughts as she forced herself to return to the hours she'd spent volunteering in the audio lab. She was surprised to realize she could barely remember it. With Spartan's death still hanging over her life, nothing else felt real.

"All right, I guess," Liv said, adding a scoop of potato salad. "Made it through."

Her mother patted her shoulder absently. "That doesn't sound good, Liv."

"Just distracted by things."

"Fandom things?"

"Er, yes." Liv shrugged. "You know how it is."

Her mother pursed her lips and pointed at Liv with a spoon. "You're not still going on about the ending of that *Starveil* movie, are you? Goodness, Liv, you don't have time to get wrapped up in the fandom nonsense."

It was an argument they'd had many times during senior year, when her mother was focused on Liv's grades, but Liv was so busy vidding at night she could barely stay awake during the day. It had come to a head almost one year ago when Liv's crash-and-burn SAT score had destroyed any chance at a full scholarship. Widow's pension and student loans it was.

When Liv didn't reply, her mother leaned forward, frowning. "Liv, I don't like the sound of this."

"But I didn't say anything!"

"You didn't have to," her mother said. "You've been moody all week. You're hardly eating." She pushed another piece of chicken onto Liv's plate. "It's like you're in mourning."

"I am!" Liv snapped. "Spartan died, Mom. It was a terrible ending."

"It's *just* a movie, Liv. And I don't want fandom to affect your grades."

"But we're on winter break. Classes haven't even started."

"You know what happened last year when you got involved. . . ."

Liv knew better than to argue. Her mother equated fandom

with Liv's dismal high school performance. Liv had thought that the university—and a tech program—would change her mother's mind about vidding.

It hadn't.

"Can you pass the fries?" Liv asked. Katherine nudged the container toward her daughter, and Liv rushed to fill the silence before the argument could restart. "So how was work?"

Katherine put down her fork. "Good enough, I guess."

Liv opened her mouth to keep the diversion going, but Katherine was faster. "Liv, about this whole Spartan thing . . . I just think you're old enough to let it go."

"Meaning what?"

Her mother's expression grew hard. "Meaning it's time to move on."

"But I don't—"

"You need to grow up, Liv. Fandom messed up your college plans already. I don't want it to—"

"I'm in college! I'm doing fine!"

"You're doing fine *now*, but what'll happen if you go off track again?"

Liv surged to her feet, chair squealing. "Then I guess that'll be my life I screw up. Not yours!"

In seconds, Liv had her coat on and was out the door, running down the street to the bus stop. She blinked in the icy air, eyes burning.

If anyone could make her feel better, it'd be Xander.

2

"I AM A LEAF ON THE WIND."
(*SERENITY*)

ander was cashing out his till when Liv arrived at Cup O' Joe.

"Give me five minutes," he said with a wave. "Just got to switch over for Marcy."

"No problem. I'll wait."

She scanned the interior, searching for spots.

Situated in downtown's Pearl Street outdoor mall, the coffeehouse was a hippie enclave left over from the sixties. Mismatched chairs and tables congregated in groups. Dark wood, textured pillows, and buttery leather chairs gave the interior an intimate feel. According to Xander, the owner had declined at least five buyout attempts by chain coffee shops, but Liv had never been inside until she and Xander became friends in early September. In the months since, Liv had become a fixture. Cup O' Joe was her personal hangout when being at home was too cloying (or too lonely).

Tonight, the café was packed. Shoppers in search of post-holiday deals filled the seats near the windows; boots and hats cluttered the coatrack. Liv's mouth turned down in irritation as Bing Crosby's voice echoed through tinny speakers:

"I'm dreaming of a white Christmas
Just like the ones I used to know . . ."

"Christmas was ruined," Liv grumbled as she spotted a pair of empty chairs. "And MRM is to blame."

She tossed her bag onto the floor and sat in the faded recliner. Feeling somewhat conspicuous, Liv pulled out her phone.

She scanned the *Starveil* posts, her mood darkening. Spartan had been a part of her life since elementary school. Losing him felt like having a piece of herself torn away. No amount of fix-it fics or alternate universes could change the fact that her one true character had died. A woman paused next to Liv's knee, disrupting her thoughts.

"Is this seat taken?"

"Yeah, it is." Liv lifted her bag and set it on the seat. "My friend's just getting our coffee now."

The woman wandered away and Liv peered to the counter, where Xander was counting receipts. She groaned. The line for coffee now stretched all the way to the door. Her gaze returned to the phone's glowing screen. In the last minutes, a new discussion had appeared on the *Starveil* board, and Liv read through it.

Post 239, @StarVeilBrian1981:

I remember how I felt when I watched Serenity, and got to THAT scene. I never thought I'd feel that sort of pain again, but losing Spartan destroyed me. I tried to go to work today, but I could barely get out of bed. Spartan's dead. He's gone. Does that even feel REAL to anyone???

I finally saw Starveil Five today. Went alone to a matinee so no one would see me if I had a breakdown. A good choice. :(Even being spoiled, the ending ripped my heart out. How could MRM set his fans up like that? All the story needed was for Spartan to have a way out. Even ONE of the damaged shuttles near enough that Spartan and the kid could make it inside. I didn't even care that Elysium got destroyed. But there was no need-NO NEED-to pull a Joss Whedon.

If I could have five minutes with MRM face-to-face, I'd . . . I'd . . . Well, it's probably better I don't have five minutes with him. I'm so angry, I can barely breathe. Fandom is the only thing holding me together. D: This is the worst day ever.

Eyes swimming with tears, Liv glanced up from her screen to discover Xander had finished cashing out. He grinned at her and mouthed *"almost done."* He traded his black apron for his signature brocade waistcoat and shook it out, a subtle transition occurring as he slid it up his arms, buttoning one-handed: The cappuccino-wielding waiter had been replaced by a Regency rakehell.

He lifted two steaming cups from the counter, weaving his way through the café to her side. Their eyes met, and Xander's smile evaporated.

"Hey, whoa! Are you okay, Liv?"

"No. Not really."

He set the cup next to her elbow, moved the purse off the chair, and sat. "What happened?"

His concern had tears prickling her eyes. She swallowed hard, forcing her voice to steady. "You saw the ending."

Xander stared at her, an expression of confusion hovering over his features. "The ending of . . . ?"

"Of *Starveil Five*."

His shoulders relaxed, and he slumped back into his chair. "Ah, yes . . . 'the ending.'" He put air quotes around it. "Dear Captain Spartan's untimely demise." He shook his head. "Seemed a little melodramatic, but I suppose it *is* space opera, after all."

Liv tried to answer, but no words came out. Her throat ached. She had no intention of bursting into tears at Cup O' Joe, but if she kept thinking about Spartan, it was definitely a possibility.

Xander's voice dropped. "I take it you're still upset over it?"

"Yes," she croaked.

He nudged the cup closer. "Would caffeine help?"

Liv gave him a wobbling smile. "Couldn't hurt."

For a minute, they sat in companionable silence, the bustle of the café mixing with the strangely out-of-date carols. Liv wasn't happy—*couldn't be happy after Spartan!*—but she wasn't alone anymore. Liv liked having someone to sit with, someone you didn't have to explain things to, someone you could be honest with without fear of judgment, someone—

The telltale sound of pinging interrupted her thoughts. Xander pulled his phone from the voluminous folds of his shirt, the device glowing like a rectangular ghost.

"Arden says 'Hello, Liv.'"

Liv rolled her eyes, but Xander—busy typing his reply—missed it.

"You want to say anything?" he asked.

"Tell her I say hi back."

22

He laughed to himself, and Liv looked up. (She hadn't meant that to be funny.)

"Oh, Arden." He chuckled, grinning down at the screen as his thumbs tapped in another answer. The phone pinged again, and he laughed louder. "You naughty, naughty girl."

Liv made a gagging sound.

Xander looked up. "What's wrong?"

"It'd be nice if my best friend could stop flirting with his girlfriend long enough to comfort me."

This time Xander rolled his eyes. "Dearest Liv . . . histrionics aside, I really think you're taking this—"

The phone pinged again, and he looked down. A giggle escaped his pursed lips. He smothered the laughter under his hand, hiding it behind a bout of coughing.

Liv glared at the other patrons in the coffeehouse. *No one understood.*

～

@LivOutLoud: FANGIRL DISTRESS SIGNAL! Send help! I need distractions. STAT.

@JoesWoes: @LivOutLoud What kind of help?

@LivOutLoud: @JoesWoes Anything. Everything! I just want Spartan back in my brain, NOW. #RLSucks

@JoesWoes: @LivOutLoud You got it, sweetie! How about my new fic? I'm already at 5K. Think I'm going to break 50 on this one! Here's the first chapter: http://tinyurl.com/Starveil1

@LivOutLoud: @JoesWoes It's awesome but I've already read it. (Loving it, btw!)

@JoesWoes: @LivOutLoud Have you read @SpartanGrrl's new fic? It's equal parts angst and smut. SO AWESOME! Let me find you the link.

@LivOutLoud: @JoesWoes Sounds perfect. *swoons* Spartan take me away!

@SpartanGrrl: @LivOutLoud @JoesWoes You rang, ladies? :) Smut ahead! http://tinyurl.com/Starveil2

@LivOutLoud: @SpartanGrrl @JoesWoes Perfect! Thank you SO much! Please send anything else you have. I want it ALL!

@JoesWoes: @LivOutLoud @SpartanGrrl Woo-hoo! Looks like Liv's back in the Starveil fandom! *fist bumps* #ItsAliveItsAlive

@SpartanGrrl: @JoesWoes Glad to have you back in the house! #SpartanSurvived fangirls FOREVER!

@LivOutLoud: @SpartanGrrl @JoesWoes Aw . . . ladies. You're making me tear up.

@SpartanGrrl: @LivOutLoud You've been quiet the last while.

@LivOutLoud: @SpartanGrrl I have. :(

@JoesWoes: @LivOutLoud Well, I'm glad you're back. We've missed you, sweetie!

@LivOutLoud: @JoesWoes I've been offline, but my heart never left. <3.

⌒

The Friday before classes began, Liv woke to the sound of voices.

"Liv?" her mother called. "You around?"

Footsteps crossed the floor in a distant part of the house. She sat up. Her forgotten laptop slid off her knees and headed for the side of the mattress, but she caught it one-handed before it hit the floor. Running a hand over sandpapered eyes, she squinted at the clock. It was twelve thirty, but with the curtains closed, she didn't know if that meant twelve thirty in the morning or at night.

"Liv?" her mother called in a tense voice. "You awake?"

Not night then. Morning. She wrinkled her nose as the scent of day-old clothing hit her. She set the laptop aside and stretched. "Hold on a sec, I'm—"

"*Liv!*" her mother bellowed from just outside the door. "*You awake?*"

Liv jerked. She certainly wasn't awake enough for *that*.

"Yeah, I'm up, I'm up," she grumbled.

The door opened a crack, Katherine's backlit silhouette appearing. "You need to get out of bed, sweetie. I know you're on winter break, but it's past noon."

Liv stifled a yawn. She'd been up half the night reading

25

Spartan fic. (All the fangirls were.) His death had unsettled the *Starveil* fandom like no other plot twist. Fan forums across the net were buzzing with grief-stricken posts.

Katherine frowned. "Are you sick, Liv?" she asked. "You look pale."

"Couldn't sleep last night. I'll be down in a minute."

"Well, hurry, please," her mother said with a sympathetic smile. "Gary brought over some lunch for us."

Liv groaned.

Gary Blodgett was Katherine's longtime boyfriend and the manager of the local printshop. Though Gary and Katherine's relationship was lukewarm at best, they'd been together since Liv was in high school. Liv avoided talking to Gary if at all possible. Gary did the same for her.

"I'm not really that hungry," Liv said. "You guys go ahead."

"Come down and have a little. I'm worried about you."

"I'm fine."

"You're not."

"I *am*."

"It's Chinese," Katherine said. "And I asked Gary to get extra cookies for you."

A grin spread across Liv's face. Chinese wasn't her favorite food per se, but Chinese meant fortune cookies, and that part she loved.

"How many?"

Her mother laughed and closed the door behind her. "Five," she called as she headed down the hallway. "But you'd better hurry up, or I'm taking them all."

Liv found yesterday's jeans and a fresh hoodie, dressing in record time. One foot was still asleep, and as she hobbled down the hallway, she heard Gary grumble: *"Running late already. Should just start without her."*

"Please do, Gary," Liv muttered.

When she reached the table, they were dressed for the outdoors. Liv's mother wore the same serviceable black wool jacket she always wore. The one that was "too good to throw away" and made Liv feel guilty for asking for anything new. Gary, on the other hand, was a real-life version of Elmer Fudd, with his hunter's cap and plaid jacket.

"You guys going somewhere?"

"We're seeing a matinee," Katherine said through a mouthful of noodles. "Hurry and you can join us."

"Um . . ."

"It's no bother," Katherine said. "We'd love for you to come. One last outing before school starts up again."

Gary grumbled something inaudible, and Liv's jaw clenched. *This* was why he annoyed her.

"I'll think about it," Liv said.

Lunch started in silence, the time-crunch giving them an excuse to keep discussion to a minimum. In a few minutes, Liv had carried her plate to the dishwasher. She reached for the Chinese food bag.

"You should thank Gary for the cookies," her mother said. "He's the one who picked them up."

"Thanks."

Liv fished out the five cookies and laid them on the counter. She ran her fingers over the plastic covers, a tingling sensation shooting through her fingertips. It was too strange for her to put into words. She'd never even told Xander, and they'd been friends for months. But there were times the fortunes weren't

27

just words. And somehow Liv always felt her father was there when she opened just the right one. It sounded crazy because it *was* crazy. But it felt true.

She tore open the first package and broke the cookie to release the paper, smoothing it between thumb and forefinger as she read: *Laughter is the best medicine.*

With a grimace, Liv set it back on the counter. Her mother lifted her brows.

"Not mine," Liv said.

"You always do this." Katherine laughed.

"Which is why I always tell you to order extra."

Her mother suppressed a grin as Liv opened the next.

A grand adventure awaits you.

Liv groaned and crumpled it up, grabbing another.

Your passions will bring you many friends.

Disgusted, Liv scowled at the remaining two cookies.

"You can have mine," her mother offered. "I don't mind."

"Thanks," Liv said, half-closing her eyes in concentration. "Just need the right one."

Nothing happened for several seconds and then . . . A faint twinge, like a single spark, ran up her arm to settle in her chest. Liv grabbed the cookie nearest her and broke it open.

It's up to you to make your happy ending.

Liv stared at it a moment, rereading the words. Did it mean life? Because if it did, then Liv disagreed. Sometimes life was downright unfair. Bad things happened to good people. Her father's death was the perfect example.

Katherine stood from the table, buttoning her coat and pulling on her mittens.

"Find the right one?" she asked.

"Not sure."

"Well, we should get going. Don't want to be late to the movie."

Liv stared at the fortune in her hand. "You guys have fun," she said in a distracted voice. "I'll get the dishes."

"But aren't you coming along?"

"I'm not feeling up to it."

"You're not still going on about the ending of that *Star Trek* movie, are you?" Gary said.

Liv's chin jerked up in surprise. Gary rarely acknowledged her presence, never mind spoke directly to her.

"I-it's *Starveil* . . . and I don't know what you mean."

"Oh, your mother told me all about it."

"She what?" Liv spun back to her mother, who was studiously avoiding eye contact.

"Hiding in your room all day. Reading fan-fic. Not giving a bit of attention to the world going on around you." Gary Blodgett wasn't known for his talking, and Liv wasn't sure if this was a joke or not. He never intervened. Rarely acknowledged her presence at all. "You've been carrying on like a spoiled kid," he added.

"I have not!"

"Sounds to me like you need a good swift kick in the—"

"Gary!" Katherine gasped. She turned to Liv. "I just want to make sure you're okay."

"I am! But I wish you'd brought this up with *me*. Gary has no business—"

He jabbed a stubby finger at Liv. "You need to stop moping!"

"I—I'm not. I'm just busy. I—I—" She felt her throat close.

There was no way she could explain to him—someone with absolutely no imagination—what it was like to lose Spartan. A man like Gary would never understand her love of the *Starveil* series. "I—I'm fine," she said. "And it's hardly your place to—"

"Your mother asked my opinion, and I'm giving it."

"Gary, *please*," Katherine pleaded. "We're going to be late to the movie."

He muttered something about "warming up the car" and headed to the front door. It closed with a bang that rattled the pictures. Liv went to leave, but her mother stepped in her way, putting her hands on her shoulders.

"All I said to Gary was that you'd been really quiet the last few days. And you *have* been." She squeezed gently. "I was worried about you, Liv. That's all."

"You don't have to be."

"Please, sweetie. Come along . . . for me."

"Not today. Okay? I'm not in the mood."

Her mother's smile faded into something careworn, and she let go of Liv's shoulders. "Another time then? Just the two of us?"

"Definitely."

When the door closed behind her mother, Liv unclenched her fists, staring down at the crumpled fortune in her palm: *It's up to you to make your happy ending.*

With those words, an idea flickered in the recesses of her mind. She smiled. Liv tucked the paper into her pocket, swept the broken pieces of cookie into the wrinkled brown bag, and brushed her hands over the sink. She grabbed her phone and tapped in a text.

> You working now, Xander?

> Ugh. YES. The Dickensian drudgery of it is slowly killing me.

> When do you get off?

> At six thirty.

> You have plans with Arden?

> Not tonight. Why?

> I'm coming by. I've got an idea I want to run by you. :D

Xander was waiting outside Cup O' Joe when Liv arrived. Icy fingers of wind dug under her coat as she trudged up the street, whereas Xander, with his long wool cloak and knee-high riding boots, was much better dressed for the weather.

Catching sight of her, he waved his walking stick. "Liv! Over here, dearest!" (As if she'd assume the Jonathan Harker look-alike was anyone *but* him.) *Dracula* was set nowhere near Boulder, she thought, but she'd be willing to bet she could match it for mood.

"I thought you would've grabbed us a table," Liv said, her breath clouding the frosty air. "It's freezing out."

Snow swirled around the streetlights, catching on Xander's hair and peppering his top hat, giving the scene a postcard appeal.

"Joe's is packed," he said. "I tried, believe me. We'll have to—" Xander's dashing grin backflipped into a look of concern as he saw her face. "Christ, Liv, you look terrible!" he said, giving her a once-over. "Whatever happened?"

Liv burrowed her nose into her scarf. "Nice to see you, too, Xander."

"I'm sorry for saying so, but you really do look dreadful."

"That is *not* an apology." She glowered at him. "You are a terrible best friend."

Xander groaned. "Oh come now, Liv. You know what I mean."

"I don't."

He waved a hand toward her mismatched ensemble. "Your hair isn't washed, your clothes are wrinkled, your shoes—"

"Not all of us live in a state of constant cosplay," Liv interrupted. Her voice dropped. "Or perfection," she muttered, thinking of Arden's long blond hair, pert body, and designer clothes.

Xander's gloved hand brushed her elbow, and he gave her a gentle smile. "But you don't look like *you*, dearest, and that worries me."

Liv knew it was true, because his words were growing into that strange hybrid of modern American and fake British upper crust. The first week of classes, Xander had gotten into an argument with their professor in the middle of class, and that same BBC-approved accent had come through. He *was* concerned.

Liv glanced over his shoulder to the window of Cup O' Joe.

Xander was right. Every seat was taken. "So where do you want to go?" she sighed. " 'Cause I'm turning into a Popsicle out here."

"Is Mickey Dee's to your liking, m'lady?"

"Perfect."

"Then your carriage awaits." He did a half bow, waiting for Liv to pass in front of him. "Just give me a minute to text Arden."

Liv headed down the street, snow crunching beneath her boots. She was annoyed again, and she couldn't explain why. She waited next to his car—a rusting orange Mazda—until Xander caught up.

"So what's going on?" he asked. "You've been radio silent for days. I thought you'd joined a nunnery or something."

"I'm actually doing a little better. That's why I'm here."

"Oh?"

"I have an idea, but I'm going to need your help."

Xander unlocked the car door and pulled it open with a flourish, his cape swinging wide. "You know I could never deny a damsel in distress."

Liv bit the inside of her lip to keep from grinning. "Is that what I am to you?"

"Not saying I mind. It lets *me* play hero." He winked. "So what's this idea of yours?"

Liv settled inside the car and smiled up at him.

"I'm bringing Spartan back from the dead."

❧

They sat in the parking lot, large fries and two drinks in the carousel between the front seats of Xander's car. For someone who dressed like a nineteenth-century gentleman, Xander Hall had a distinct love of processed food.

"Tom Grander is very much alive," Xander said for the third time. "I saw him in the Atlanta airport once. The man dresses like a slob."

"Yes, Tom's alive, but Spartan is dead," Liv said. "And that's just wrong."

Xander sipped his iced tea. "You talk to the coven about it?"

"You *know* I don't like it when you call us that."

"Sorry. I'll come up with a better sobriquet."

"Or *don't*. I'm fine without one, thanks."

Xander tapped his lip with his forefinger, his gaze drifting over her as if searching for clues. Liv squirmed under his inspection.

"Hmm . . . How about *the posse*?"

"We're not cowboys."

His eyes widened. "*The ton*?"

She grabbed another fry. "I don't even know what that means, Xander. But no."

"*Inner sanctum*," he breathed.

Liv snorted. "That one sounds illegal."

"I've got it!" He plucked the french fry from her waiting fingers. "*The coterie!*"

Laughing, she stole the french fry back before he could put it into his mouth. "How about *the* Starveil *fandom*? It's self-explanatory, and it doesn't sound like I've joined a cult."

"Well, yes. That's a bonus," Xander said. "But it's too blasé, dearest." His hands swung up, knocking the complicated knot of his cravat askew. "You deserve something that captures your essence!"

Liv reached out, straightening Xander's necktie. "Essence, hmmm?"

His face flushed, and he looked away, smoothing the tie's folds. "Exactly."

Outside it was snowing again. Flakes dotted the dark windows like a star field. Liv picked up another fry, twirling it between her fingers before popping it into her mouth.

"Xander," she said after a moment. "I was hoping you'd help me with something."

"Aha!" He brushed off his hands. "Now we're getting to the heart of it. What nefarious escapades have the cov—" he cleared his throat "—have *the fandom* been up to?"

"Nothing yet, but I want you to help me with a little project."

"I'm all ears."

"In the last movie, Spartan dies." Liv took another fry. "But I'm going to change it."

"The film's already released. You can't change it now."

"I think I can."

"But . . . it's canon." He took another sip of iced tea. "The countdown clock was on."

"Screw the clock," Liv said. "I'm changing it."

"How?"

Liv rubbed greasy fingers on the side of her jeans. "I'm not a writer, Xander, but I've been in fandom long enough to know how much influence the fans have. It's way more than most people realize."

Xander smothered laughter behind his hand.

"They do!" Liv insisted.

"Give me one example."

"In the second *Starveil* movie, there was a mention of the

colony on Io. Two seconds of film, max. But the fan-writers picked up the idea and ran with it. When the third *Starveil* came out, Io was one of the key destinations in Darthku's plan for domination. It was the *writers* who influenced the plot of the movie; they made it what it became."

"That seems like a vague reference to me. I mean, how many *other* fics were out there, besides the ones about Io?"

"Fine. Then how about the relationship with Tekla? There wasn't even a hint of romance in the first two movies, but the SparTek ship became so popular, they added it."

He smirked. "Perhaps, Liv, but I doubt that—"

"For goodness' sake." She laughed. "They practically used the same 'pretending to be married' setup that appeared in one of SpartanGrrl's fics!"

A grin tugged the corners of his lips.

"They *did*, Xander. I know they did, because I read that story first." She reached for another fry. "I've been part of the *Starveil* fandom since day one. You haven't."

"All right then, so what's your plan to revive our dear Mr. Spartan?"

"You're an actor, right?"

He raised an eyebrow. "Among other things."

"I need to build a character. A persona." Liv opened the online forum on her phone. "I need someone to act for me."

Xander's eyes narrowed. "Why do I get the feeling this is going to require a degree of embarrassment?"

"It might, but only a little bit. I'll pay you back."

He set his cup back into the holder and crossed his arms. "How? I want details before I agree to anything."

"God, I'm not asking you to sell your soul to the devil." Liv laughed. "Besides, I'll help you sew your new outfit. You need a sewing machine to finish the last piece of your cosplay, right?"

"Cosplay. Why, you just said the magic word," he drawled. "Count me in. So what kind of acting do you need?"

Liv tapped in a username and hit Find.

"I need an actor, a voice for the revolution. Someone to say 'the fans haven't given up, and neither should you.' You'll be the star, Xander, and I'll be the director who brings it all together."

On her phone's screen, a reply appeared: *Username AVAILABLE.*

Liv hit Accept. When she looked back up, Xander was grinning, and suddenly she was, too. He lifted the fry box, offering her the last one.

"You're serious about this, aren't you?"

"Absolutely." Liv pointed at him with the end of the fry. "So are you in or not? The revolution can't start without you."

He winked. "I always had a soft spot for Che Guevara."

～

Spartan Forum, 2:15 a.m.

New thread, topic: Spartan Rescue Mission

@SpartanSurvived:

ATTN: All members of the Starveil Rebellion. Many of you have heard that Captain Matt Spartan, commander of the Star Freighter Elysium, has been reported missing in action. Surveillance footage from the final escape pod shows the

Elysium being destroyed, but in the last hours, there have been multiple reports of an unidentified transceiver messaging in the Omega Quadrant.

We need you, soldiers. Spartan needs you. Look for evidence. Find reports, word-of-mouth testimony, footage if you can. If we have any hope of finding Spartan alive, it will come down to your ingenuity and determination. This rescue message must spread far and wide. Post your findings on all fandom platforms using the hashtag: #SpartanSurvived

THIS IS YOUR CALL TO ACTION.

@SpartanSurvived

Liv chewed her lower lip, rereading the text once and again. Leaving a post like this on one of the busiest *Starveil* forums was a call to arms. It was so outrageous—so arrogant—she couldn't doubt the potential for ridicule. Trolls loved tearing apart things like this. And if they decided to start flaming her post, they'd burn her idea down to the ground. But if she didn't post it, she'd never know.

Her fingers drummed on the armrest. *Post or not.* That was the big question.

Liv lifted her phone, scrolling through her texts. There was one from Joanne. It had arrived while she was out with Xander.

@JoesWoes: So upset over that stupid ending, Liv. How do you get over losing a character you love? Spartan's REAL to me. He's my baby, you know? :(

Liv *did* know. He was her baby, too. He was everyone's! And by killing off the character, the creators had wounded an entire community of fans. She reread Joe's text, her finger hovering over Reply for a long moment.

She set the phone down again.

Her gaze darted back to the computer screen. *THIS IS YOUR CALL TO ACTION.* If she posted this, it needed to be real. She needed people to believe Spartan could come back. They needed to trust that he'd made it out of the ship. It couldn't just be fangirl to fangirl, writing *Starveil* AUs that never really happened. This would be the guerrilla warfare of character ships. The fans would have to reweave the details they had into a new explanation of those last seconds of film. They'd take no prisoners, leave no wounded fans behind. But, as in any war, that meant the intel behind the revolution had to stay secret for as long as possible.

Fandom had to *believe.*

Liv released her breath, heart beating in her temple. *It's up to you to make your happy ending.*

She hit Post.

3

"I SOLEMNLY SWEAR THAT I AM UP TO NO GOOD."
(HARRY POTTER AND THE PRISONER OF AZKABAN)

Saturday morning Liv woke to the sound of the garage door closing. Her mother had the day off, but she went in for a few hours each weekend and had done so for as long as Liv could remember. The house was cold, and an icy wind rattled the bedroom windows. Liv rolled over and pulled the covers over her head, waiting for sleep to retake her.

Heady warmth spread through her limbs. Behind closed lids, images flickered: the video she'd done for her final project last semester, the girl in the audio lab who always asked Liv for help with the anticrackle effect, Xander dragging her through fabric stores so he could pick out "the right brocade," the new ONLY ONE MAN CALLS ME DARLIN' T-shirt Liv wanted to buy.

"You ready, darlin'?"

The alien bug crouched, ready to attack.

"G'bye, Spartan."

Liv's eyes snapped open. With a groan, she whipped off the covers and swung her legs off the bed. No point in sleeping if *that* was what she'd dream about. Twenty minutes later, she was back in bed, albeit showered and dressed, with a cup of tea on the bedside table and her laptop balanced on her knees. Out of habit, she opened her e-mail.

Three hundred eighty-seven messages.

Liv blinked in confusion. "What the . . . ?"

The hundreds of messages had one source: her Spartan post from the previous night. With shaking fingers, she scrolled through them. Tweets, replies, likes, and, most exciting of all, "evidence posts"—at least fifty of them—filled the screen. These were getting their own reposts and replies, too. She leaned back against her pillow, heart pounding.

#SpartanSurvived had taken off.

Liv fumbled for her phone and flicked off airplane mode. It began to vibrate in her hand, four separate tweets from Joe, Brian, and two other fangirls appearing.

@JoesWoes: @LivOutLoud OMG Liv-GET ONLINE! Something's going on with Starveil. O_O

@StarVeilBrian1981: @LivOutLoud Check out the new manip I just posted:

New Spartan post, btw. You should do a vid or
something.

@**SpartanGrrl:** @LivOutLoud Liv! LIV! LIIIIIIIVVVVVVVV!!!!
Where ARE you??? There's a Spartan revolution about
to begin!

@**VeilMeister:** @LivOutLoud Check out this post, bb.
http://tinyurl.com/Starveil3

"Oh my God!" Liv gasped as the realization hit her. "I'm
trending."

Liv started to type an answer to Joe's tweet, then stopped
and deleted it. It felt important she keep anonymous, at least
for now. It wasn't supposed to be a joke. It was a call for action.
She flicked back to VeilMeister's tweet. Not just a call to arms,
a Spartan revolution.

Grinning, she finally decided on Xander. Besides being her
friend, he had absolutely no connection to the *Starveil* fandom. Even if he accidentally said something online, it wouldn't
matter. The only people who really knew him were the steampunk crowd. Besides, he *needed* to be in the know, since they
had a vid to film. She wrote half a page of text, then deleted it
after all, calling instead. The phone rang three times before a
sleep-laden voice answered.

"Liv?" Rustling echoed in the background. "You all right?"

"I'm fine. I just need to talk to someone."

"So text me," Xander mumbled. "Goodness. What century
were you born in?"

"But I need to talk to you *now*, not three hours from now!"

"I cannot imagine anything that can't wait three hours."

The sound of yawning came through the phone. "There are reasonable ways to wake a person in the morning, you know."

"From someone who prefers an inkwell to a Sharpie," Liv said, giggling, "you are a surprising technology snob." She peeked down at her computer screen. Forty-six new notifications had arrived in the time since she'd woken. "So are you awake yet?"

"Mrrrph. I'm trying . . . I really am."

"I'll take that as a yes. I need you to go online, Xander."

"As in right now?"

"Yes, now."

"But I'm so tired," he moaned. "Can't this wait?"

"No."

"Honestly, Liv. How are you awake at all?"

"Please, Xander," she pleaded, "just do it."

"All right . . . let me grab my tablet." He yawned again. "Okay, I'm online. This better be good."

"I need you to go to the *Starveil* wiki."

There was a pause. "Are you joking? You know how I feel about *Star*—"

"Just GO."

"Fine . . . But only because it's *you* asking, dearest." Liv heard him moving around, the phone being shifted. "All right. I'm over on the dark side. You'd better have the cookies I've been promised."

Liv giggled. "Now find the list of Spartan forums."

"Where? I don't see it," Xander grumbled. "This is really the *worst*-designed fan page I've ever—"

"They're over on the left side of the page. You see them now?"

"Um . . . yeah. Yeah, I got it. Which one?"

"Just click on the search box at the top of the list and type in Spartan Survived."

There was a pause.

"Okay," Xander said. "I've got about a hundred different results. Which one?"

"All of them!" Liv laughed. "That's me! I'm trending."

There was a pause of several seconds.

"That's . . . *you*?"

"Yes! That project I was telling you about last night? I kind of started it on my own. I put out a post. It should be the first one on the list."

Liv heard him moving about, sheets rustling. Xander's voice returned, brighter than before. "Is this the Spartan Rescue Mission post?"

"Exactly! It's trending. I've got like . . ." She refreshed her e-mail browser, eyes widening at the new list. "Close to five hundred replies already."

"Are you kidding me? This is for freaking *Starveil*. Unbelievable!"

Liv choked back laughter. "Don't be mad," she teased. "I'm sure steampunk will have its day."

She could hear the grin in Xander's tone. "It already does, Liv dearest. You just have to meet *real-life* people at cons to truly experience it."

"So you keep saying."

"Then why don't you come with me this summer? Dragon Con is something you must experience to understand. Arden and I are already planning our dual cosplay."

Liv rolled her eyes at the mention of Xander's girlfriend. "Wouldn't that be . . . kind of weird?"

"Why would it be weird?"

"I dunno . . . With Arden and you, and then . . . me?" Liv laughed. "I'm not excited to be a third wheel."

"Pfft! Arden adores you. Besides, every room is packed that weekend. That's just how Dragon Con works. My cousin's coming, too. We could find room for you, if you wanted."

"I don't think so. But thanks."

"Not a problem," Xander said. "And seriously, Liv, this whole thing you did with the *Starveil* post is fantastic. Bravo, dearest! Five hundred overnight is . . . It's amazing! I'm in awe."

"Thanks, Xander. That means a lot." She grinned. "So are you ready to start a revolution?"

He chuckled. "I think it's already started."

~

"Where does the belt go?" Xander's irritated voice came, disembodied, from the other side of the door.

"In the belt loops." Liv laughed.

"Not *that* belt," he said. "The other one. The, er . . . fancy one."

Liv frowned in confusion. There *was* only one belt on the costume she'd handed him. She closed her eyes, ticking through the different parts of the resistance uniform.

"Can you describe it for me?"

"It's got these, um . . . silver things glued to it?" Xander made a snorting sound. "I don't know, Liv. This is all a bit showy, if you ask me."

Liv began to giggle. "That's not a belt. That's a bandolier

for your blaster." Her laughter grew. "It goes across your chest."

The bathroom door opened a crack. "Blaster as in a gun?"

"Yes, Xander. Just throw the strap over your shoulder and . . ."

Liv's words disappeared as the door opened the rest of the way.

Xander stepped forward. Only it *wasn't* Xander at all, it was a *Starveil* resistance fighter. His hair was no longer pomaded into a smooth coiffure, but hung loose into brooding eyes. The signature coat of the Rebels hugged muscular arms, and rank pins twinkled on his lapel.

"Well," Xander said, lifting a brow. "Do I look rebellious enough for you?"

Liv couldn't speak. The words literally wouldn't move past her slack lips. Xander's hooded eyes suggested wicked deeds about to be unveiled, and her heart was in overtime with the mere thought of what they'd be. Liv had seen many people's cosplay, but none had affected her like this. Her gaze moved from head to toe and back up, absorbing details like parched soil drawing in rain.

"I . . . you . . ."

"How does the rest of it look?" Xander turned in a circle, the ragged coattails swirling. It was like seeing a character from a movie alive and well in her living room. Liv's mind just couldn't put together Xander—with his old-world charm and debonair good looks—and this smoldering Rebel leader. "Does the jacket fit all right?" he asked. "I can't see the back."

Liv turned away. "I-it's good, Xander." She cleared her throat. "Really good. You definitely have the Rebel look."

"I didn't shave today. You notice?" He caught hold of Liv's fingers and rubbed them across the edge of his jaw. "See? Truth in art."

Her breath caught in her throat. She was standing far too close to Xander, and she wasn't certain how she'd gotten there. "Yeah. I guess so." She forced a smile as she stepped back. "So are you ready to film?"

Xander grinned. "Let's give Arden a sneak peek, first."

He pulled out his phone and placed it in her hand, but the second Liv lifted it, Xander stepped up next to her and slid an arm over her shoulder. His scruff brushed the edge of her cheek as he leaned in for the picture.

"Ready for a selfie, m'lady?"

Liv pasted a grin on her face and clicked.

⁓

Hours later, their video was finally coming together.

"You're doing it again." Liv laughed.

Xander moved back from the computer screen and settled into the chair next to her. "Apologies, dear. Just watching."

"Sitting would help. You make a better door than a window, you know."

Xander put his hand over his heart and dropped his chin. "If you want me to leave you in peace, just say the words. I'll go."

Liv's eyes were starting to blur, but she had every intention of finishing the editing before she crashed for the night. She'd expected Xander to leave after they finished filming, but near midnight he was still at her side, watching as the raw footage transformed.

"I'm fine either way," Liv said, expanding the video's time-line. "But I need to be able to see the screen."

He nudged her with his elbow. "I'll be good. I promise."

"You'd better be."

"Or what?"

"Or this will never get finished!"

The footage Liv had ripped from illegal online downloads was now hashed into a montage that looked surprisingly real. She'd matched the colors of the original movie's background with those from other sources. Kubrick's *2001* might be half a century old, but it pulled off the look of space better than most sci-fi action movies Liv had seen. Combined with some bits that Brian had sent her the previous year—when Liv's vidding had been her driving passion—she had what looked like a very realistic (if actorless) segment of *Starveil* footage.

"The first part was just a warm-up, are you ready to jump into the fun stuff?" Liv asked.

"Most definitely."

"Then watch and learn. . . ."

Liv pulled up a shot of Xander in costume as Major Malloy. He stood against the background of a blue tarp hung on one wall of Liv's bedroom. She placed it onto the timeline above the combined shots.

"That's me!" Xander shouted.

"Shh! My mom's asleep." She giggled. "And it's Major R. C. Malloy if you're on-screen."

"Yes, yes. I look *so* good in that role."

"You'll look even better when we put you into the film."

Xander leaned closer, the lace of his cuff brushing her arm. "Wonderful," he breathed. "You're *really* good at this, Liv."

"Thanks."

"So what's next?"

Liv popped open the effects panel. "Well, I'm going to use chroma key here"—she dragged it onto his raw clip—"to select the color behind you." She popped open another panel, using quick keys. "And then we'll pull the blue color out so the montage we just made is right behind you."

Xander frowned. "Google translate that please."

Liv grinned. "You'll be *on* Io, Xander." She selected the color, moving to the effects control panel. "Right about—"

Xander's phone buzzed, and he dropped his eyes from the screen, scrolling through a text. He sighed.

"Gotta go?" Liv asked.

"I don't want to, but I kind of have to. Arden's on her way over right now and . . ." He looked back up. "Wait—WHAT?!" He leaned closer. "What did you do?! I'm—I'm on Io! Like I'm *actually* standing on the surface of the moon." He jumped to his feet, the phone forgotten in his hand. "Wait show me how you did that!"

Liv smothered a fit of exhausted laughter. "Hold on, hold on. I'll undo." She clicked the effect off and on, and Xander flickered back and forth from blue screen to Io. "See? A bit of vidding magic and . . . ta-da! You're there."

"Unbelievable," Xander said. "You really have a talent with this, Liv. Someday you should—"

Another text buzzed his phone. He groaned.

"You should go," Liv said. "It's late, and I kept you all day." She forced a smile she didn't totally feel. "Tell Arden I say hi."

Xander stared longingly at the laptop screen. "Are you sure?"

"The rest is just a bit of polishing. I'll show you the finished vid tomorrow, all right?"

"Fair enough," he said, gathering his embroidered jacket and pulling it on. "Arden should be here in a few minutes. She got off work hours ago."

"Thanks again for the help, Xander. You look awesome." Liv stretched her arms over her head, a series of pops running up her spine.

"That is utterly disgusting."

Liv shook her head. "Don't say vidders don't suffer for their craft."

"Wouldn't think of it." He took two steps toward her door. "I'll just head outside and wait for Arden to—" Xander spun back around. "Hey, do you mind if I show her?"

Liv frowned. "Show her what?"

"The film."

"But it's not done."

"It looks so good already!"

"Um . . . I don't know if—"

Xander's phone interrupted, followed almost immediately by the shrill peal of the doorbell. "Shit!" Liv hissed. "My mom's sleeping!"

"Sorry! My fault. Should've warned her." Xander sprinted for the door, phone in hand. "I'll get the door. Arden's waiting outside."

Two pairs of footsteps returned. Liv swiveled away from the computer, pasting a smile on her lips and bracing for the attack. Encountering Arden was like tangling with a very perky, fit-bodied hurricane. After the storm passed, Liv found herself picking up the detritus—the pink lip-stain on her cheek, the cloying body mist clinging to her clothes, the tangled hair and lost earrings. Arden's demonstrative nature made Liv anxious.

"Liv! How've you been?!" Arden threw her arms around Liv's neck, hugging tight. "Can't wait to see this! Xander's been texting me about your project all day."

"He has?"

"It sounds amazing!"

The trouble with Arden, Liv thought, was that she was almost *too* likable.

"So scoot over," Arden said, sliding half onto Liv's lap. "I want to see this!"

Liv moved over until only half her bum gripped the edge of the chair. "There's not that much to see," she said, stalling.

"Not true," Xander tutted. He pulled a second chair out and offered Arden his hand, assisting her to her own seat. "Liv has done a remarkable job. I've no idea what the finished version will be, but the B-roll, on its own, is spectacular."

"That's an exaggeration, Xander."

"It's not. Now show us, please."

Arden squeezed her arm, smiling. "Please, Liv? I'd really love to see."

With a sigh, Liv hit Play. The *Starveil* theme began, interspersed with bits of footage. When they arrived at Io, Xander abruptly appeared.

"Oh my God, it's Xander." Arden laughed. "That's fantastic, Liv." She turned to him. "You look great, babe!"

Xander preened under her attention as the remaining clip played. Liv flicked it off as they reached the last scene.

"And that's it."

"That's just amazing!" Arden said, applauding. "You've got some mad skills, Liv."

"Thanks."

"And you"—Arden slid her arms over Xander's shoulders—"are looking particularly sexy as the major."

"Thank you, my sweet."

Liv flinched as the distinct sounds of kissing came from behind her. "If it's okay," she said, not looking up, "I'll just get back to work then."

"Of course, dearest." Xander chuckled. "We'll see ourselves out."

Liv peeked back over her shoulder. Xander caught Liv's eyes as they headed out the door. "Until tomorrow, I bid you adieu!"

"Later."

The front door closed behind them, and Liv was alone once more.

She cracked her knuckles and turned back to the screen. The challenge post was burning up the Internet. Her @SpartanSurvived Twitter account had ten times as many followers as her private account, and her online friends had no idea who the force behind the challenge was.

"And it's going to stay that way," Liv muttered to the empty room.

If #SpartanSurvived failed in its efforts, no one would be the wiser. There was no risk to her online persona. No backlash from haters. Anonymity's cloak both protected her and kept the torch of Spartan alive. Because as much as fandom *knew* a fan had created the post, the faceless message held the faint promise of authenticity. And if people believed it, then the magic was real. They could change Spartan's fate because they *thought* they could, and tonight's video would cast the first spell.

She opened the After Effects program, waiting for it to load. "And now, the magic *really* begins. . . ."

⌣

Channel: https://www.youtube.com/user/SpartanSurvived

Home page-Video 1: Call to Arms

The video opened with a flickering black screen. It crackled and buzzed, shimmering with interference. In seconds the static coalesced into militaristic black text against a grainy background: Surveillance Photos from the Space Probe Janus, Omega Quadrant. With a final crackle, it flicked to what appeared to be a black background, but which was, on closer inspection, the void of space.

On-screen, a single escape pod passed in front of the camera. (Though layered with textures, the image was recognizable as the final scene of *Starveil Five*.) Partway across the screen, the image jittered, the video feed ignoring the distant pod in order to return to the floating detritus of the destroyed Star Freighter Elysium.

Bits of broken metal floated past on a backdrop of stars, until—in time to the first strains of the well-known Starveil Rebellion theme—a single blip of light appeared in the distance. Was it a probe? A distant satellite? The light sparked once, twice . . . The camera zoomed forward into the flashes, footage growing increasingly pixelated until it dissolved into a lens flare, then snapped out entirely.

The music rose in crescendo on the black screen.

The camera pulled back from an extreme close-up of a man's jacket. Black-haired and unsmiling, an unknown resistance fighter filled the screen. His major's rank was emblazoned across his tattered jacket, a carbon-smeared blaster tucked nonchalantly into his belt. The man's posture was stiff despite his ragged clothes, his jaw clenched as he stared daggers into the camera. A Rebel code flashed across the top of the screen, and a robotic voice announced: "Rebellion leader, Major R. C. Malloy. Previously of the Rebel Base Io."

Called to attention, the man strode forward, and the gentle swell of music dropped as he spoke. His voice carried the lilt of Old Terra, educated and icily controlled.

"Attention, comrades. This message is for Rebels across our star system and beyond. As you've no doubt heard, Captain Matt Spartan, commander of the Star Freighter Elysium, has been reported missing in action. Until this footage was acquired by Rebel command a few hours ago, Captain Spartan was assumed dead." The man's voice crackled with contempt. "That assumption is incorrect!"

The man disappeared as the video jumped to another scene, this one taken from inside the hangar of the Star Freighter Elysium in its final moments. It showed Spartan throwing himself through the open hatch of a shuttle while flames washed the screen. (It was a clip only die-hard fans would recognize as a behind-the-scenes shot taken from the collector's edition of the second *Starveil* film.) Tongues of flame burned up the sides of the shuttle as an electronic voice shouted a countdown: "Five . . . Four . . . Three . . ." The camera cut to a point-of-view shot of Spartan's hands, tapping in a jump-code as explosions filled the air.

The screen went white.

The unnamed Rebel leader reappeared, and the jaunty trill of the original *Starveil* theme filled the air. The man's fists were poised on his hips. He stood in front of a map, which marked the many Rebel bases from all quadrants of the galaxy. (The image was a fan-created graphic borrowed from the current *Starveil* wiki.) The camera whizzed into a close-up of the major's face. His straight-edged jaw was brushed by a blue shadow of stubble, disheveled strands of black hair hanging into brooding eyes.

"Your determination. Your research. Your proof of Spartan's whereabouts are the only hope we have for his safe return." The camera cut to a medium shot—showing the ragged edge of the Rebel coat, light glittering on the metal barrel of a blaster—and then back to a close-up of his face. A wide shot of the Rebel base on Io (recognizable from the fourth *Starveil* film) appeared for a moment. Two men—Matt Spartan and someone who might have been Major Malloy—stood side by side, laughing in the foreground.

"Matt Spartan fought alongside me on Sardis. He saved my life, and I intend to do the same for him."

The on-screen image switched back to a rendering of the solar system, the major posed in front of it. He pointed to a glowing spot on the screen, and the map swirled in response.

"There are other people in the Rebellion—other troops and resistance fighters—who may have seen Captain Spartan . . ." More pointing, more points of light across the solar system. "These people have given us the first hints of his whereabouts. It is my utmost hope *you* are one of them.

"We need to take up Spartan's fight, no matter what the personal risk." The man glared into the camera, and the music's tempo shot up. "Join us!" he shouted. "Show us where you've seen Spartan alive. Tell us the rumors you've heard. And the Rebels will bring him back for you . . . alive!"

The #SpartanSurvived hashtag appeared, and the screen went black, music dying on its final pulse.

Xander burst into applause, the lacy cuffs of his shirt a blur. "Holy shitballs, Liv, that's motherfucking fantastic!"

Liv broke into a peal of laughter. "Jeez, Xander. You kiss your mom with that mouth?"

He grabbed her arm. "Can I use it in my acting portfolio? Can I? Please? Please! I've gotta use it!" His grin was contagious.

"Sure, I guess." Liv giggled. "Though you should know that all those scenes are ripped. I lifted them from the *Starveil* films, so it's not totally legal."

"So what? You made me look . . ." Xander shook his head. "Like a Hollywood heartthrob or something."

Liv burst into another peal of laughter, and he shoved her arm, his smile fading.

"Thanks for the vote of confidence."

"No, wait!" she choked, unable to breathe. "That's not what I mean at all, it's just . . ." She caught sight of Xander's face and the white collar starched beneath his chin. He looked so irritated and prim she couldn't stop. Giggles popped free from Liv's chest. "I can't—I meant—I—"

One brow lifted scornfully. "If this is supposed to be making me feel better, it's not working."

She pressed her hands to her mouth, chest quaking. "I'm sorry. Really I am."

He shook his head and looked away.

"Seriously, Xander. I'm not laughing at you." She caught hold of his arm. "I'm laughing because you just don't get it."

"No," he grumbled. "I don't."

Liv's giggles faded as she realized he wasn't exaggerating; he was upset. "I'm sorry, Xander. I was only laughing because you *are* that person. The Hollywood heartthrob look just gets lost under the lace and brocade."

He gave her a seething look.

"Don't get me wrong—I love it! Your stellar eighteenth-century fashion sense is fantastic."

"It's nineteenth century, actually," he sniffed.

"Fine, nineteenth." She looked down, realizing she was still clinging to his arm, and pulled back her hand. "But the problem is, most people don't appreciate it. I'm sorry I laughed before. It *wasn't* about you."

He waved away her words. "Nothing to be sorry for. I misunderstood." He tapped the laptop's screen. "Oh! And I'm definitely taking a copy of this for my drama portfolio."

Liv hit Send. "Just don't say I never helped you with your homework."

"Never." He hit Play again, and the music restarted. "But you're still going to help me sew the rest of my cosplay, right?"

Liv frowned. "But I thought it was just a new waistcoat."

"I've got another jacket I want to finish. Breeches, too. I need both of them by midterm."

Liv turned to Xander, just as he appeared on-screen. "Hey now. This cosplay's part of your upcoming costuming course, isn't it?!"

"Maybe. Maybe not. . . ." He smirked. "CU posts all course

outlines online now. You could get ahead on your projects, too, you know."

"But that means I'm doing your homework for you!" She crossed her arms. "No way!"

"You'll do it if you want an actor for your next vid," Xander drawled.

"You blackmailing bastard!"

Xander gave an enigmatic smile. "I prefer Major R. C. Malloy, Rebel leader."

⌣

The spring semester began with a rush of preparations. New classes meant new people, and new people meant anxiety. Liv spent her first day back on campus slumped in the back of the classroom, hoping her terrified silence passed for aloofness.

Her course load involved two postproduction classes that seemed interesting; a history of film class she'd taken with Xander, which ran two nights a week; a math class so redundant it felt like a rehash of high school; and one sociology class, which she utterly loathed. By the end of the first day, she was utterly exhausted by the effort to seem sociable when all she wanted to do was curl up at home and read fic. Interacting online was so much easier!

Liv's phone was out of power by the time she got home, but it began buzzing the moment she plugged it in. She glanced at the screen, brows rising in surprise.

@StarVeilBrian1981: @LivOutLoud GET ONTO THE STARVEIL WIKI NOW, LIV!!!

Liv tossed her bag onto the floor, slumping onto her bed and kicking off her shoes. She couldn't keep the smile from her face as she typed in a reply one-handed:

@LivOutLoud: @StarVeilBrian1981 Sure, Brian. Why?

She struggled out of her winter jacket, moving her phone—with its plug tether—from one hand to the other, then briefly getting it caught in her sleeve. By the time she untangled it, another message had appeared. Liv settled back onto the pillows of her bed, reading.

@StarVeilBrian1981: @LivOutLoud There's a video posted this time! It's bloody unbelievable! 1/2

@StarVeilBrian1981: @LivOutLoud Do you remember that clip I sent you of the cut scenes from SV 2? THAT WAS IN IT, I'm 99% sure. WATCH IT. WATCH IT NOW!!!!! 2/2

Liv's grin widened until her cheeks ached. She tapped an answer with shaking fingers.

@LivOutLoud: @StarVeilBrian1981 Looks pretty cool! So are you going to do a manip for it?

@StarVeilBrian1981: @LivOutLoud Are you kidding? I'VE DONE EIGHT OF THEM. Hold on.

@StarVeilBrian1981: @LivOutLoud This one's my fave.

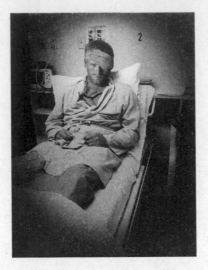

@LivOutLoud: @StarVeilBrian1981 LOL-that's awesome, Brian. :D Has @JoesWoes seen it?

@StarVeilBrian1981: @LivOutLoud @JoesWoes Seen it? She's already started a new #SpartanSurvived fic. She's using the manip as her fic header.

@LivOutLoud: @JoesWoes @StarVeilBrian1981 AWESOME!

@StarVeilBrian1981: @LivOutLoud So what are YOU doing for the rebellion?

@LivOutLoud: @StarVeilBrian1981 I'll think of something. ;)

Liv's gaze rose to the posters that covered her room's walls. In one, Spartan posed atop the ruins of Io. In another, he and Tekla stood back-to-back, blasters raised. *Yes,* she thought, *I'll definitely come up with something.* But first, Liv needed inspiration. She grabbed her laptop and turned it on.

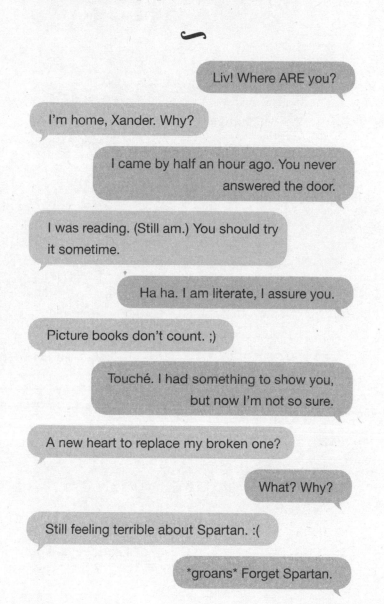

Liv! Where ARE you?

I'm home, Xander. Why?

I came by half an hour ago. You never answered the door.

I was reading. (Still am.) You should try it sometime.

Ha ha. I am literate, I assure you.

Picture books don't count. ;)

Touché. I had something to show you, but now I'm not so sure.

A new heart to replace my broken one?

What? Why?

Still feeling terrible about Spartan. :(

groans Forget Spartan.

Then what?

I found the right velvet for the smoking jacket. Amazing pile.

Pile?

Pile-as in the lushness of the fabric. (Do I need to pick up new needles for your machine?)

Not sure, Xander. I'd have to see it first.

Which is why I TRIED to stop by. Why didn't you answer the door?

Already told you: I was reading.

Yes, but WHAT, dearest?

I should probably show it, rather than explain.

Show? O_O

Definitely something I'll clear my history after. LOL

Oh! I'm intrigued!

It's er . . . a little NSFW.

This sounds delicious!

Let's just say I'm not used to thinking of you this way. ;P

Liiiiiiiivvv . . . stop torturing me and TELL ME what you found.

OMG OMG OMG-I can't do this by phone.

O_O I WANT DETAILS NOW.

LOL-Like what?

ALL OF THEM.

You may change your mind when you read it. But it makes me feel better. Oh god, I'm thinking about Spartan again. D: Seriously, X. I can't get past this.

Get on the bus. NOW. I want to read your story.

It's not my story. It's a friend's.

Fine, but I want to read it. Stop by Cup O' Joe. I'm off at 9.

I will, but you may regret it.

I only regret things I haven't done, Liv.

Not sure you've done this. ;)

You'll never know unless you ask me though, will you?

4

"SO SAY WE ALL!"
(BATTLESTAR GALACTICA)

When Liv arrived, Xander was waiting in one of the twin wingback chairs near the front door.

"My imagination is in overdrive," he said. "Where's the book?"

"It's not a book." She slid into the chair next to him. "It's a Spartan fic."

Xander's nose wrinkled as Liv pulled out her tablet and connected it to the café's Wi-Fi. She handed it to him.

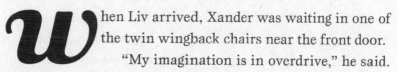

Title: **Shadow Soul**

Author: **JoesWoes**

Word Count: ~ 6,000 words

Primary Characters: **Spartan, Tekla, Malloy**

Pairing: **SparTek**

Rating: NC-17 for sexuality (NSFW)

Warning: Mentions of suicide, death, and war atrocities.

Tags: **#SpartanSurvived #SparTek #Malloy**
#ShadowSoul #Hurt/Comfort #JoesWoesFic

Xander looked up. "Your friend Joanne wrote this? Does she know about us? The vidding, I mean."

"Doesn't know a thing," Liv said. "She just writes because she's JoesWoes. She's been a fic writer since the very first *Starveil* movie. Joe's Internet famous."

"More famous than you are?"

"God yes! Or at least more than my LivOutLoud account for sure. I have my own group of followers, but I don't write, I vid. There just isn't the same following for that. Joe has thousands of people who wait for her every post."

"So she's one of the grande dames of fandom? The Madame de Staël of the *Starveil* world?" Xander teased.

"You could say that," Liv said. "Joe's been around forever. Everyone follows her. Though if I keep gaining followers with our vids, I think my SpartanSurvived account might give her a run for her money." Liv poked the tablet. "JoesWoes has more than five hundred Spartan fics."

"Five hundred," Xander muttered. "She's quite prolific."

"But this one's different. Joe never writes anything but canon. Never. But in this one she includes *your* character: Malloy. You're not actually in the movies, but if you've got JoesWoes writing about you, it *seems* like you are!"

"This feels . . ." Xander glanced back down. Summary: *Leaving the memories of the Fight for Io behind is harder than Spartan had believed. Malloy helps him come to terms with the horror.* "Really weird."

Liv snorted with laughter. "At least it's not RPF."

"You're speaking code, Liv."

"Real person fic . . . as in fic about *you*, Xander Hall, not the character you play." She broke into choking laughter as his eyes widened into saucers. "Joe's fic is much tamer. Promise."

Liv looked over at the counter. Two hipsters with matching beards were arguing over the last muffin in the tray. "You said you wanted to read the story, so read it. I'm gonna go grab myself a—"

"Already got it for you," Xander said, nudging a cup on the nearby coffee table. "Decaf latté, soy milk, whip on top rather than froth, right?"

"Exactly."

Liv grinned as Xander sank back into the chair's cushions, his attention on the screen. She could see part of the text and wondered if he'd stop at some point, suddenly realizing what he'd been dragged into.

Liv took a sip of latté, watching over the rim of the cup. Xander's lips moved when he read. Not like a little kid, she decided, but as she did when she was fighting to get a particularly difficult After Effects render to work. Liv wondered why she hadn't noticed before.

Ten minutes passed in silence. Liv emptied her cup as Xander scrolled the story a paragraph at a time. She could follow the progression of the story—one of Joe's angst-ridden best—by the jump and drop of Xander's eyebrows. The ending was dark, different from Joe's usual fare, but Liv loved it more than she could say. It also meant Xander as Malloy had just gone from an unknown actor to a living, breathing character in the *Starveil* saga. Liv knew Joe's stamp of approval would bring even more fans over to #SpartanSurvived.

Xander's brows disappeared into his hairline, and Liv giggled. He'd just reached *that* part.

He glanced up, catching her staring.

"So *this* is what you've been reading about me, hmmm?"

Liv looked down at her cup, hoping the café was dim enough to hide her flushed face. "Um . . . yeah."

"It's interesting." He leaned closer, eyes twinkling with mischief. "But, I can promise I've done all of this so far."

Her eyes jerked back up. "Wh-what?"

"I'm keeping a tally."

Her face heated up five degrees.

"Oh, Liv, my sweet innocent." Xander threw back his head and laughed. "You're blushing, dearest!"

"Am not!"

"Are too." He smirked. "Not saying I mind or anything, but I feel like you've been spying on me en déshabillé."

"If I've been spying on anyone, it'd be Malloy."

"And how did Malloy measure up to your dear Spartan?"

Now her cheeks were definitely on fire. In fact, her entire face felt like it was in flames. "I have history with Spartan," she said archly. "But you're holding your own."

"Good." Xander grinned. "Now give me a minute to finish this, shall we?"

Xander resumed reading, and Liv to watching. His teasing had left a residual flicker of awareness that hummed beneath her skin. Whom had she been rooting for when she'd read this fic? It may have been, Liv thought, Xander's Malloy, not Spartan after all.

"Oh dear," Xander muttered. He didn't look up.

He scrolled the fic higher, eyes flickering. Liv's fingers tightened around the cup, waiting for the moment when he realized Malloy—his character—wasn't just caught in the battle, he was already dead. She'd read it this morning and had spent twenty minutes fixing her teary mascara because of it. Hurt-comfort fic was her favorite. Somehow imagining Xander as Malloy made it more poignant.

Liv took another sip, watching Xander unawares. He was glued to the screen, eyes scanning. A muscle jumped in his jaw, and Liv wondered if he was reading the final scenes.

Xander looked up so quickly it startled her. He was breathing fast, his cheeks utterly white except for two bright dots of color.

"Holy shit," he said with a nervous laugh. His gaze skittered to the screen and back up. "She—She killed me."

"Not *you*, exactly. She killed Malloy."

"Yeah, but . . ." He ran his fingers through his hair. Tufts of it stood on end, so different from his usual smooth coiffure. "That's a messed-up fic, Liv. Sheesh! Like watching a horror movie in reverse and finding out it's actually about you." He shuddered. "I'm going to have nightmares about that."

Liv snorted. "Hurt-comfort fic is big in the *Starveil* fandom. Spartan loses his best friend, but Tekla gets to ease his pain." She took another sip of her latté. "It's got over five thousand hits and six hundred kudos already. Joe's one of the most popular *Starveil* writers around. And she just made *you* Spartan's best friend."

For a moment, she thought Xander would argue about it or, worse yet, refuse to take his place in the second trailer she was planning. Instead, his face split into a wide grin. With his hair askew, he looked every bit the Rebel leader she'd imagined.

"Five thousand hits?!"

"And that's only one fic," Liv said. "There are new stories

posted every day on the Spartan Survived tag." A mischievous smile spread over her lips. "You're more popular than some of the canon characters."

"I'm a star!" Xander crowed. "A real one!"

Liv tipped her cup toward him. "I'll drink to that."

Xander leaned back, steepling his hands on his chest. With hair rumpled and cravat loose, he looked like an English lord thinking about colonial domination. All he needed was a ship and a flag.

"So what's our next move?" he asked.

"Next, we finish sewing your drinking jacket—"

"Smoking jacket," Xander corrected.

"—and then I have a little cosplay project of my own." When Liv's mother had insisted Liv learn how to mend her own clothes, it had been an embarrassment rather than a lesson in frugality. Today, being a seamstress felt like a secret superpower few people Liv's age possessed.

"Cosplay?" His eyes skimmed down her body. "Do tell."

"Not for me. For you!"

"Pity . . . you'd be a sight. I'll get you into a costume sometime, you know."

"Sometime will be sometime *later*." She giggled. "This one's for you."

"Do tell."

Liv tapped the tablet's screen. "If you're leading the search mission for Spartan, you're going to need a freighter captain's uniform. Any dark pants you have will do, but the jacket needs to be handmade."

"Do you have pictures to work from?"

"Better than that. SpartanGrrl has a pattern she bought

70

at an online auction. She sent me JPEGs last year." Liv drummed her fingers on the arm of the couch. "But are *you* going to do your part, too?"

Xander smirked. He doubled over in the leather chair, performing a courtly bow, made awkward by the fact he was already sitting.

"At your disposal, madam," he said in his BBC drawl. "I shall be honored to cut and pin and act as haberdasher, if you're willing to serve as seamstress."

"Seems fair."

Xander grinned. "Don't say I didn't help you with any of *your* homework."

~

The first weeks of January spun past before Liv realized it. She hadn't considered the sheer amount of time that an online revolution would require, and now every minute of every day was eaten away by obligations, every night by vidding. Any free time was spent replying to posts and building excitement online, all the rest taken up by schoolwork. She lived, ate, and breathed *Starveil*.

Even Xander noticed her distraction.

"I can't believe you're bailing on Mickey Dee's. Who am I supposed to share trans fats and fandom woes with? My blue card still hasn't shown up from Dragon Con yet. I'm getting anxious!"

Liv barely looked up from her computer. She had a @SpartanSurvived Twitter account to maintain!

"Sorry," she muttered. "You want to get food?"

Xander's hands rose to his hips. "That's what I just said!"

"But it's not even . . ." She squinted at the time on her computer. "Whoa! It's ten thirty. When'd that happen?"

"You've been online for hours." He twirled his pocket watch. "C'mon, Liv. For me. I *need* fries. They're an addiction."

"Why don't you take Arden?"

"Arden's working," he said in a melancholy tone. "Besides, she hates fried food. And I want to go with *you*." He knelt beside her chair, hand over heart. "My dear, sweet Miss Walden, I hope you will excuse the liberty I take in interrupting your vidding, but I know our bosom friendship will excuse any faults in my character." He fluttered his lashes. "Please, Liv? I need fries. Please, please, please, please?"

"Fine," Liv sighed. "Five more minutes, and I'll come."

He flashed a winning smile. "It's a deal."

Xander wasn't the only one to notice Liv's change of schedule. Late-night vidding began to compete with family obligations, too. Takeout became the rule. Her mother seemed determined to hold Liv to her promise of a movie night; and when Liv swore she didn't have time to go out and see one, Katherine found an oldie station playing *Gone with the Wind*.

"We've seen that movie a hundred times, Mom."

"Exactly. It's our 'thing,' Liv. A mother-daughter tradition."

"Not tonight, okay?"

"Fine. I suppose you have better things to do." Her mother sighed as she headed to the kitchen.

"Mo-om," Liv groaned. She hated it when her mother guilted her into doing things. "I've got to film some new clips, but Xander can only come over tonight. He's working the rest of the week."

Her mom stopped in the doorway and turned back

around, mouth half-open. She looked like she'd just noticed something expensive in a store window. The glitter in her eyes was unnerving.

"You two have been spending a lot of time together. Is there something . . . ?" Her mother let the unspoken question hang in the air, and Liv felt her face light on fire.

"Oh God, no. No! Jeez, Mom. There's nothing between us."

"You certain? Because it doesn't look like nothing to me."

"Xander has a girlfriend."

Her mother put her hands on her hips. "A friend who's also a girl, or one who he dates?"

"That he dates."

"Well, it can't be very serious then. I mean, you two spend almost every minute of the day together."

Liv scrambled for a way to explain. "Xander's helping me with a video project."

Her mother's face fell. "And you need to finish filming it."

"And editing, and postproduction, and sound checks. I've got a lot to do. It's a project for my film class," she lied. "I have an extension to the end of the week."

Her mother wilted. "You better finish it up then."

Liv tamped down her guilt and forced a bright smile. "Thanks for understanding."

"I do," she said. "And I'm glad to see you're doing better, Liv. You look . . . happy again."

"I am."

"And," her mother added, "you're focused on school again. That's so good to see."

Liv forced her smile not to waver.

"Thanks."

The anticipation building online more than made up for the

lack of sleep. A month into the project, hundreds of posts were coming in each day. Some of them had even been retweeted by a few of the secondary cast members of the *Starveil* franchise. (Tom Grander hadn't mentioned it once. Liv knew; she'd been watching his online feed for weeks.) Nonetheless, Liv was certain the revolution had begun to have an effect, for each new day meant more buzz for the *Starveil* fandom. When Liv was finishing the tailored breeches for Xander's latest cosplay (and Xander's costuming project), Joanne sent Liv an online article that speculated the *Starveil* stars themselves were the forces behind the #SpartanSurvived movement.

@JoesWoes: @LivOutLoud Do you think it's true?

@LivOutLoud: @JoesWoes Do I think WHAT is true?

@JoesWoes: @LivOutLoud That it's Tom Grander behind #SpartanSurvived. That he's trying to raise himself from the dead!!! Wouldn't that be AMAZING?

@LivOutLoud: @JoesWoes But it's not really Tom Grander who is dead, Joe. It's his character, Spartan. #GetYourFactsStraight

@JoesWoes: @LivOutLoud Fine, Liv-but do you think it's HIM doing it? OMG could you imagine Tom reading my fanfic??? I'd die, Liv!!!! Literally, DIE.

Liv giggled at the reply. For a second, she considered telling Joe the truth—they'd been fandom friends for years—but Liv had kept the ruse up for so long, it felt like she'd be undermining #SpartanSurvived if she did. This was real because fandom *believed* it was. She couldn't risk the success of it now.

@LivOutLoud: @JoesWoes Trust me. Tom Grander has nothing to do with this.

@JoesWoes: @LivOutLoud Bet you ten bucks you're wrong.

@LivOutLoud: @JoesWoes Ten dollars? You got a deal. ;P

❧

"You're going to the CU Mixer," Xander insisted.

"Am not."

"Are too."

"Xander," Liv warned.

"We've been back in classes for a month. How many times have you gone out in that time?"

She stuck out her tongue rather than answer.

"Exactly." He threw open the doors of her closet and reached inside. "Enough of the hermit act. You're coming dancing with me."

"But I'm reading."

"You mean moping." He peered back over his shoulder. "Don't think I can't tell the difference."

"Difference?"

"You're pining for someone who isn't real, dearest. That worries me."

"I'm not pining, I'm . . ." Liv wanted to laugh, or cry. (Or both, she thought dismally.)

"I don't like seeing you like this." If he wasn't at that exact moment rummaging through her wardrobe, Xander's concern would have been touching.

"I can't help it. I miss Spartan. And masterminding a revolution is a time-suck."

"Exactly." Xander nodded as if a decision had been made. "And a dose of reality is in order."

"This advice from a college freshman carrying a cane?"

"It's a walking stick, I'll have you know."

"Same difference."

"Hardly. It's fashion. Now, get ready. I'm taking you out."

Liv groaned as Xander pushed his way into the overfull closet. T-shirts and jeans tumbled to the floor. "Sweet Jesus, Liv," he sighed from the depths. "You realize this is a fire hazard, right?"

Liv peeked out from behind her laptop long enough to glare at him.

"Honestly, dearest, where are your dresses? Your heels? A body as lovely as yours requires adornment."

"Don't own any," she grumbled, sinking lower in her bed. She'd been in an unpleasant mood all day, and Xander wasn't helping. His impromptu makeover was making her feel like a freak.

"But you can't go out in a T-shirt and jeans. You're partying, not housecleaning!"

"I'm not doing either," Liv argued, but Xander talked right over her.

"You need sparkle. Dancing demands it!"

"If I looked like a stick, I'd wear something nice, but big breasts make it hard to dress up."

A slinky black T-shirt she'd worn once then hidden away hit her in the face. "Pfft! Your figure's perfect."

"Not perfect for this century." She wadded the shirt into a ball and whipped it back at Xander, hitting him in the head. He paused next to the mirror, smoothing his pomaded hair.

"I think you're beautiful."

Liv's catty retort died on her tongue. "Y-you do?"

"Yes, of course I do," Xander said, his reflection winking at her. "You ever seen the painting of Madame X?"

"I don't think—"

"That's you to a tee, Liv." He picked the shirt off the floor and tossed it back at her. "Now move. It's almost eleven, and I promised Arden we'd be at the club half an hour ago."

"Arden's coming, too?" Liv hated feeling like a third wheel.

"Uh-huh. She's probably already there." He disappeared entirely, and his voice came from the layers of fabric. "Should be lots of fun . . . dancing's always a good idea, and you need a break from the computer. . . ."

Liv looked at the screen. *Five hundred reblogs.* Her e-mail was clogged with replies, but tonight the thought of it made her sad. So many people missed Spartan. She turned off the notifications.

From the closet came a shout of triumph; Liv looked up just as the wall of clothing surged and Xander burst from between the folds, dragging what looked like a shimmering silver face-cloth. He held it victoriously aloft.

"A skirt! You've been holding out on me."

Liv stared at it in confusion. She could vaguely remember

the sparkly sequined miniskirt from some foggy middle school dance, which Liv had spent hiding in the washroom, overcome by anxiety. She hadn't worn it in years. The skirt was far too small, the hem far too high.

"Uh-uh," Liv said, pushing her computer off her lap and onto the bed. "No way. I'll never get in it."

Xander crossed his arms, the skirt dangling from his fingers. His jaw was clenched. "I'm not going out with someone dressed like my eight-year-old brother. Just try it on before you decide."

"And if I refuse?"

"I'll remind you that you owe me one." A devilish smile curled his lips, his shock of dark hair and white shirt channeling mad, bad Lord Byron. "*More* than one, if you're serious about filming another video."

Liv snapped the laptop closed. "Fine."

With a laugh, Xander dropped the skirt on the bed and stepped outside. "I await your return."

⌣

Liv stood in front of the narrow mirror, frowning at her reflection. Long brown hair that hung smooth and flat, a body too curvy for her own comfort, and a face so average as to be bland. The shirt was okay, but the skirt left far more of her legs showing than she felt comfortable with. Tears welled, blurring her vision.

"Wrong century, that's for damned sure."

"Liv," Xander called from the hallway. "Can I see?"

The line between her brows grew deeper. If it were anyone

else, she'd have said no, but Xander was Xander. Ever since their first CU class together, when they'd been two outcasts, they'd clung to each other for comfort. Where most people made Liv feel weird, Xander was strange enough in his own right that she felt like the normal one.

"Nothing to see," she snapped. "I'm not going dancing."

The door opened a crack. "Are you decent?"

Liv laughed. "Keep talking like that and you're really going to get my mom's imagination going." She tugged at the skirt, inching it lower. "Yeah, come on in."

Xander crept back inside, his eyes widening.

"Oh God," Liv groaned. "I told you I didn't—"

"It's perfect!" He grinned as he inspected the outfit from one direction, then the other, nodding to himself. "I knew, of course, but to finally see you out of your T-shirt-and-jean cocoon is quite refreshing."

"So you like it?"

Xander's eyes caught hers in the mirror. "Of course I do! Good lord, Liv," he said with a snort. "I wouldn't have suggested it if I didn't. This is hardly daring, but it's a start!"

"I dunno, Xander. . . ."

His hands rose to his hips. "You don't know what?"

She chewed her lower lip, staring uncertainly at the not-this-century woman in the mirror. The clothes fit, but there was so much skin. "I don't know about this. I feel . . . exposed."

Xander's laughter suddenly faded. "Oh, Liv," he said gently. "I'm so sorry I've upset you. I didn't realize—"

"It's not you; it's me." She let out a tired laugh. "I just don't know how to *be* this."

She could feel tears threatening to fall, her image in the

mirror blurring. Xander stepped up next to her. She expected him to make a joke, but his words were quiet and sincere.

"You're breathtaking. Seriously, Liv. Absolutely beautiful." His vowels had softened, the nervous inflection slipping back into the conversation. "Truly, dearest, you are."

"Thanks. I needed to hear that." Liv grabbed her jacket off the bed and forced a smile. "Now, if we're going to the mixer, then let's go before I change my mind."

Xander swung open the door and bowed. "After you, m'lady."

﹏

Breathtaking.

That was the word, Liv decided, that had persuaded her to wear the ludicrous outfit, because no one—not the one, solitary boyfriend she'd had during high school, or the leering frat boys she avoided at college parties—had ever spoken to her with such reverence. Although her mother's borrowed heels made her as unwieldy as a newborn moose calf, with Xander beaming down at her, she *did* feel beautiful. Hopefully she could make it through the night without breaking her neck.

By the time they'd arrived, Arden was gone. She'd stepped out for only a minute, Arden's friends assured Xander. But when she didn't return his first, second, or fifth texts, the truth became clear. She'd bailed on them for being late. Xander had looked so let down by his girlfriend's abandonment that Liv had finally asked him to dance.

"Like dance here . . . ?" Xander asked. "For real?"

"Yes, for real," Liv snorted. "I wouldn't have asked you otherwise."

"I know, but—"

"But what?" she asked defensively.

He grinned. "I'm just surprised you dance. I thought it was against your religion or something."

Liv laughed. "Philosophy, yes. Religion, no." She shoved him toward the dance floor. "Now hurry up before I change my mind."

He grabbed her hand. "Not a chance."

Xander's obsessing over nineteenth-century fabrics was the person Liv knew; Xander's breaking it out to the latest alternative-rock song was a sight to behold. Liv couldn't help but giggle as he tugged her out with him song after song, grinding to the beat, while the press of partyers grew into a mob. They were completely mismatched—Liv in her silver skirt and black tee, and Xander in his nineteenth-century garb— but she didn't care. She floated on a bubble of pleasure. This *had* been a good idea (though she'd die before she admitted that), and the gloom that had hung over her since Spartan's final moments seemed to fade.

Xander grinned and said something, but it was lost under the thudding bass.

"What?!" Liv shouted.

"Are you having fun yet?!"

"Absolutely!"

"Good!"

He grabbed her hand and spun her in a circle, the two of them laughing aloud as the song reached a fever pitch. Liv was smiling so hard her cheeks hurt. She couldn't remember the last time she'd felt so alive, so happy, so—

"Xander! Liv!" a familiar voice called. "I've been looking all over for you!"

Xander's face broke into an even-wider grin. "Arden!" He laughed. "The prodigal girlfriend has arrived!"

"My roommate lost her keys," she said with a shake of her head. "Just got back. Sorry for ditching."

"No problem," Liv mumbled.

Arden grinned at Liv before turning to Xander. Her hand slid possessively up his chest. "You ready to dance?"

Xander slipped into her embrace, Liv forgotten at the side. "Of course, m'lady." He leaned closer. "You look utterly ravishing, you know that?"

"Mmm . . . thank you." Arden pressed a kiss to his mouth. "You do, too."

Liv turned away. She really wished they would wait until they were alone to do stuff like that. She had no idea where she was supposed to *look* when they were wrapped in each other's arms.

She scanned the room. There were numerous acquaintances, but no one she felt comfortable enough to talk to. Without Xander at her side, she was lost. She dropped her gaze to the floor, her eyes catching on the silver miniskirt. There was no way she was spending *another* night sitting in a bathroom in this outfit.

She tried to pick up the rhythm of the music. (Girls could dance alone, couldn't they?) But the motion of her body— supple seconds earlier—had grown wooden. The jerky bouncing finally disappeared altogether, and she stood alone, jostled by the sea of moving bodies. She peeked over at Xander and Arden. They moved as one, pressed together from hip to chest.

Liv stumbled as someone slammed unceremoniously into her back. She turned to find another couple pushing into her space. The man's elbows and kneecaps were moving targets, and Liv jumped back as his heel grazed her shin.

"And . . . I'm done," she growled. A wall of college students blocked her way. "Excuse me," Liv grumbled as she wobbled off the dance floor. "I need to get past."

A laughing young man with a bottle in hand stepped in front of her. He bumped her shoulder, and beer slopped onto her arm.

"Watch out!" she snapped.

"Hey, no harm, no foul." He laughed as he continued on by, followed by a throng of girls.

"Excuse *you*," Liv said, stepping around them.

It felt like wading upstream, and the crowd grew with each step. She reached the edge of the dance floor. Now she was caught between tables and leering frat boys who thought nothing of ignoring her face to admire her bosom. Liv crossed her arms and walked faster, pushing her way through the ever-thickening mob. The whole outfit was a nightmare.

"Excuse me, pardon me. Coming through." Her jaw clenched. "Move!"

Finally, she reached a wall. She leaned against it, panting. Her eyes roamed the room. No friends, just "others" who filled the classes she attended. Her gaze returned guiltily to the dance floor. Xander shone like a beacon: an out-of-time character in a sea of nameless extras. As Liv watched, he swept Arden across the floor. She threw her arms over his shoulders, pulling him down to meet her lips. Liv couldn't look away. The embrace could have been from an old Hollywood movie. Xander dipped Arden low, her hair a waterfall of silver draping over his arm to brush the floor.

With a resigned sigh, Liv looked away. She plodded to the coat check to retrieve her coat and purse, then stepped outside. It was snowing again.

"Just my luck."

The cold settled into her limbs as she stomped her way to the bus stop, her mood dropping with the degrees. There was only one thing that could match her emotions: *Starveil Five*.

5

"THIS IS MY TIMEY-WIMEY DETECTOR. IT GOES DING WHEN THERE'S STUFF."
(DOCTOR WHO)

*I*t was three a.m., but Liv couldn't sleep. She dabbed tears from her eyes and restarted the streaming vid. The *Starveil* theme rose, the opening sequence appearing amid a barrage of music. Spartan appeared, grinning broadly at the camera. Seeing him, her sobs redoubled, fresh tears tumbling down her cheeks. If she could just go back to this moment when she'd seen it in the theater, she could believe it would all be okay. But she *knew* how it ended. How Spartan died. The pain was unbearable, and yet she couldn't stop watching.

She hit Pause, then grabbed a wad of tissues to blow her nose. She reached to hit Play at the same time her phone buzzed. She frowned as she read the screen.

Liv-you around?

Yes. Why?

Goodness! I thought you'd run off with someone. (Not that I disapprove of that behavior at all! ;)

I went home early.

Oh, Liv . . . :(I'm so sorry for abandoning you when Arden arrived. I am a terrible friend.

It's fine, Xander. You have a gf. I get that.

It's not fine. It's the behavior of a cad. (I do hope you're willing to ignore my reprobate character in view of my other attributes.)

Your character is just fine.

I do wish you hadn't left. I thought you were having a good time. (Weren't you?)

I was . . . and then I wasn't. Sorry. You're probably busy with Arden right now. I'll let you go.

Arden's already home. (She works in the morning.)

. . .

Liiiiiiv. What's wrong, dearest?

Nothing.

Not true. I can hear it in your voice.

Text.

Same difference. :) Seriously, though. Are you okay?

Not really.

Liv, is this about me forcing you to wear the skirt? *WHICH YOU LOOKED AMAZING IN* I apologize. But I don't regret it. You enchanted the masses.

Not about that.

Was it Arden's PDA?

Er . . . not really.

Good. Because I've kissed my fair share of girls and boys before. It shouldn't be a big deal.

Boys?

Yes, boys.

Really?

A few. Why?

Um, I just didn't realize . . .

Liiiiiiiv, you know I'm bi. I told you that when we met.

Yes, of course. I forgot. That's cool, Xander. It is.

And Arden's rather . . . demonstrative. ;)

Agreed. But that's not it.

Didn't think so. Do go on.

Nothing important.

It's you, so it is important. Tell me everything.

It's nothing.

It's not.

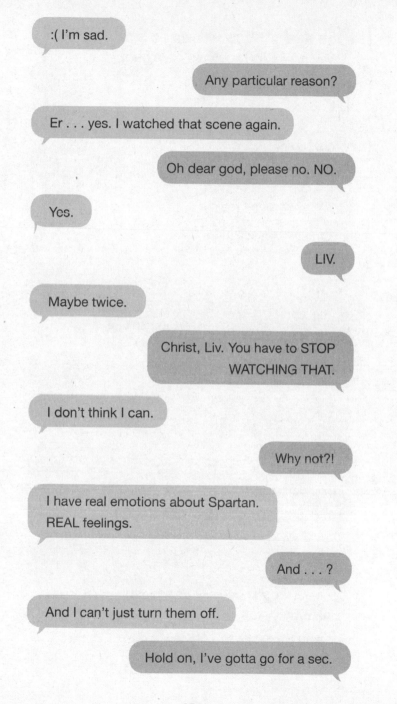

:(I'm sad.

Any particular reason?

Er . . . yes. I watched that scene again.

Oh dear god, please no. NO.

Yes.

LIV.

Maybe twice.

Christ, Liv. You have to STOP WATCHING THAT.

I don't think I can.

Why not?!

I have real emotions about Spartan. REAL feelings.

And . . . ?

And I can't just turn them off.

Hold on, I've gotta go for a sec.

I'm starting SV5 now. I'm going to watch for a while before I go to sleep.

Are you back yet?

Xander? You still there?

I'm sorry. I shouldn't be texting so late.

Talk to you tomorrow?

:(((((

Alright I'm going to say goodnight, X. Sorry if this was too weird. I just needed someone to talk to. I shouldn't have vented.

It's fine, Liv. Relax, dearest.

God! I thought you were mad at me.

At you? Never.

Shit!

What?

Nothing. Forget it. It's too late. I'm ignoring it.

Go answer.

What?

Someone's at your door. Go.

Wait. Hey-how did you know that?

Because it's ME, Sherlock. Now hurry up. It's bloody cold out here.

WTF?

Grab a coat. We're going to do something OTHER than rewatching Starveil 5. Now, get dressed. Please. For me, dearest.

Okay.;)

Seriously, L. I'm freezing. Answer the goddamned door.

Hold on. I'm dressing. Where are we going exactly?

Mickey Dee's has a 24 hour drive through. It's 4:00 a.m. and I want fries.

LOLOL On my way.

\o/ *and the villagers rejoiced* \o/

Mid-February brought an explosion of work. Although Liv's life revolved around Spartan's survival, the universe seemed indifferent to the amount of work on her plate. Her sociology professor believed in research. Not doing it per se, just digesting it. Liv had never read such tiresome articles. And it was for this reason alone, she assured herself, that as midterms neared, she'd started to make small talk with the people around her. . . . A behavior decidedly *not* her norm.

Liv wasn't good at making friends. (Not in real life at least.) But in sociology the blond guy with the plaid jacket and the "Save the Trees" button walked up to her when the professor forced them to work in groups to dissect yet another theory on social status. Seeing the man's hiking boots and broken-down jeans, *granola* was the first word that went through her mind. But as soon as he looked up, another word replaced it: *Spartan!* The man could've been his twin.

"Great to meet ya," Granola said cheerfully. "I'm Hank." He held out his hand and gave her a blinding grin. He was so blond, his teeth so white and even, Liv was momentarily stunned. He really *could* be Spartan's taller, younger brother. The thought left her breathless.

She gave his hand a cursory shake. The toothpaste-ad smile carried on and on. He'd definitely had braces at some point, Liv decided. And maybe highlights, too. You weren't just *born* looking like that. Were you?

"Sorry, I never caught your name," Granola said. If he wasn't staring right at her, she would have assumed he was talking to someone else.

"Oh, right. I'm L-Liv," she stammered.

"As in Olivia?"

"No, Liv. Just Liv." The floor didn't open up and swallow her, but she wished it would.

"Well, it's great to meet you, Just Liv," he said with another enthusiastic nod. He pulled out the chair next to him and tossed his bag onto the floor. "Grab a seat!"

His bag, Liv noted, had a TAKE ONLY PHOTOS, LEAVE ONLY FOOTPRINTS sticker on the side. Liv rolled her eyes and wondered what sarcastic comment Xander would come up with if he saw *her* wearing it.

Granola leaned in, and Liv automatically recoiled. It was a natural reaction. People who looked like him didn't talk to people like her. But Granola didn't seem to notice. "Looks like we're stuck together for the next while," he said in a stage whisper. "Hope that's okay with you, Liv." He winked, but unlike Xander, it didn't feel like a punch line. This time it felt like flirting.

Liv peered over her shoulder. No one else there.

She turned back.

"Do I have a choice?" She winced at the sharpness of her tone.

"Probably not. Profs like this like being in control." Another grin. "We could do sociological research on them." He laughed at his own joke, and Liv smiled warily.

"Um . . . yeah. But I don't think she'd sign off on it. Ethics and all that."

"Probably not, but if she did, she'd assign it as reading to her next class."

"Of course she would," Liv snorted.

Granola leaned forward, pointing his pencil toward the professor, who was handing out photocopies of the assignment. "Here we can observe the common Colorado professor, genus *Academia professorantus* in her natural environment," he whispered. "She gathers her clippings the way animals gather twigs for a nest, sharing them with dogged determination."

Usually, Liv ignored people, but Hank's outgoing nature broke through her sense of self-preservation. By the time the papers were spread throughout the classroom, Liv was the one grinning as Hank made jokes. As impossible as it seemed, his smile had even grown by a few kilowatts until his face practically glowed.

"I'll carry my share," he added as the professor started up the projector. "Don't you worry. I'm not a slacker."

"I didn't think you were."

94

"Wasn't sure. You never talk to anyone in class." He grinned again. Perhaps, Liv thought, there were some people who just didn't know how to be awkward. She definitely wasn't one of them. "You just seem really focused."

"About some things, I guess."

"I love sociology," he said. "Want to be a social worker someday, or maybe do some volunteer work overseas. You know. Change the world. How about you?"

"I—I . . ." But other than her occasional daydream of escaping the doldrums of Colorado, the only answer that came to mind was her #SpartanSurvived project, and there was no way she was going to admit to that. "I'm a freshman, so right now I'm just trying to get through the year without a meltdown."

"Fair enough. But what gets you riled up? What's your passion? Your dream?"

"I don't . . ." Liv felt her cheeks begin to burn. She had no idea how to talk to strangers without a tech interface. She was 100 percent sure Granola did *not* follow the *Starveil* story line, and that made her feel even more exposed. "I've never really thought about it," she answered lamely.

"But there have to be things that get you going," Granola prompted. "The arts? Human rights? Feminism?"

Liv was saved by the professor starting her presentation. The lights in the classroom dimmed in response, and then all Liv could see was Hank's smile, a Cheshire cat in the darkness.

"Tell me when you think of it," he whispered. "I'd love to hear."

"Okay," Liv choked.

The half circle of his smile grew dim and then faded altogether as the professor started to speak. Liv lifted her pen, ready for notes. Her mind buzzed. What *was* she passionate about, other than *Starveil*?

Someday she'd have an answer for Hank, but it certainly wasn't today.

ᕙ

The semester slowly crawled past. Sociology became the class Liv looked forward to the most (subject matter notwithstanding). It was clear Liv's inability to come up with a "defining passion"—or one she could admit to—wasn't going to be an issue. Hank was passionate about everything. And that left her out of sorts. She found herself doing bizarre things: giggling like a moron when he made a joke, touching his arm for no apparent reason, walking with him to the student union building during break to grab coffee, and, worse yet, dreaming about him at night. Hormones, it seemed, were making a much-delayed appearance in her life.

Liv was horrified.

"My brain is making me crazy," she told Xander after their Wednesday-night film class. They'd watched *Nosferatu*, and Liv felt sympathy for the vampire in the film, at the mercy of his uncontrollable bloodlust. "I just need it to stop overthinking everything. To just turn off and chill about things."

"Is this about Spartan again?" Xander groaned. "I thought you'd dealt with that, Liv."

He wore tails tonight, and he slid on the silk jacket slowly, smoothing it over his chest. Liv, with her oversize parka and long knit scarf, felt like a hobo next to his old-world perfection, no matter how many odd looks passersby gave him.

"I wish it was. This is something else." They walked down the hallway side by side, the rush of students moving past in a steady stream. "I think I've got a . . . fixation."

Xander raised a brow. "Opium, I hope."

She swatted him with the end of her scarf. "Hardly, I—"

"Cocaine perhaps? No, wait! Absinthe. It has to be absinthe." They reached the door, and he tugged it open, a blast of icy mountain air hitting Liv in the face. "All the best delinquents—and nineteenth-century artists—are drinking it."

"Stop it, Xander." She burrowed her nose into her scarf as they headed out into the winter night. "I'm, well, I'm . . ." She stole a nervous look at him. "Obsessing over a boy."

Xander grinned. "Liv, dearest, Spartan has been my dear companion for these many long months—"

"It's *not* Spartan."

His eyes widened. "Really?"

"Yes, really."

His pace didn't slow, but his smile faded until he stared at her in apparent confusion. "As in a *real-life* boy? Like . . . a live one."

"Flesh and blood."

He tapped a gloved finger against his lips. "Will wonders never cease."

Cheeks burning, she punched his shoulder rather than answer. "Careful of the jacket," he tutted. "It's raw silk, dearest. The fabric alone cost me a month of tips."

"You're not funny, Xander."

"I am, but that aside, I'm . . . Well, I suppose I'm a bit surprised."

Liv glared at him. "Why?"

"Because you've never been attracted to anyone who wasn't fictional before." He smirked. "So what happened?"

"Nothing."

He raised an eyebrow.

"Honestly. There's nothing to tell."

"Liar."

"Okay, there's a little bit to tell, but not much."

"I don't care how little," Xander said, waving her concerns away. "I want to know what's happening."

By the time they reached the end of the parking lot, she'd done a recap of the sociology project, and late-night work on Bristol board, and Hank's obsession with double-checking references, and his summer volunteering for an equal-pay-for-equal-work focus group. Xander seemed a little quieter than usual—certainly not his usual outgoing self—but Liv was relieved to have him to confide in. She just wished she knew what he was thinking.

"I've never had a serious boyfriend," Liv sighed. "I mean I dated one guy when I was in high school, but that was different. It was just a teen thing. We hardly even kissed, never mind did anything else."

Xander stared at her. "Are you joking?"

"No. He just . . ." Liv squirmed. "I don't know. He didn't seem interested."

"Mmph. Too bad for him."

"But this thing with Hank feels just different, you know? Like it might go somewhere."

Xander opened the passenger door for Liv before heading to the driver's side and climbing into the frozen car. He started the engine. It whined and moaned, the two of them forced to sit in the icebox while the fan struggled to spread heat through the air. For a long time, Xander stared out the window, frowning.

"I know you're thinking something," Liv said. "So you might as well say it."

Xander rubbed his gloved hands rather than look at her. "I'm not actually."

"You are."

He didn't answer.

"So . . . what would you do?" Liv asked.

"You should do whatever you want."

"But what if you were me?" Liv said. "What would you do then?"

Xander sighed. "I suppose I'd probably ask him out."

"But I can't do that!" Liv gasped. "Dating's stressful. I'd have to dress up."

Xander gave an exaggerated sigh as he popped the car into drive and eased it onto the snowy streets. "My dear Liv, I've dated plenty, and I honestly think it comes down to mind over matter."

"Please don't give me that stupid 'if it doesn't mind, then it doesn't matter' line."

Xander chuckled. "I don't think that particularly applies to dating. You *should* mind what someone does. But you shouldn't let your fear stop you." He slowed for a passing truck, then turned off campus and onto the main drive. "If I never went onstage when I was scared, I'd never act. If I never asked someone out if I thought they'd say no, I'd always be alone." He nudged her with his elbow, though his eyes stayed on the road. "If I never trusted you could make me into an Internet sensation, I'd never be the star of a YouTube video with half a million hits."

Liv sighed. "I just . . . I don't think I can."

"It's up to you whether you want to try or not, but you've got to decide what you want from life. You're a freshman. You should be living a bit." He grinned. "Granola sounds nice, albeit a bit boring."

"I should never have told you that nickname," she grumbled.

"I think it's a lovely nickname." He laughed. "Fitting even."

"Xander . . . that's just mean."

He snorted rather than answering.

Liv stared out the window as they drove. Xander was an actor. It was easy for him. But the thought of asking Hank out left her panicked.

Xander cleared his throat, drawing Liv back to the present. "What's on your mind, Liv?"

"What if I ask him and he says no?"

"He'd be stupid to do that." Xander patted her hand. A tiny gesture, but it nearly brought her to tears. "Trust me. It'll work out."

"How do you know?"

His smile faded into something softer. *Sadder*, Liv thought afterward.

"Because you deserve to be happy," he said quietly, and then the light changed, and they drove on. Just the two of them, one warm car, in an endless swath of night.

"Maybe," Liv whispered.

6

"MY 'PEOPLE SKILLS' ARE 'RUSTY.'"
(*SUPERNATURAL*)

@StarVeilBrian1981: @LivOutLoud Have you heard the news, Liv?

@LivOutLoud: @StarVeilBrian1981 News?

@StarVeilBrian1981: @LivOutLoud There's a rumor #SpartanSurvived isn't Grander at all. It's MRM!

@LivOutLoud: @StarVeilBrian1981 Doubt it, Brian.

@StarVeilBrian1981: @LivOutLoud But what better way to prop up a sagging fandom? It's the perfect plan to create a surge of popularity!

@LivOutLoud: @StarVeilBrian1981 It's a good theory. I just don't think that's it.

@JoesWoes: @LivOutLoud @StarVeilBrian1981 I'm with Brian on this.

@LivOutLoud: @JoesWoes @StarVeilBrian1981 Maybe . . . maybe not. ;)

@JoesWoes: @LivOutLoud I think MRM killed Spartan on purpose, then started #SpartanSurvived. Think about it-fandom's together like it never was before.

@StarVeilBrian1981: @JoesWoes @LivOutLoud Only one way to know for sure.

@LivOutLoud: @JoesWoes @StarVeilBrian1981 And that is?

@StarVeilBrian1981: @JoesWoes @LivOutLoud Have to ask him personally.

@LivOutLoud: @JoesWoes @StarVeilBrian1981 Well, I don't live in LA, so that's not an option.

@JoesWoes: @LivOutLoud @StarVeilBrian1981 Neither do I, but that's not the only place you can talk to MRM.

@StarVeilBrian1981: @JoesWoes @LivOutLoud You still thinking about this summer, Joe?

@JoesWoes: @StarVeilBrian1981 @LivOutLoud Better than thinking. I'm saving for it! Liv, you should think about coming too.

@LivOutLoud: @JoesWoes @StarVeilBrian1981 Coming where?

@JoesWoes: @LivOutLoud @StarVeilBrian1981 To Atlanta. MRM just announced he & cast will do the con circuit this summer. Dragon Con is top of the list.

@LivOutLoud: @JoesWoes @StarVeilBrian1981 Er . . . probably not.

@JoesWoes: @LivOutLoud @StarVeilBrian1981 C'mon, Liv. It'd be a fun escape from RL.

@LivOutLoud: @JoesWoes @StarVeilBrian1981 Wish I could, but I can't. I just don't see it happening.

@StarVeilBrian1981: @LivOutLoud @JoesWoes Never say never.

"My God, I look like Tom Hiddleston in this!" Xander laughed.

"Better than Hiddleston," Liv said.

"Better?"

"You look like one of the *Starveil* cast. You're gorgeous!"

"Gorgeous, hmm? I do like the sound of that." Xander squinted at the screen. "Who did you say made this?"

"StarVeilBrian1981. He's been in the fandom forever. He's got mad Photoshop skills."

Xander glared down the length of his nose. "I meant his *given* name, Liv. Not his username. Good lord, I'd never remember StairMaster Nine—"

"StarVeilBrian1981." Liv giggled. "And his first name is Brian."

"Well, tell Brian I'm very impressed."

"Oh! I can't."

Xander looked up from the screen. "Why not?"

"No one knows I'm behind Spartan Survived."

"Really?"

She gave a one-shouldered shrug. "It just seemed simpler that way."

Xander nodded. "I guess that could work."

"What do you mean *work*?"

"Well, your fandom is mostly online. It's interaction-free. You don't have to even know someone's name." He snorted. "I know my friends. In the physical world, I mean."

"So you like to remind me." Liv grumbled. She pulled the laptop toward her, but Xander grabbed hold of it before she could take it away, the two of them caught in an impromptu tug-of-war.

"Hey now!" Xander complained. "I'm not done with that!"

"Then be nice about my friends. I don't troll your steampunk buddies."

"True. You don't. And I'll play nice. Promise."

Liv let go, and Xander slid the laptop to his side of the table. "It's a very good manip, though. I look absolutely amazing!"

"And you're oh so humble about it." Liv laughed, her irritation fading.

"Thanks to you," Xander said, nudging her with his elbow. "You were right about the captain's jacket."

"Told you so."

For a few more seconds, Xander examined the screen. Liv expected this, like so many of their other projects, would be added to his acting portfolio. Suddenly he spun back toward Liv. He grabbed her arm.

"Why don't you make yourself a costume? I'd help you!"

"A costume for what?"

"For whatever you want, Liv! There are cons all over the place." Xander's voice was breathy with excitement. "I'll go with you!"

"I don't know. I'm not one for dressing up."

"But think how fun it would be!" He tapped Tekla's image. "We could even go together. Dual cosplay, if you will. It'd be great!"

"Xander . . ." Liv groaned. "I don't think—"

But Xander was already sizing her up. "Yes, yes. You could totally pull off her outfit. You have the bust . . ." Liv crossed her arms over her chest just as Xander reached for her booted foot. He pulled it up. "But her legs are longer than yours." He waggled his eyebrows. "You're built for comfort rather than speed."

Liv kicked her foot away from him. "Stop it!" she hissed. "You're embarrassing me."

He laughed. "You really do have an amazing figure."

"Enough!" She could feel the heat rising from her chest to her face.

Xander chuckled and leaned back in his chair. He waved away her words with an indolent gesture of dismissal. She never knew how he could pull off the whole "cosplay as a way of life"; just thinking about one day of dress-up terrified her.

"When I convince you to come to Dragon Con with me, I'm going to insist you try it."

Liv purposefully ignored his suggestion. "You know there's a bunch of people from the *Starveil* fandom going to Dragon Con this year. Apparently MRM's making some big announcement."

"And are *you* coming with the Spartan entourage?"

"Don't think so."

"Any chance I could change your mind? There's even a parade, you know. We go right through downtown Atlanta. They film it and everything." Xander grinned. "DC is a cosplayer's paradise."

Liv's palms went sweaty at the mere thought. "I don't really think that's for me."

"You don't know unless you try," Xander insisted. "It's better than Comic-Con. The stars are much more accessible. And I have every intention of convincing you to come along."

Liv snapped the laptop closed. "Coercing me, you mean."

He smirked. "All a matter of opinion, dearest."

"Sometimes," she sighed, "I think you take the whole Byron thing way too seriously."

"You're the one who cast me as the Rebel."

Liv smiled despite herself. "If the shoe fits."

⌒

March disappeared.

April began.

The posts to the #SpartanSurvived tag grew. Liv and Xander made another vid, which made YouTube's top ten video picks of the week. Rumors on several websites suggested that the Spartan Survived movement had drawn the attention of Hollywood itself, and *Entertainment Nightly* did a feature on the "grassroots movement" to bring back America's favorite Rebel. In it, they interviewed Mike R. Miles, the creator of *Starveil*, about the fan movement, and he spoke of "reassessing fan interests" and "projects in the works." As crazy as it sounded, Liv had to admit her death-defying enterprise was doing exactly what she wanted. People really *were* wondering if Spartan had survived. And if Liv ignored the last ten minutes of *Starveil Five* and just read fic, then she could convince herself he hadn't really died.

She read Spartan. Vidded Spartan. Dreamed of Spartan.

If only, Liv thought morosely, *my real life were as thrilling as my dreams.*

Her crush on Granola Hank had grown worse, not better, over the last weeks. *He looked so much like Spartan!* She found herself arriving at class early, offering to work late on projects, her body thrumming with desire whenever he smiled at her.

"You need to ask him out," Arden announced the afternoon she stopped by Liv's house to pick Xander up after filming.

Liv jerked like she'd been burned. "Wait—what?"

"That guy in your socio class," she said, flopping onto Liv's bed. "The guy you like."

Liv gave Xander a seething look. "You *told* Arden?!"

Xander paled until he matched his shirt. "I . . . I didn't know it was a secret."

"Why wouldn't it be?!"

His eyes widened until there was a ring of white around the irises. "I—I'm sorry, Liv. I—I never—"

"So why haven't you asked him out yet?" Arden said. Liv turned to discover she'd thrown herself across the pillows of Liv's bed, making herself at home. "The longer you wait, the more likely someone else will snap him up," she said. "There's no time to waste."

Liv had the sudden urge to scream. Arden had no right to meddle.

"I'm not even sure why *you* care," Liv said.

"I care because I'm your friend," she said in a hurt voice.

Liv wilted. Why was Arden always so goddamned *nice* to everyone?! It made it hard to hate her.

"It's obvious you need to get out," Arden said with a sympathetic smile. "C'mon, Liv. It can't be fun being cooped up all the time. I'm worried about you. We both are."

Liv glared at Xander, who was looking increasingly uneasy.

"We just want you to be happy, Liv," he said.

Arden sat up. "The first step is to ask this guy out," she said in a cheery voice. "You like him. He likes you. End of conversation."

"But I can't!"

"Why not?" Arden asked. "It's not 1950. A girl can ask a guy out if she wants. I asked out Xander."

Liv knew Arden meant well, but she hated the comparison to Arden's picture-perfect social life: Arden, the sorority sister, fun-loving and outgoing, at ease in every situation, versus Liv's overall dorkiness and lack of social graces.

"I know, it's just . . ." Liv groaned. "It's terrifying."

Arden gave Liv a pained look. "I know this might be hard to hear," she said gently, "but with all your worrying, you're sabotaging yourself before you even begin. It's a date you're suggesting. Not marriage."

"It's not 'just' anything."

"It *is*."

For every argument she came up with, Arden had another. Eventually Liv was too tired to fight.

The cinema downtown was hosting a midnight showing of the first *Starveil* movie. It had been filmed more than a decade before, when Tom Grander was a fresh-faced unknown, and Mike R. Miles a washed-up television director. The dialogue was cheesy, the special effects second-rate. But it was the start of the empire, the beginning of the franchise. Besides, Liv rationalized, if she was to have any chance at all with Hank, he would have to know about her *Starveil* obsession.

It was a make-or-break proposition.

The day was sunny. A good sign, Liv decided, as she waited outside the sociology classroom. She and most of the other students had exited the room, but she could see Hank next to their professor, his arms swinging as he argued animatedly about today's topic. He was the physical embodiment of a *Starveil* AU. Liv's chest tightened in response. Hank had no right to make her feel that way, but in the last few weeks, it was like her brain and hormones had parted ways.

From inside the classroom, Hank suddenly looked up. He gave her a brilliant smile as their eyes met. Liv's knees went weak.

"Oh God," she muttered. "I'm hopeless."

But it was too late to run. Hank was walking right toward her. No, she thought, not walking . . . striding. Whereas Xander strolled through life, Hank walked with determination, as if he were about to start up a farm collective or carry an orphan baby to an inoculation station in another village. A smile insisted on resting on Liv's mouth—spreading the closer Hank got—and as much as Liv fought it, she couldn't make the expression go away.

"I thought you'd already gone," Hank said.

Liv shifted from foot to foot. "No, I . . . I wanted to talk to you."

"Is this about the notes I borrowed? I've got 'em in my bag. I can bring them back next class. Just need to copy them."

"No, not that." She swallowed with a dry mouth. "I . . . It's something else."

He nodded, his grin unchanged. "What then?"

"I was . . ." Liv cleared her throat. "I was wondering if . . ." She squeezed her eyes shut, focusing on the sounds caught in her throat. "I mean, I was trying to . . ." The words simply wouldn't come.

She opened her eyes to find Hank watching her with an expression of concern. "Are you okay, Liv? You look like you're gonna throw up." He caught hold of her elbow, steering her to the side of the hallway. "Here. There's a garbage can."

"Nope. Fine," she choked, pulling from his grip.

"Seriously, Liv. You look awful. You're green."

She gave a high-pitched laugh, forcing herself to smile, though it was really just a reflex, the way a dog did before it vomited. "No," she squeaked. "I'm . . . I'm good. Had something caught in my throat."

Hank smiled again. (Hank always smiled.)

"I, um . . . I was wondering . . ." she said. "That is, I was thinking . . . about you. Well, not about you exactly . . . but about . . ."

He tipped his head to the side.

"If you were, maybe . . . I don't know—" Her gaze skittered to the door, where the next class's students were arriving. "If you weren't busy . . . that is . . . didn't have anything happening . . ."

Suddenly Hank—who always had a smile on his face—frowned at her. It was the strangeness of the expression that pushed her to blurt it out.

"If you wanted to go out to a movie sometime," she gasped. "Like . . . Like a date or something."

The bomb dropped.

She waited, but Hank didn't move. He stared at her for a long time. Liv felt like she was caught in a movie, and everyone else had switched into slow motion, but she hadn't. She was certain at least thirty seconds passed before he blinked, like the film he was in had been on pause and he had abruptly caught up to her.

Hank smiled, but this time it was a different sort of smile. A weaker one. "Liv, I . . . I don't know what to say." He beamed down at her, but it wasn't the toothy grin she knew. This was something else. Something that hurt the inside of her chest. "I'm flattered. Really, I am. But I have to say no."

"What?" The word was the sound of someone kicked in the gut.

Hank's smile faltered. "I can't. I mean, I'd love to, if I didn't have a girlfriend." He winced. "And if I felt that way about you."

Liv turned away from him. Her stomach roiled. The only possible way this situation could get worse was if she *did* throw up. "Oh my God." She pushed past a gaggle of girls lingering outside the doorway and headed down the hall. She needed to get away!

"Liv, wait!"

She walked faster, vision tunneling down. Now she felt like she might pass out. *Oh God*, her mind screamed. *What have I done?*

"Liv?"

She couldn't answer.

Hank jogged up next to her, keeping pace. "Please don't get me wrong. I'm really flattered, Liv. I am and I—"

"You already said that," she snapped.

"But I am. It's just that I have a girlfriend. Hayley doesn't live in Boulder, but we've been together since we were in high school. I couldn't say yes and just—"

Liv came to a sudden stop. "I get it!"

Hank's perma-smile faded to nothing. "I just wanted to explain. It's me, not you. You're a cool chick, and if I wasn't with Hayley, then—"

"Oh my God, please stop!" Liv shouted. "Just stop talking! You're making it worse!"

Hank's face looked all wrong when he was sad. Like something had broken inside, and the parts she recognized weren't working anymore.

"I'm trying to be cool, Liv," he said quietly. "I want to stay friends with you."

The hallway swam beneath a layer of unshed tears. "I want to die," she croaked. "But thanks anyhow."

She turned and sprinted down the corridor.

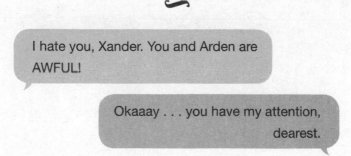

I hate you, Xander. You and Arden are AWFUL!

Okaaay . . . you have my attention, dearest.

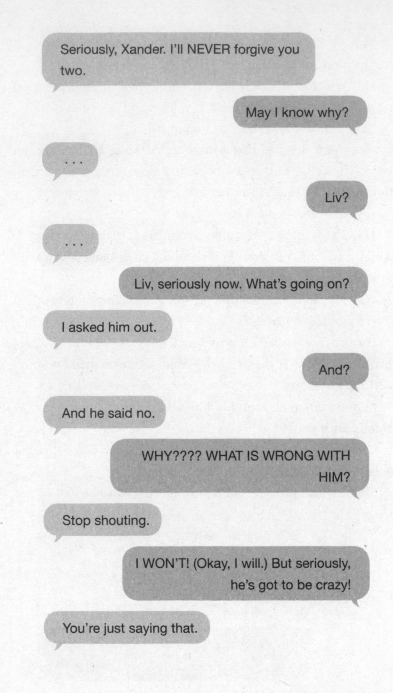

Seriously, Xander. I'll NEVER forgive you two.

May I know why?

. . .

Liv?

. . .

Liv, seriously now. What's going on?

I asked him out.

And?

And he said no.

WHY???? WHAT IS WRONG WITH HIM?

Stop shouting.

I WON'T! (Okay, I will.) But seriously, he's got to be crazy!

You're just saying that.

I'm NOT just saying that! What in seven hells is wrong with him?

He has a girlfriend.

BASTARD.

No. He's nice.

He's a disgusting, pox-addled fool. How dare he insult you!

He didn't. He just said no. (Also, no one in Boulder has pox.)

He besmirched your honor. I'm challenging him to a duel!

Stop it, Xander. You're making me laugh.

Good. ;) What else can I accuse this nefarious fool of? Necromancy? Flatulency? Other "y's" I've yet to list?

Nothing. :) I don't want to laugh. At least not yet.

I'm sorry it didn't turn out, Liv. That isn't fair. You liked him.

Life's never fair.

Do you want me to come over? Arden's working tonight, but we could hang out.

I dunno. :(

You want to go out somewhere?

Definitely NO.

What if I took you to see the first Starveil? Hmmm? Is your steam-powered Spartan-o-meter humming?

But . . . you hate Starveil.

True, but I know Starveil makes you happy.

You don't have to do that.

Come on. Let's go, Liv. I want to go. Truly.

Oh god, I'm crying again.

Don't. Granola isn't worth it.

I'm not sure.

I am. Now dry your eyes and remove yourself from the boudoir. We have a cheesy movie to attend!

I'm going to lure you over to the Starveil fandom. You know that, right, Xander?

You can try. But I doubt you'll be successful.

I will. Guarantee it. And thanks, Xander. I mean it.

Any time, dearest.

～

Liv and Xander sat in the theater, the room humming with excited chatter. Almost every seat was taken, a surprise for a decade-old rerelease. Liv squinted into the semidarkness. She recognized a couple of die-hard fans, people she'd seen standing in line for the Christmas Eve, midnight release of *Starveil Five* alongside her months earlier. Others were new, younger fans: middle schoolers who bounced in their seats like balloons about to release. The room was packed, and Liv wondered how much of that was due to the buzz over #SpartanSurvived. It was unbelievable what a difference three and a half months had wrought. She flashed to the moment when Spartan had died in the last film, her brow creasing in pain. It hardly felt like canon anymore, and that moment—sitting alone in the theater crying—felt like it had happened in another lifetime.

Xander slouched at Liv's side, one leg thrown over the arm of the chair next to him.

"You'll get kicked out of the theater if he sees you doing that again," Liv said. Xander had already been warned by the exasperated theater attendant, but he'd put his feet back up as soon as the young man had walked back up the aisle.

"No, I won't," Xander drawled. "I'm Major Malloy. I've been spending months trying to bring Spartan back. I've earned more than one seat."

"That only works if he recognizes you," Liv said. "You look more like a fop to me."

"Wrong century. I'm a *flaneur*, if anything." He brushed his fingernails against his jacket. "I do like the sound of that, by the way."

"Well, whatever you want to call yourself, your foot's still on the seat. That's a theater rule, and you've been warned."

Xander waggled his fingers at her. "Ah, but the leader of the Rebellion doesn't care about rules." He glanced back at the crowd. "Besides, I like legroom."

"Don't say I didn't warn you."

Liv's smile faded as a group of young men entered, jostling one another as they headed up the aisle. "Just my luck," she groaned, slumping until the back of her chair blocked the group of men from view.

Xander sat up, following her line of sight. "Is that the fabled Granola I've heard so much about?"

"No," Liv sighed. "But they're all his friends, and that

means he's probably here, too." She slid down until her chin rested on her chest. "Dragnat all! This was a terrible idea."

"No," Xander said. "It's not. And who cares if he sees you out? That's good, right? You're not pining for him. You're moving on." He slid his arm over her shoulders and winked. "Moving *up*, in my opinion."

"Not helping," Liv fumed. She refused to turn around to see where Hank's friends had gone.

"My dear Liv," Xander said in his best "Colin Firth trying to be rational" tone. "You're worrying about this far too much." His words were clipped, inflection decidedly upper-crust.

"I wouldn't care," Liv sighed, "except I thought he actually liked me."

"And perhaps he did. A 'no' could have many reasons for it."

"He didn't like me, at least not in that way." Liv took a surreptitious peek over the back of the seat. Hank's friends were there, but there was no Spartan look-alike among them, no glowing smile. She turned back, catching Xander watching her. "I'm just one of the guys to Hank. I could have been anyone. You, even."

Xander's mouth twitched in amusement. "I'm sorry, dearest. You may be many things, but you are *not* one of the guys."

"Yes, I am. That's exactly how guys think of me. It's my role." She nodded to a passel of young women dressed in yoga pants and too-tight T-shirts. "I don't know how to do that."

"Good lord," Xander said with a shudder. "Who'd want to? That's about as unfeminine as I can imagine."

Liv giggled.

"Your problem, dear, is that you trap yourself by overthinking."

"What's that supposed to mean?"

Xander's lips curled mischievously. "You could become a Siren, luring men to their deaths." He leaned forward. "I'd follow you onto the rocks."

"Just so you could laugh when I drowned."

"Pfft! Flirting's like acting. Even fools get onstage."

"But flirting depends on timing, and not sticking your foot in your mouth," Liv argued. "I suck at it."

"Rubbish!" Xander said in a sharp voice. He sat up, looking around the theater. "You're overthinking again. Choose someone. Anyone here."

"Wh-what?"

"Choose someone. Anyone in the theater. Right here and now."

"I am *not* going to talk to them."

"I know," he said with a wink, "but I am. And I'll show you what I mean."

Liv peered up and down the aisles, catching sight of Hank's friends. Xander snapped his fingers.

"Hurry up, Liv, the movie's going to start. Wouldn't want to miss Spartan, would I?"

It was his jibe that made her do it.

"There," Liv said, pointing. "The one in the gray jacket. His name's Jason, I think."

The look on Xander's face was totally worth it. "Very funny," he said sourly. "But I'm fairly sure I'm not Jason's type, lacking breasts and"—he winced—"those horrific yoga pants."

Liv gave a catlike smile. "But you said choose anyone. Who's overthinking now, Xander?"

For a moment, Liv thought he was going to chicken out,

but then he slid off his jacket and rolled up the French cuffs of his shirt. Now, instead of a nineteenth-century duke, he looked like a French exchange student overdressed for a night at the movies.

"Christ almighty, woman. You'd better applaud when I'm done."

He rolled his shoulders and stood.

"Jacket," he said, reaching for Liv's parka.

"No way!"

"Yes, way," he said, grabbing her coat and pulling it on. The French exchange student was abruptly replaced by a somewhat emo-looking college freshman with killer looks. "Dressing for your role is all part of it," Xander said.

Before Liv could answer, he jogged up the aisle, a transformation taking place before her eyes. Xander's posture changed. His limbs grew looser, movements less refined. Liv did her own double take. The Xander she knew and loved was gone, replaced by someone completely different.

"Jason!" he shouted.

Hank's friends turned as one.

Xander reached them and began to chatter, arms swinging in time to whatever he was saying. Liv watched the scene, openmouthed. Jason's expression was stiff and wary, but the longer Xander talked, the more relaxed he became. Suddenly one of the other friends interrupted, and Xander laughed. Jason nodded and smiled, pointing to a seat near the end of the row of young men. Xander shook his head and waved bashfully before turning around and jogging down the aisle to Liv's side.

As if on cue, the lights in the theater dimmed.

"What the hell was that?" Liv laughed.

Xander grinned devilishly. "I take back what I said. Jason might be a tiny bit interested in me—not that he'd ever admit it in present company—but honestly? He's not really my taste."

The first strains of the *Starveil* theme rose around them, but Liv hardly noticed. "But what *was* that?"

"What do you mean?"

"That thing! That thing you did right there!"

"That, my dear Liv, was confidence. Talk to someone. Make jokes with them. Seem interested in what they are saying even if they're dull as mud." He shrugged. "Anyone . . . anyone at all, can be glamoured if you know how."

The music faded, opening credits beginning. "But how?" she mouthed.

He leaned in, until his mouth was almost against her ear. "You pretend hard enough and *they* believe it," he whispered. "That's the key to casting a glamour. Byron had a clubfoot. No one cared. Every man and woman in the ton wanted him for their lover. It was all in how he carried himself."

Liv shivered. They were too close, and maybe she was feeling a little glamoured herself.

"But I—I can't do that."

"You can."

On-screen, Captain Spartan appeared. He was young and fresh-faced. Most days this image left Liv swooning, but tonight, sitting in the dark with Xander at her side, she could barely concentrate.

"Confidence is something you're born with." Liv turned to look at him, their faces so close they were only a hairsbreadth away from a kiss. "You have it. I don't."

A smile ghosted over Xander's lips, his eyes dark with the suggestion of something Liv wasn't sure she wanted to understand. "Then I'll teach you."

Heart pounding, Liv nodded and lifted her gaze back to the screen, but with Xander beside her, Spartan was the last thing on her mind.

Liv was surprised the lights were on when Xander dropped her off at her house. Her mother made it her policy to be in bed by ten most nights because she got up at five each morning and left for work long before Liv even rolled out of bed. Seeing the glow from the windows, Liv felt a frisson of fear run the length of her spine. She unlocked the door and tiptoed inside.

Her mother sat on the couch in her bathrobe, a cup of tea cradled in her hands, her work laptop and a scattering of papers in front of her.

"Hey, Mom," Liv said warily. "You're up late."

"I was waiting up for you." Her mother closed the laptop and pushed it aside. "Can you come here for a minute?"

With those words, the panic Liv had been feeling ever since Hank had given her the "it's not you, it's me" speech came surging back. This was how her mother had looked when she'd told Liv her father had disappeared. This was how her mother looked when the police broke the news that they'd found his body. This was her mother, stoic at her husband's funeral.

This was Katherine Walden steeled for bad news.

"O-okay."

"Sit down, Liv," her mother said, patting the couch.

Liv's hands were icy claws as she slipped off her boots. *Oh my God*, her mind chanted. *Something's wrong!* She hung her jacket on the hook by the door and came into the living room slowly, watching her mother's face for clues. Katherine's lips were a slash, her arms crossed over her chest.

"What is it?" Liv asked.

"We need to have a talk." Her mother pointed to the empty cushion next to her. "Sit."

"Mom, you're worrying me. What's this all about?"

"I was doing laundry today, and I found something in your room."

Liv frowned. "Oh?" Whatever *this* was, it couldn't be good.

"I think we need to talk about it."

Her mother reached past the laptop and picked up a paper. Liv's breath caught in her chest as she read it:

Liv Walden
Midterm Exam: Calculus
46%

7

"DON'T TALK OUT LOUD. YOU LOWER THE IQ OF THE WHOLE STREET."
(SHERLOCK)

Every muscle in Liv's body tensed to run.

"Mom, I can expl—"

"No," her mother said in a hollow voice, "I don't want to hear it."

"But—"

"I went online after I found your exam. I looked up your @LivOutLoud account and started searching."

Liv blinked. "You did *what*?"

"I googled *all* of it. You're back at it again, Liv. You and Xander haven't been working on school projects at all." She opened the laptop back up, the screen blinding in the dim room. "Watch," her mother commanded.

Xander, as Major Malloy, stood in front of the burning remains of the colony on Io (which Liv had carefully lifted from the last *Starveil* trailer). The text "Spartan Survived!" rippled across the screen, disintegrating into a shower of sparks that rained down onto the colony's pockmarked surface. As fire spread from building to building, the screen cut to a series of fan-generated images and video. These played in snippets on a holoscreen, while Xander begged the resistance to send more evidence of Spartan's survival. *"Your determination. Your proof has given us hope that Spartan still—"*

Her mother closed the laptop with a snap. Xander's growling voice and the *Starveil* theme disappeared. "The crap you pulled in high school was one thing, but this is something else entirely. You're going to flunk out of college at this rate."

"It was only a couple of vids."

"I don't care. You said you were keeping up your grades, and now I find this?" She picked up the midterm exam and shook it at Liv. "You *lied* to me. You're failing already."

"Mom, I can handle—"

"No, Liv. You *can't*." Her mother pinched the bridge of her nose. "We saw that in high school, didn't we? You have college riding on your grades now. I never thought you'd fall back into your *Starveil* obsession. Fandom . . ." Her lips curled on the word. "I hate it! And let me tell you, Liv, as long as you're living under my roof, you'll live by my rules. This is going to stop!"

Her mother's voice had that crackling sound like she was about to cry, and that sent Liv's emotions into an uproar. She blinked away wayward tears. *Starveil* had been one of the connections between Liv and her father. The fact that her mother had never understood it had been a thorn in their relationship for years.

"It's just one project, Mom. Just one." (*With any number of side projects*, she thought but didn't say.)

Her mother took Liv's hands in her own. She looked worn

and tired, and Liv felt a sudden wave of guilt for putting this on her shoulders.

"You're going to stop," Katherine said grimly.

Liv jerked her hands away. "What?!"

"It's *over*, Liv."

"But I can handle it! People in the *Starveil* fandom really care about these vids! You can't just—"

"Yes! I can and I *will*! You are done with this nonsense! Fandom is destroying your future!"

Liv's eyes brimmed with tears. "But, Mom—"

"After that stunt you pulled last year, I know *exactly* how this will turn out! School matters, Liv. Real life matters. This"—she pointed to the closed laptop—"doesn't! Fandom is a waste of time and talent."

"It's not!"

Her mother caught Liv's hands again, and this time she held them so tight Liv couldn't get away. Her tone grew cold. "Let me be perfectly clear: You *will* give up fandom, Liv. No ifs, ands, or buts about it."

Tears rolled down Liv's cheeks. She couldn't breathe let alone speak.

"It's over," Katherine said in a weary voice. "Focus on school this semester. Promise me."

Liv hung her head, chest aching. "Fine."

"And, Liv, I want you to know that I'm only saying this because I—"

But Liv stood from the couch and sprinted away before her mother could finish.

You sleeping, Xander?

Soundly. I'm dreaming of Orson Welles's time machine.

Don't you mean H. G. Wells's time machine?

Right. But more importantly, I'm dreaming about how I can use it to go back in time and prevent Tom Grander from EVER agreeing to make that atrocious movie.

Sorry for waking you. I'll bug you tomorrow.

I'm kidding, Liv. Christ! It's barely 11. I'm a Victorian gentleman, not an octogenarian.

. . .

How are you doing, dearest?

Awful.

Why? I was kidding about the time machine BTW. (At least the Tom Grander part of it.) Now, what's going on?

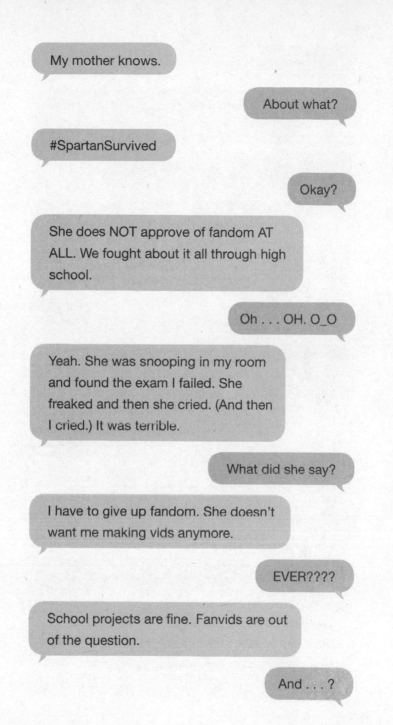

My mother knows.

About what?

#SpartanSurvived

Okay?

She does NOT approve of fandom AT ALL. We fought about it all through high school.

Oh . . . OH. O_O

Yeah. She was snooping in my room and found the exam I failed. She freaked and then she cried. (And then I cried.) It was terrible.

What did she say?

I have to give up fandom. She doesn't want me making vids anymore.

EVER????

School projects are fine. Fanvids are out of the question.

And . . . ?

And what?

And what are YOU doing about it? This is your choice, Liv. Your life.

Ugh. I can't imagine giving up fandom.

That's your choice then, right there.

No. It's not.

Why?

Because I live at home. Mom's widow's pension helps pay for college. She holds all the cards on this. I can't win. :(

I'm sorry, dearest.

I have to focus on school and give up fandom. I wish I didn't but that's the deal.

I can help you study, you know.

Thanks, but you're on her radar too. (She was furious you were helping me vid.) I should probably just lay low for a while.

Fair enough. But I expect that coffee dates and Mickey Dee's are still acceptable?

Of course. Ugh. I just hate fighting with my mom. :(

Sometimes you have to.

Thanks. I'm glad you were awake, Xander.

Me too, dearest.

⌣

With midterms over and the spring semester barreling toward finals, Liv's entire purpose at school became to avoid a confrontation with Hank, who seemed determined to bravado his way through the stilted awkwardness that followed their encounter. More than once, Hank tried to talk to Liv during sociology, and several times he offered to grab a coffee at break, but her panic in the wake of recent events quickly ended the last semblance of a relationship. It was better that way, Liv told herself the day Hank moved to sit on the opposite side of the classroom. Easier. She just wished it didn't hurt to see him laughing and talking. Unlike Liv, Hank found it easy to make friends.

The problem was, Liv's hormones hadn't gotten the message that Hank was out-of-bounds. And as days moved into weeks, the dreams began. They featured Hank as Spartan, caught in the dying Star Freighter Elysium. She woke frustrated and upset, more disturbed by her brain's refusal to give up on Hank than by his rejection. And with fandom off-limits, there was nothing to distract herself with.

Days trundled past. Usually she would have invited Xander over and thrown together another #SpartanSurvived vid, but she was determined to keep her promise of "no fandom" to her mother. Trouble was, fandom was more than a hobby, it was a support system. Without it, Liv had no one to talk to when she was lonely. She had nothing to look forward to after school, and no outlet for creativity. Liv found herself spiraling back into melancholy.

She got up.

She went to classes.

She came home. . . . And then did it all over again.

Sleep became the escape that fandom had once been. She would have happily locked herself in her bedroom forever, if Xander and Arden hadn't arrived early one Saturday morning.

"Rise and shine!" Arden said in a chirpy voice. "It's time to go."

Liv glared at her. (Who in their right mind straight-ironed their hair on weekends?)

"No, thank you."

"Liv, dear. Get up," Xander said drily. "You've hidden in this dusty mausoleum long enough." He kicked a rumpled pair of pants out of his way, wrinkling his nose. "In this state, your room isn't fit for human occupation. Arden and I are here to abscond with you to the outside world. Now let's go!"

"Don't want to," Liv grumbled.

Arden gave a long-suffering sigh. "Xander and I aren't leaving until you move. This behavior isn't healthy. I'm serious, Liv. You need to get out of the house once in a while."

Liv retreated under the covers. Perhaps if she fell asleep, they'd leave. (Why *was* Arden here, anyhow?)

"Liv, are you listening to me?" Arden said. "I'm not leaving till you—"

"Go AWAY!"

"No!" Arden jerked on the covers, and Liv's fingers tightened. "You are getting up." Arden tugged again, but Liv refused to let go. "Xander," Arden said through clenched teeth. "A little help here?"

"Oh, no." He chuckled. "You seem to have that all firmly in hand."

Xander stood at the end of the bed, hands on hips, the jacket Liv had helped him sew thrown open, a gold-threaded waistcoat glimmering underneath. He was the Regency hero today, but she didn't feel like being saved.

"Why are you guys bugging me anyhow?" Liv snarled.

"Because you're in a melancholy funk," Xander said.

"I'm not."

"No? Then get out of bed," Arden said sweetly.

Most days, Liv didn't mind Arden's chipper attitude. Today she fought the urge to smother her with a pillow. Xander wandered to the dresser and picked up a Spartan action figure that had fallen sideways, inspecting it with a bemused expression.

"Leave my stuff alone," Liv ordered.

He put the figure down. "Only if you prove to me that you're still alive. C'mon. Arden and I are taking you out for breakfast."

"And then we're—"

"Breakfast," Xander said, giving Arden a warning look. "Out of the dark is an important step." Xander brushed a place clear at the edge of the bed and sat next to Liv. "This room isn't healthy."

"Nobody's making you stay." Liv's voice cracked. "Hank sure didn't."

Xander rolled his eyes. "For goodness' sake, Liv. It was one guy—and not a particularly interesting one at that. He is *not* worth this reaction."

"So, what? I'm just supposed to keep asking guys out until one says yes?"

Arden grinned. "Yes, exactly!"

"I don't need your help," Liv snapped.

"Come on, Liv," Xander said, patting her knee. "You're already dressed. We're just offering breakfast." He glared at Arden. "That's all."

"I'm tired."

Arden had cleared a path to the door with the efficiency of an infomercial host. She spun back around, surveying her work. "Then let's get coffee. C'mon, Liv. Just an hour."

"Fine," she grumbled. "But only if you guys are buying."

Xander began to laugh. "Lord, if I'd known that was the key, we could've saved all the dramatics."

❧

Half an hour later, they sat in Cup O' Joe, three espressos on the table between them. Liv was determined to sulk, but Xander and Arden's cheerfulness was hard to resist.

"Hank wasn't the one," Arden said with a gentle smile, "but that doesn't mean we can't find you someone. There are plenty more fish in the sea. You deserve to be happy."

Liv grimaced. "I don't want to be your pet project, thanks."

"Why?" Arden said. "Xander's already yours."

Xander had been watching the repartee from behind his cup, but at Arden's barb, he dropped his voice to Malloy's growl: "Your perseverance, your courage, is what we need to conquer this dating disaster."

"Ha-ha," Liv said. "Very funny."

"Well, I thought so."

"What we need to do is get you some momentum," Arden said. "Get you exposed to a few dozen—"

"Dozen?!" Liv gasped.

"—men and then figure out what you like. Once you've got that down, you're fine!"

Xander rolled his eyes and returned to his espresso.

"Maybe I don't have someone out there," Liv said. "Maybe he drowned when he was five."

"God, Liv. Try not to be so creepy," Arden snorted. "That is a definite turnoff. How are you supposed to find a soul mate if you chase them all away?"

"I don't believe in soul mates," Liv grumbled.

"Me neither," Xander said, "but I tend to think there *are* people who you can click with. You just have to spend enough time with them to find out."

Liv took another scalding sip of espresso. She could feel the caffeine making its way into her bloodstream. Sitting here in the café made her feel like she'd been asleep for days and was finally starting to wake up.

"Look, you guys," Liv said. "I know you mean well, but I don't know how to talk to men."

"You talk to me," Xander said in a hurt voice.

Liv shook her head. "You don't count." Xander made a choking sound of exasperation. "It's different with you. It's just . . . easy."

Arden's gaze moved from one to the other, her eyes narrowing. "So if you can talk to Xander, then you *can* talk to men. We just need to find you the right ones."

"I don't know, Arden. I'm not sure I'm ready."

Arden grinned. "Oh, you're ready all right! It's like a dating rule: Freshman year is the time to mingle."

"Maybe . . ." Liv set her coffee back on the table and blinked. The room seemed brighter, sounds clearer. Maybe coming out had been a good idea.

"Soul mates and dating rules aside," Xander said, "it's a truth universally acknowledged, that a young woman of your intelligence and stature may consider dating, if only for her own enjoyment. No other reason, dearest."

A smile brushed Liv's lips. "Universally acknowledged, hmm?"

"It is." Xander loosened the tight knot of the cravat at his throat and looked away.

Liv sighed. "So how's that supposed to work if I've vowed never to ask a guy out again?"

Arden gave her a scheming grin. "You let *me* play matchmaker."

❧

@LivOutLoud: @JoesWoes @StarVeilBrian1981 Guys, I need some good vibes. Date night tonight! O_O

@JoesWoes: @LivOutLoud Liv??? Where have you BEEN, girl? I haven't seen you online in ages! *frowns* You jumped ship? Spartan NEEDS you!

@LivOutLoud: @JoesWoes Just some family drama going down. I'd never leave Starveil behind. You know that.

@JoesWoes: @LivOutLoud Glad to hear it! Have you been keeping up with the #SpartanSurvived tag? There is SO MUCH going on right now!

@StarVeilBrian1981: @JoesWoes @LivOutLoud MRM has a "big announcement" coming soon. I'm not saying it . . . but I'm going to say it: HE'S BRINGING SPARTAN BACK.

@LivOutLoud: @JoesWoes @StarVeilBrian1981 OMG- REALLY??? How do you know??? *screaming internally* THAT WOULD BE AMAZING!

@StarVeilBrian1981: @LivOutLoud @JoesWoes There's a livestream on Friday night. MRM is WAY past promos at this point. It's something else.

@JoesWoes: @LivOutLoud @StarVeilBrian1981 Actually, MRM has booked the entire Starveil cast for a bunch of cons. It's happening! SPARTAN'S COMING BACK.

@StarVeilBrian1981: @JoesWoes @LivOutLoud I'm doing CC and DC for sure. First question I'm asking is

WHO came up with #SpartanSurvived? I owe him my firstborn.

@LivOutLoud: @StarVeilBrian1981 LOL

@StarVeilBrian1981: @LivOutLoud What?

@LivOutLoud: @StarVeilBrian1981 Who said it was a guy? ;)

~

The agreement was that all first dates would happen at Cup O' Joe. That way Arden and Xander were there for backup, and Liv had a limited amount of time to tolerate the embarrassment, should things go wrong. The first was a man named Ken, whom Liv vaguely remembered having seen at the café any number of times. Arden ushered Liv forward as she arrived.

"He's over there," she said in a stage whisper. "Go!" And then shoved Liv forward.

Liv stumbled to the table, anxiety rising.

"Hi, I'm Liv."

The guy glanced up and down again. "H'lo," he muttered.

Liv stood for several long seconds, uncertain if this really *was* the guy she was supposed to be on the date with.

"I, um . . . Are you Ken?"

His eyes scuttled up, and he nodded.

Liv sat, hands clutched in her lap. Ken didn't look at her. He stared at his coffee.

"So, um . . . tell me about yourself," Liv said, then winced at how stupid the opener sounded. (It didn't matter. Ken was still staring at his coffee.)

". . . immachemmiss . . ." he whispered.

Liv leaned forward. "Could you repeat that?"

His voice dropped lower still. ". . . achemmiss . . ."

Liv leaned in until she was almost forehead to forehead with him. "I'm really sorry, but I can't hear what you're saying. Could you—"

His chin jerked up, and he recoiled at the sight of her so close. "A chemist," he said in a hoarse whisper.

He looked utterly terrified. His forehead was dotted with sweat, chest heaving.

"Well, that's great," Liv said. "I'm a student."

He nodded and dropped his gaze.

A full minute passed in silence.

Liv glanced up to find Xander staring at her, his face caught in an expression of abject horror, Arden grinning at his side. She mouthed: *"Talk!"* Liv turned back to the table and Silent Ken.

He was still inspecting his coffee.

"So . . . what do you like to do . . . other than chemistry?" Liv asked.

". . . iliketoread . . ."

Liv leaned forward. "Sorry, could you repeat that?"

An hour later, Liv sat, Arden and Xander bookending her. Arden had a moleskin and was making notes into it.

"My God," Xander said, "Was that as awful as it looked?"

"Worse."

Arden snorted. "It would've helped if you took my advice to get him to talk about himself."

"I tried!" Liv said. "But he was so shy he wouldn't answer

me. I swear to God, Arden, less than twenty words passed between us!"

"You're exaggerating. I watched."

"It looked horrible to me," Xander said.

"Some level of hell." Liv laughed.

Arden smirked. "Then they can only get better, right?"

The second date made Liv reassess that level of optimism. Jimmy was a bodybuilder, but his personality clearly needed work.

"So you're Arden's friend, huh?" he said, avidly admiring Liv's chest.

She crossed her arms. "Um . . . yeah."

"She was right," he said with a chuckle.

"Right about what?"

"You're stacked."

"I—I'm what?!"

He winked. "They real ones? Actually, doesn't matter. I'm not fussy. I like both."

Liv felt her cheeks light on fire. "I—I can't believe you just said that!"

But Jimmy wasn't listening. He untucked his too-tight T-shirt. "Check this out, babe."

"Oh sweet Jesus. What're you doing?"

He nodded to his own reflection in the café window. "Check out my back," he grunted.

"Sorry—your what?"

He pulled his shirt higher and tensed. "My back," he repeated. "Check that baby out." He twisted so that the muscles rippled into high-def. "Yeah, that's right. That doesn't happen overnight. Anyone can get a six-pack, but you gotta put some real time in to get your wings to show."

Liv smothered a fit of giggles under her hand. "You must be . . . so proud."

She looked over at the counter. Xander was red-faced and laughing, while Arden stared at her with fury. *"TALK TO HIM!"* she mouthed, but Xander's mirth proved too difficult.

"Something in my throat," Liv choked, stumbling away from the table, "gotta go!" She made it halfway to the bathroom before she exploded into a gale of laughter.

Arden was not amused.

The next attempt at matchmaking was a volatile management student who claimed Liv's state-provided scholarship was the slippery slope toward communism. When he started grilling her on her political views, Liv faked an attack of food poisoning and walked out, glaring daggers at Arden and Xander the entire time.

The fourth was a new experience.

Liv was the first one to arrive at Cup O' Joe. It was a Wednesday night, and the café was mostly empty. Xander had the espresso machine half-disassembled, steam hissing in the background.

"Where is he?" Liv asked.

"Just have a seat," Arden said, not holding her eyes. "I'm sure the bus is just late or something." She pushed a coffee into Liv's hands. "Here. I got you this."

"Thanks, Arden."

Liv was halfway through her coffee when a fresh-faced young woman with a short mop of hennaed hair sat next to her.

"Hey, Liv!" she said, offering her hand. "I'm Mona."

Liv's eyes widened. "Hi . . . ?"

Mona shook Liv's hand. "You're Arden and Xander's friend, right?"

Liv nodded. Her gaze jumped to Arden, who was staring at her with the intensity of an Olympic gymnast about to mount the high beam. Her gaze jumped to Xander. Only his hair was visible behind the coffee machine.

"I . . . yeah. I am." Liv frowned. "Sorry, but I'm supposed to be meeting someone right now."

Mona's smile faltered. "That'd be me, actually."

Liv's eyebrows shot into her hairline. "Oh God. Sorry! I didn't realize—" She sent Arden a withering glare.

"It's fine," Mona said. "Good to meet you, Liv."

There was a long, awkward silence. Liv stared at her coffee feeling a sudden kinship to Ken, the chemist. Maybe if she didn't look up, Mona would disappear.

"So, how did you meet Arden?" Mona finally asked.

"Through Xander."

There was another silence.

"And how'd you meet Xander?"

Liv's gaze flicked up. Mona was looking at her with a pained expression. This was just as horrible for her, Liv realized.

"We met in a college class." Liv gave a weak smile. "I didn't have any friends, but Xander sort of took pity on me."

Mona nodded to the counter where Xander had reappeared, working through the nozzles of the disassembled machine. "Xander's a great guy. I heard you helped him sew his new jacket. That's pretty cool, Liv."

Liv frowned. "You know Xander well?"

Mona grinned. "We dated for about six months back in senior year." She dropped her voice to a whisper. "It was actually Xander who suggested we might click."

Liv's mouth fell open. *Xander had set her up!*

Mona began to giggle. "Don't worry about it." She laughed. "There's no fireworks for me, either. But it's always cool to meet Xander's friends. He talks about you a lot."

"He does?" Liv glanced back to the counter. Arden's penetrating gaze hadn't wavered, but Xander was studiously avoiding eye contact.

"Uh-huh. We don't hang out that much anymore, but we're still friends. Xander's a good guy. One of the best."

Liv grinned and turned back. "I know, right?"

And for the rest of the "date," Liv and Mona chatted about Xander: his likes and dislikes, facts and foibles. By the time Mona stood to go, Liv felt she'd struck out where dating was concerned but gained a friend despite it.

"Well, I should go," Mona said. "It was good to meet you, Liv."

"It really was."

"If you want to hang out sometime," Mona said, "you just need to call."

Liv smiled. "Thanks, Mona. I think I will."

After that, the dates blurred into one another, until Liv could barely keep the names straight. The last week and a half felt like she'd been on a roller coaster, peaking at high hopes only to barrel back down into reality. While she was too busy to have the deep lows of depression, she could barely keep her grip as she spun from one person to another.

At the end of yet another failed coffee date, Arden sat next to Liv. "You've gotta give me something to work with, Liv," she said grimly. "I can't do this on my own."

"How about *not* working with me," Liv grumbled. "I'm just fine."

Arden turned back to where Xander watched from behind the counter. "Xander, you talk to her," she said wearily, then walked away. "I don't have time to deal with this tonight."

Liv winced as Arden slammed the door behind her.

Xander sauntered over to the table with two lattés and set one before her.

"A peace offering?" Liv said drily.

"Something like that. Was it as bad as it looked from afar?"

With a dark look, Liv lifted her cup. "Worse." She blew across the top of the cup, watching the surface ripple and swirl. "I think Arden has terrible taste in men"—Xander opened his mouth to argue—"present company notwithstanding," Liv amended. "Everyone else has been horrible."

"Mona was nice."

Liv choked, the latté sloshing over the edge and onto her fingers. "You set that up to be mean," she said, putting the cup back on the table.

Xander smirked. "I didn't actually. She's a cool chick."

"Then why don't you date her?"

Xander's grin widened. "I did, dearest. That's how I know."

"But I'm not gay!"

"But you might be bi," Xander said. "You never actually said." He waved away Liv's protesting gasp. "I just thought you should check Mona out. Sexuality is a spectrum, Liv. Never know until you try."

"I'm not sure Arden's buffet approach is working."

"Ah, but you're out. You're meeting people."

"The *wrong* people," Liv said with a bitter laugh.

"But that's still progress."

"How, exactly?"

"Tell me what you *don't* want," he said with a nod. "Tell me all the things that annoy you."

"That's going to be a long list," Liv grumbled.

"Ah, but now you know what you don't like, it's only a matter of finding what you do."

"That is a twisted sense of logic."

"You sure?"

"Pretty sure." Liv lifted her cup and took another sip. "I think Arden should stick with acting. Matchmaking may not be her forte."

"Probably not," Xander sighed. "But you're not scared of making small talk anymore, are you? I've seen you do it. You know the tricks of faking calm. Feigning interest. You might not like it, but you can do it. That, dearest, is the start of glamour." He was watching her with an intensity that made her pulse quicken.

Liv paused, the warmth of the cup pressed against her lips. He was right. She *hadn't* been scared tonight. She'd said hello, she'd made small talk. She'd realized her date was no one she'd ever want to spend a lot of time with, and they'd parted on amicable terms.

"I guess."

"You can do it now. You can't say you've never dated, because you have. A lot of people, actually." Xander gave her a mischievous grin. "You've leveled up, dearest. You're an expert on dating compared with Liv of six months ago."

Liv lowered her cup, a slow smile dawning across her face. "Yeah. I suppose I am."

The corner of Xander's mouth twitched. "Now we just have to get you out of the convent and into the real world."

8

"I'D JUST AS SOON KISS A WOOKIEE!"
(*STAR WARS*)

*T*he first Saturday in May found Liv wandering the downtown streets that made up the Pearl Street Mall, en route to Cup O' Joe. She'd spent all morning studying for her upcoming finals. Heavily caffeinated coffee and a pastry—rather than Liv's go-to support of fandom—would be her much-deserved reward.

The sky was bright and cloudless, blotches of vibrancy appearing in the newly budded trees and spring flowers. Nearing the intersection, she stepped from the shadows of the building onto the sun-bleached sidewalk.

"Liv! How are you?"

She turned, squinting, to discover Hank jogging up to her. His hair was even blonder than she'd remembered, his teeth a perfect porcelain white, and that smile. *Oh God! That Spartan smile!* She felt her skin warm in his beaming presence.

"Wasn't sure it was you," Hank said with a laugh. "It's good to see you."

Liv shifted nervously. "Y-you, too."

"So what're you doing downtown?"

"Coffee," she choked out. "Food."

Speak in sentences! her brain commanded, but all her body parts had gone rogue. Liv's lips refused to create the sounds she wanted, and her heart was beating so fast she could hear it in her ears. Hank waited patiently. Like Spartan, he was blindingly beautiful: tall and athletic, with a smile so bright it hurt her eyes to look at it.

Hank smiled (again). "That's cool, Liv! Where at?"

She nodded down the street. "Cup O' Joe."

He grinned down at her like that was the best thing he'd heard. "Great! Mind if I join you?"

Liv had read the term "blindsided" in any number of fandom fic, but she'd never really understood it until this moment. "Wh-what?"

"Coffee, y'know? Just you and me."

"Why?" She couldn't help the accusatory tone.

His smile dropped to a 60 watt gleam before bouncing back up to 120. "'Cause you're here and I'm here. And there's a coffee shop at the end of the street."

"You want to go for coffee," Liv repeated. "With me. Alone." What in the world was happening?

Hank rolled onto his heels, tucking his hands into his pockets. "Yeah, I do." He dropped his voice. "I've really missed talking to you. It's weird not sitting with you in class every day."

She couldn't think over the rush of emotions, all her rebellious feelings fighting to get out of the cocoon where she'd hidden them over the last two weeks. If her heart pounded any faster, it would burst. She'd die here—*right here!*—on the street, and Hank would have to deal with the body. That, Liv decided, was worse than humiliation. In hopes of keeping herself alive, Liv started walking.

"All right," she said. "Coffee."

Hank fell into position at her side, walking with her the way he'd done so many times after sociology, earlier that spring. Body tingling, Liv could barely talk, but it didn't matter. Hank always had a thousand things he was passionate about, and he launched into a diatribe about the effects of chemicals on bees and his plan to go tree-planting in Washington later this summer. She watched him through the veil of her hair, trying to put on the confident glamour Xander always swore was the key.

It wasn't working!

In minutes, they were inside, at the counter. Xander stood at the cappuccino machine, focusing a hissing jet of steam into a silver urn. He glanced up as they neared.

"Hey, Liv," Xander said with a smile. "I didn't expect you to—"

His eyes widened in shock for half a second, then his face turned into a mask of icy contempt. Liv knew the look. She and Xander watched the BBC version of *Pride and Prejudice* in their film class; and if there had ever been an image of Mr. Darcy, haughty and annoyed, it was Xander at that moment. His lip curled. His jaw clenched. And he drew himself up to his full height, which would have been more impressive if he wasn't a good six inches shorter than Hank.

"Xander," Liv said nervously. "This is Hank."

"Hey, buddy," Hank said amicably, extending his hand. "Good to meet you." Xander glared at the proffered fingers as if he'd been offered a soiled handkerchief. He nodded, but his grip stayed on the urn full of frothy milk, ignoring Hank's gesture.

"My pleasure," Xander said, though his tone belied his words. "Liv's told me *all* about you."

Hank glanced at Liv in confusion. "Oh?"

"About the project we did," Liv rushed to explain. "I—I talked to Xander about the sociology project."

"Well, any friend of Liv's is a friend of mine," Hank said.

"Mmph," Xander snorted. He caught Liv's eye, and she gave him a pleading look.

"Coffee," Liv said.

"Two coffees would be great, man," Hank chimed.

Xander rolled his eyes. "I'm not your man."

"Xander!" Liv hissed.

"And how would you like your coffee . . . *sir.*" Xander curled the word on his tongue like a curse.

"Lotsa cream. Two shots of hazelnut syrup, too."

"Delightful," Xander sneered, his nostrils flaring in disgust. "I'll bring it out to you right away. Please . . ." He gestured to the café. "Do make yourself right at home. I'm sure you know how."

Without waiting for a reply, Xander turned away from the counter, where the cappuccino sat steaming, and stalked, stiff-backed, into the back room. Hank smiled at Xander's retreating back, but the expression looked more like bared teeth than kindness.

"You know that guy?" he asked stiffly.

"Yes," Liv grumbled, heading to the farthest table, by the wall.

"Seems like a dick."

Liv spun, and Hank stumbled to a stop.

"Xander's my friend," she snapped. "My *best* friend. And I'd appreciate you remembering that!" From over Hank's shoulder, Liv could see Xander gaping.

"Sorry, Liv. I didn't realize."

Hank's eyes were worried, and guilt joined hands with her annoyance. She stormed over to the table near the far wall, hoping the distance would keep them out of Xander's radar. Coffee had been a terrible idea.

It wasn't Xander who brought their drinks. The other server—Marcy, if Liv remembered correctly—brought out two steaming mugs. She placed a bill in front of Hank, but when Liv reached for hers, Marcy shook her head. "Xander covered it."

Liv peeked over to where Xander stood behind the counter, but he was studiously refusing to look at her. "Tell Xander I said thanks."

Liv took a sip and sighed. Hank watched her, smiling.

"What?" Liv asked.

His grin spread. "What do you mean, *what*?"

"Why'd you want to have coffee?"

Hank's chin dropped down, and he fiddled with the handle of his cup. "I—I missed you, I guess."

"Oh."

The admission sat between them. Liv didn't know how to answer, and Hank didn't take it back. Seconds passed as Liv's pulse shot back into overtime. She stared at the surface of the coffee swirling in her mug. Tiny universes rose and fell in the liquid depths as the moment dragged out into uncomfortable territory. *Oh God!* her mind screamed. (God didn't answer.)

"So tell me what you've been up to," Hank said.

"I dunno," Liv muttered. "School, I guess."

"That last sociology assignment was killer."

"I think I did okay." Liv's eyes flicked up and back down, taking in the open face, the warm grin.

Hank laughed. "I would've done a lot better if I'd had you to work with. Hope the final's a little easier." And suddenly they were talking again, the calm returned. Maybe, Liv thought, this was the start of something. Maybe Hank *did* like her after all. The thought that maybe—just maybe!—he'd broken up with his girlfriend in the last few days surged like a bird trapped in her chest, but it felt too crazy to be true.

An hour later, their coffees were finished, Hank loose-limbed and grinning, Liv warily returning his smiles. Every once in a while Liv could see Xander eye them from behind the counter, but he made no move to intervene.

"I should probably get going," she said, reaching for her purse and standing. "It was good talking, Hank."

"It was," he agreed, following her to the door. He didn't touch her, but he was closer than he needed to be—closer than anyone stood, except for Xander—and he pushed open the door for her, waiting as she passed.

Liv's heart was pounding as they reached the street. She kept expecting him to head off on his own route, but Hank followed her until she reached the bus stop. He stepped into the shelter alongside her, his bulk blocking the midafternoon light. Hank's blond hair had a golden halo, his grin that of a beatific god.

"This was really nice, Liv."

"Yeah, it was."

He reached out, running a finger along Liv's cheek and stopping whatever else she had intended to say. She was frozen in place. That gesture was *not* just friendly. That meant something. But before she could figure out *what*, Hank spoke again.

"I was thinking about what happened," he said. "I feel bad about how things ended." Liv couldn't think past the screaming of her brain. Hank's hand stroked her jaw as he leaned closer.

"I think you're a really cool chick," he said. "I like hanging out with you." He moved in, his other hand circling her waist. "And I thought maybe we could do it more."

His hip bumping into hers dislodged a single word: "W-what?"

Hank grinned down at her—so close by now all she saw were teeth—and then the distance disappeared entirely. They were kissing, Liv realized in shock, in the bus shelter, and anyone could see! It was so crazy she couldn't think. He tasted sweet and syrupy, and his lips were soft—puffy almost— and Liv was distracted by the sudden fear Xander would see this.

What am I doing? her mind shouted.

Hank let her go, and she stumbled back, catching herself against the wall. His smile grew wolfish.

"Liv," he said quietly, "I had this crazy thought."

She took a gasping breath. "O-okay?"

"And I'm only saying this to you 'cause you're really cool, and I like you." He brushed her hair from her eyes, and Liv let out a soft moan. His smile grew. "I like you a lot."

Liv nodded. She had no idea what was happening, but she knew she wanted Hank to kiss her again. Her entire body was humming, a panicked fervor centering on the brightness of his smile.

Hank caught hold of Liv's hand. "I was wondering if you'd be interested in meeting Hayley sometime."

Liv blinked. Her brain wasn't adding things together. She glanced down at their twined fingers and then back up. "Hayley?" The name didn't make sense.

Hank nodded. "I told Hayley about you—how awesome you are, and how you asked me out that time—and she said she'd be cool if you were interested in hanging out with us, if you catch what I'm saying." He tugged at her hand, but this time Liv didn't move. She frowned.

"Sorry, but who is Hayley?"

"My girlfriend."

The word was a bucket of ice water. "Your girlfriend?" Her breath was gone, air sucked from her lungs.

"I thought that you might be interested in hanging out with us." Hank's gaze dropped down the length of Liv's body, and she had the sudden urge to cover her breasts. His leer made her feel naked. "Maybe get to know each other better. I think you two would really get along. We've done it before, you know. Two's fun, but three's better." He chuckled.

He reached for her again, but Liv got her hands up at the same time. Instead of the kiss Hank had been expecting, Liv shoved his chest. It felt like hitting a brick wall. The impact shot up her arms, jarring her shoulders.

"What the—?"

"I need to go," she cried, pushing past him.

"Where?"

She shot him a fierce look. "Anywhere away from you!"

Hank's smile faded. "But I thought you liked me."
She turned to run.
"Not anymore!"

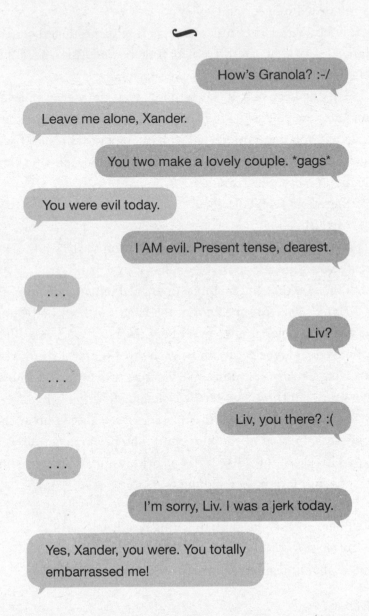

How's Granola? :-/

Leave me alone, Xander.

You two make a lovely couple. *gags*

You were evil today.

I AM evil. Present tense, dearest.

...

Liv?

...

Liv, you there? :(

...

I'm sorry, Liv. I was a jerk today.

Yes, Xander, you were. You totally embarrassed me!

I apologize, dearest. But Granola irks me.

I'm still not talking to you.

I'm sincerely sorry. (To you, that is. Not to him. Loathsome creature!)

. . .

Sorry. Sorry. Sorry. Sorry. Sorry. :(

. . .

Have you forgiven me yet?

Nope.

Now?

No.

How about now?

NO.

I'm very cute, you know. And I'm not sure you've heard, but I have five thousand pounds a year. I've taken a place in Boulder for the season. Miss Dashwood and her sister will vouch for my parentage.

Go away, Xander. I hate you.

Forever? :(

No. But tonight I do.

Ugh. I was horrible, Liv. I'll admit it. He just looked so damned smug.

If it makes you feel better, I hate Hank more than I hate you.

Well, that doesn't bode well. O_O What happened?

I don't want to talk about it right now.

But you're okay? Like-physically?

Yes.

Tell me about it later?

Maybe.

Promise?

Yes, but only if you don't bug me about it.

You have my word as a gentleman.

Call me tomorrow, Xander.

I will.

. . .

Feel better, Liv.

Liv knew something was up the moment she came in the door. A wall of odor hit her. Fried chicken pervaded the air, one of the few foods Liv truly hated. She kicked off her shoes, irritated she hadn't gotten home in time to attempt cooking (or at least ordering) something healthier. Even soup would have been preferable. The thought of soggy fillets of breaded chicken boiling in oil turned her stomach and always had.

"Liv?" her mother called. "That you?" Her voice sounded unnaturally chipper.

Liv dropped her bag by the door. "Yeah, it's me."

"Come on up. Gary and I just started to eat."

Liv groaned. Gary didn't eat anything unless it was an animal. He didn't enjoy it unless it had been fried. The smell should have been a dead giveaway of his presence.

"I'm not sure I'm hungry," Liv lied. If she got away now, she could grab something downtown with Xander, or eat cereal after her mom went to bed. She reached for the door handle.

"Come up and visit then," her mother said. "You haven't seen Gary in ages."

Liv's shoulders drooped. After their last run-in, Liv had no intention of making small talk. "All right. But just for a minute."

With leaden feet, Liv trudged into the kitchen. Gary was already elbow-deep in a plate of fried chicken, his lips and fingers shiny with fat. Liv's stomach clenched in revulsion. He didn't stop eating; he just nodded to her as she came through the doorway.

"How was school?" Katherine asked warmly.

Liv slumped down in her chair. "School was fine."

"You get that final math assignment handed in?"

"Did that yesterday. Today was review."

Gary watched the interaction with docile interest, fleshy jowls swinging as he chewed.

"So it's just exams now?" Katherine prodded.

"This week is still classes, then finals begin. And on that note . . ." Liv pushed back from the table, forcing herself to smile. "It was great seeing you, Gary, but I should get back to studying."

"You still doing that make-believe stuff?" Gary grunted.

He wiped his fingers on the paper napkin and dropped it onto the tabletop beside him.

"A-am I what?" Liv stammered.

"The online stuff," he said, waving shiny fingers at her. "The movies and such."

Liv felt her stomach contract, the smell of fried chicken mingling with her horror. She glanced at her mother, who was staring at her hands. "Mom?"

No answer.

"Your mother tells me you've been fooling around with that whole *Star Trek* thing for years."

"*Starveil*," Liv said.

"That you almost flunked high school because of it, and you'd picked it up again."

"That's hardly . . . that's—" Embarrassment and fury seethed under her skin, prickling like sparks.

"Katherine said she tried to talk sense to you, but that you wouldn't listen."

Liv spun on her mother. "That's not fair! I haven't vidded at all since we talked!"

"And she thought we should sit down and talk about it," Gary finished.

Liv stared at him: the balding head, stiffly pressed shirt, the sweat rings under his arms. "Like you and I should talk?" Liv coughed. "What would *that* accomplish?"

"Liv, please," her mother said quietly. "I thought with another perspective we'd be able to find a way to get along and—"

"I just can't believe you told him!" Liv shot back. "You and I talked! I'm doing *exactly* what you asked me to. I gave up fandom for you! Why is Gary involved at all?"

Her mother's lips trembled. "Because it's hard, Liv—*really hard*—to parent sometimes. And I can't do it alone."

"I don't know what that's even supposed to mean. I told you I'd stop, and I've stopped. I'm passing all my classes!"

"But that's only the start," Gary said. "Freshman year's a cakewalk compared with real life. You think of that?"

Liv bolted from her chair, the glasses rattling as her knee smacked the edge of the table. "Who asked you!?" she shouted. "What makes you an expert? You don't even have kids! You've never been married! You're the manager of a—a goddamned printshop!"

"Liv!" her mother gasped.

Gary stared at her with his dull, colorless eyes. "So what's your game plan?"

"My what?"

"What are you doing after college?" Gary asked. "Where are you going with all this tech stuff? What's the plan?"

"I don't have to answer that."

"It's a legitimate question, Liv," her mother added. "What *are* you planning to do with your life?"

For a split second, Liv couldn't answer. With fandom gone, she had no idea what she wanted anymore. And that was something Liv could never explain to her mother, never mind Gary.

She stormed from the kitchen.

"You wouldn't understand!"

⌣

Liv glared at the laptop screen, the cursor pulsing in time to her thoughts. There was footage on her hard drive: unused segments from the bonus features of the various *Starveil* films and twice as many outtakes with Xander, music and audio clips. It was all there, ready to make another #SpartanSurvived vid.

She just needed to break her promise to do it.

"Liv?" her mother called from outside her bedroom. "Can we talk?"

"No."

Liv slid her chair over to the door and locked it.

"Liv, sweetie," her mother pleaded, "I know you're angry I talked to Gary, but if you'd just listen you'll—"

Liv put on her headphones and hit Play.

The well-known trill of the *Starveil* theme flooded her ears, and she let out a sobbing laugh, overwhelmed by emotion. This was it. This was where she felt at home. Not at the dinner table with Gary! Not doing stupid school projects that didn't matter. The sound of her mother's knocking faded, and Liv sighed in relief. She needed this the same way she needed air. The last few weeks, she'd felt trapped, but now she was free.

Decision made, Liv opened the video editor and smiled.

It was time to bring that passion back to fandom.

9

"ONCE MORE, WITH FEELING."
(BUFFY THE VAMPIRE SLAYER)

Channel: https://www.youtube.com/user/SpartanSurvived

Home page-Video 3: Sitrep

The video opened up to a grainy black screen, buzzing with interference. With a blare of trumpets and flashing lights, a line of military text shot forward into center screen, breaking through the haze. It read:

EVIDENCE MOUNTS! SPARTAN IS ALIVE AND PLANNING A RETURN TO TERRA!

The trumpets faded into the iconic Starveil theme as the screen cut to Major Malloy. He wore the same military uniform as in the previous video, his hair combed similarly, lighting identical. In fact, if not for the change in background—a star freighter's dingy interior—you would almost think it was the same shot. A robotic voice announced him: "Rebellion leader, Major R. C. Malloy, en route to Terra, addresses Rebel Troops."

Malloy nodded once at someone off-camera then, lifted his chin. "Attention, comrades," he growled. "This is a message for Rebels across this star system and beyond." The screen swung on a dolly, and a new image appeared on top of it: a fan-made manip of Spartan in a military hospital. A time stamp ran across the screen while Malloy's voice continued.

"This footage was acquired by Rebel command a few hours ago."

The screen snapped with static, the star freighter abruptly replaced with video of the smoking ruins of a Rebel holdout (clips that most die-hard fans would have recognized as behind-the-scenes shots from the second and third *Starveil* films). In the short segment, posters of Darthku's face insolently plastered the side of random buildings, burning in the wake of an apparent attack. The footage shot forward through the flames, showing the face of a young man. It was Spartan—incongruously laughing at something or someone—alongside a lounging group of Rebel soldiers. With a buzz of interference, the footage ended.

The music switched to the thudding bass of Darthku's theme. From the black background, Major Malloy emerged from the shadows like a wraith.

"Captain Spartan was assumed dead," he said. "That assumption is incorrect!"

The robotic voice returned: "Rebellion leader, Captain Matt Spartan, as seen in the Rebel-controlled freehold of Adonis."

Another (fan-created) clip began. This one featured spliced footage of a young Tom Grander, in another, lesser-known science-fiction role, deftly interspersed into later *Starveil* shots. Offscreen, Malloy's voice rose.

"Your determination," he said grimly. "Your research.

Your proof of Spartan's whereabouts is the only hope we have for Spartan's safe return."

The musical theme changed as another fan-generated video clip ran. This was followed by a series of photo manipulations showing Matt Spartan in various situations: flying a shuttle, fighting Darthku with a sword, saving a child from a burning building, drinking with a pixelated Malloy. With each new image, the beat of the drums rose until—with a blinding flash of light—both audio and video abruptly ended.

From the inky darkness, the first hint of an image appeared. Pixels? Stars? For several seconds, it remained murky black splotched with gray, then the scene faded into a wide shot of the galaxy. This cut to a medium shot of Major Malloy. He stood on the top step of a war-damaged colonnade, the filtered light falling in glowing bands around him.

"People in the Rebellion"—the screen jittered—"have seen Captain Spartan." The image cut to a close-up of Malloy's face, grooved with determination. "These people have given us the first hints of his whereabouts"—another jitter—"there is proof of his survival!"

The screen brightened until Malloy's face seemed to glow. His gaze—directly into the camera—was hypnotic. "We will bring him back . . . alive!"

The #SpartanSurvived hashtag appeared, and the screen went black. For a few more seconds, the music trilled on, fading into the sound of static before disappearing altogether.

Liv leaned back from the computer and rolled her shoulders, wincing at the telltale pop of her back. The vid wasn't as smooth as her others had been, and some of the viewers would certainly notice she'd reused a number of scenes of

Major Malloy. (Thankfully, with Xander's laughter, they had plenty of outtakes.) She smiled bleakly. The process of hashing this vid together from bits and pieces had wrung her out, but seeing it finished left her with a sense of accomplishment. Her smile faded. Now if only she could spread that emotion beyond *Starveil* to the rest of her life.

Liv opened the Spartan Survived YouTube channel, trembling fingers hovering over the Upload button. If she posted this latest video to the net, her mother would most certainly find out, but if Liv didn't, she'd essentially given up, rolled over, and called it quits. She frowned, undecided. A sacrifice would be made either way, but Liv had felt alive the last two days, and that was more than she could say for the weeks of depression before. Taking a deep breath, Liv hit Upload.

She'd just thrown gasoline on the fire. Now it was up to fandom to keep it burning.

~

@JoesWoes: @LivOutLoud Liv! LIVVVV!!!! Have you checked the #SpartanSurvived tag yet? THERE'S BEEN ANOTHER POST! *shrill fangirl screaming* WATCH IT!!!

@LivOutLoud: @JoesWoes Cool! :) What'd you think of it?

@JoesWoes: @LivOutLoud OMG-LOVE LOVE LOVEDDDDD IT!

@LivOutLoud: @JoesWoes Sounds pretty good! ;)

@JoesWoes: @LivOutLoud Better than good! AMAZEBALLS!

@LivOutLoud: @JoesWoes LOL

@JoesWoes: @LivOutLoud I swear this whole Spartan Survived thing feels like a spin-off! MRM was vague in his livestream, but I KNOW there's more!

@LivOutLoud: @JoesWoes Spin-off for what?

@JoesWoes: @LivOutLoud For another franchise! MRM can't ignore the fans anymore! My gut says this means MORE MOVIES COMING!

@LivOutLoud: @JoesWoes OMG Could you imagine? :D X 100000

@JoesWoes: @LivOutLoud I am SO excited to see MRM's panel at Dragon Con this summer. I WILL ASK HIM OUTRIGHT!

@SpartanGrrl: @JoesWoes @LivOutLoud Joe-I never knew you were going to D*C. I'm going to Atlanta too! Oh Liv, you have to come with us! PLEASE!!!

@LivOutLoud: @SpartanGrrl @JoesWoes I wish I could, Kelly!

@JoesWoes: @LivOutLoud Why CAN'T you?

@LivOutLoud: @JoesWoes I can't afford it with school and everything. :(

@JoesWoes: @LivOutLoud Get a job. Get a loan. Do whatever you need to do, just GET THERE!!!

@LivOutLoud: @JoesWoes You are an enabler, Joe. :P

@JoesWoes: @LivOutLoud For Spartan, I'd do more than enable!

@LivOutLoud: @JoesWoes Hee! ;P

@JoesWoes: @LivOutLoud Just keep it in the back of your mind, all right?

@LivOutLoud: @JoesWoes Deal. :)

Liv heard her mother's staccato heels cross the hallway outside the bedroom, and she quickly opened a second tab to hide the Spartan forum. A tentative knock interrupted.

"Liv?" her mother called. "You in there?"

"Uh-huh. Why?" Liv struggled to her feet, grabbing clothes off the floor and throwing them into the hamper.

"Is your stomach feeling better, sweetie?"

"A little."

There was a longer pause.

"Can I come inside and talk?"

Liv glanced warily at the chaotic jumble of her room. "Sure, I guess. I was just cleaning up."

The door opened a crack. Her mother peeked in but made no move to enter. Liv rushed from bed to basket, sweeping dirty clothes into piles and throwing them aside. On impulse, she grabbed the edge of the sheets and tugged them free.

"Wow. You really *are* feeling better," her mother said. "Haven't seen you cleaning in ages."

"Think I had a touch of the flu," Liv lied. "Feeling better now."

"Xander called while you were asleep."

Liv's hand faltered on the edge of the sheets, losing the fabric. It sprung back, flinging crumbs overhead. "He did?" That made no sense at all. Xander didn't use phones. Texting was his form of communication. "Did he say what he wanted?"

Her mother shook her head. "I asked if he wanted to leave you a message, but he said not to bother you." Katherine's voice softened. "Are you guys fighting about something?"

"No, not at all." Liv jerked the sheet one last time, and it sprang free from the mattress, coiling into a ball. "I can't imagine why he didn't just text." When she turned back, her mother was watching, her narrow brows knit together.

"Was there something else?"

Her mother's expression tightened. "I've been monitoring the *Starveil* fandom the last couple of weeks. I . . . I saw the new video, Liv."

Liv took a breath, waiting.

The lines on Katherine's face grew deeper. "So are you going to say anything?"

"Like what?"

"An explanation, for one. What were you thinking?"

Liv lifted her chin, heart thudding heavy in her chest. "There's nothing to say. I did it. You saw it. End of story."

"Oh for Chrissake, Liv," her mother snapped. "I'm really getting tired of this teenage angst crap!"

"You don't understand!"

"No, Liv, I don't. I never have."

Liv sat on the unmade bed. "Fandom is part of my life. A *good* part. I have friends—"

"Not real friends."

"Yes, real friends! Just because you can't walk to their house doesn't mean a relationship is any less real."

"Liv . . ."

"Fandom's something I love! And I won't let it affect my grades, but I *am* going to be part of it."

Her mother's hands rose to her hips. "Liv, you're so close to finals. I won't allow this."

"I'm studying, Mom! There's no reason I can't vid, too." Liv forced her voice to be steady. "You can't stop me."

"How could anything good come of this?! If you get wrapped up in fandom again now, your grades will suffer."

"Fandom is *good* for me, Mom!" Liv said, voice rising. "And just because you don't understand it, doesn't mean it isn't true."

Her mother scowled at the action figures standing at attention atop the dresser, the posters lining the walls. Her father had hung the first one. Liv knew they seemed juvenile to her mother, but she couldn't bear to change them. To do that would mean the end of an era, another loss.

"Liv, this obsession of yours . . . It's just not normal."

"You're wrong."

Her mother turned back around. She no longer looked patient. Steeliness filled her gaze. "I want you to stop," she said firmly. "You need to move on!"

"No!"

"But, Liv—"

"It's my life!" Liv shouted. "Not yours. And I wish you'd remember that."

Her mother gasped, her mouth opening and closing again. "I—I've never tried to control your life. I want you to do what you want. I want you to be happy."

Liv stood from the bed, pushing past her mother and heading for the door.

"Then let me live it for once!"

⤙

Liv's newly washed hair was half-dried by the time she reached downtown Boulder. Sunshine warmed her face as she stepped off the bus. She breathed in the scent of the mountain city: pine needles and car exhaust and hot asphalt and fast food, but on top of all this, the odor of summer waiting just around the corner. In the last few days, spring had exploded to life. Bright splashes of green unfurled on dark branches. Where there had once been tentative buds of flowers, upended paintbrushes filled window boxes and buckets with a riot of color.

Reaching Cup O' Joe, Liv peered down the street. The orange Mazda was nowhere to be seen. She pushed open the door and squinted into the dim interior. The café was quiet, not a surprise for midweek. A few patrons hid in darkened corners, nursing mugs of coffee and perusing newspapers; others hid behind books. Jazz filtered through the speakers. On the far side of the shop, a solitary writer sat in the corner, pecking at her laptop. She looked up as the bell on the door chimed.

Liv scanned the counter, but Xander wasn't standing behind it. No one was. Frowning, she made her way to the cash register, catching sight of Xander's down-turned head. The black waves of his hair were tangled across his forehead, his lower lip caught between his teeth as he fiddled with the steam valve of the machine. He stood up as Liv's footsteps neared.

"How can I help—" Xander's words ended midsentence. He smiled, but it didn't make it all the way to his eyes. "Liv," he said tiredly.

"Hey, Xander. What're you up to?" She grinned. "I mean, other than school and work."

For some reason, he didn't join in her laughter. He didn't smile.

"Nothing else," he said. "Just that."

"You have a minute to talk?"

He shook his head. "Sorry, no. I'm a little busy," he said. "We're shorthanded today."

Liv glanced at the nearly empty interior and then back. Something felt off, but she didn't know what. She took a step back from the counter.

"All right then, I'll just—I'll go." She started toward the door. "Sorry for bothering you, Xander."

"Stay."

Liv peeked back at him, her long hair giving her the half second when Xander couldn't see her, but she could see him. It was enough time to read his face. He looked frustrated. More than that, he looked *sad*. But by the time Liv turned the rest of the way and pushed her hair behind her ear, the mask had come back down: Had she imagined it?

"Are you sure you want me to stay?"

"Yes, of course." He ran his hand over his face. "So how about you, dearest?"

"Mom and I had a fight."

"Oh?"

"She was snooping around online and . . ." Liv's words faded as she caught sight of the pale shadows under Xander's eyes, the wan smile. Her chest tightened. "Xander, what's going on with you?"

The fake half smile slid from his face. "Arden and I broke up."

Liv's breath caught. "Oh my God."

"She said she didn't think it was working anymore."

"But . . . but why?"

He shook his head. "There were a lot of reasons, but in the end, Arden said she didn't think we fit anymore." He gave a bitter laugh. "And now I'm stuck with an extra ticket to Dragon Con, and I've got to find someone to take her place in the room, and . . ." He ran his fingers through his hair. "Goddamnit! This wasn't supposed to happen this way!" His voice seethed with British inflection.

"I'm really sorry." Liv stepped closer to the counter. She wanted to touch his hand, but some part of her knew this wasn't the right thing. Not now. Not after this.

"Are you?"

"Yes, I am. You two were good together. And you seemed . . . happy."

He wiped his fingers on the dish towel he held. "Some of the time," he grumbled. "But not always. And when she said it was time to move on, I . . . I didn't try to stop her, Liv. I knew it wasn't working out."

"I'm still sorry."

His brows drew together. "Why?"

"Because you're hurting, and I hate to see that. But you'll be okay, Xander. You will."

He gave her a weak smile. "Thanks, dearest. That means more than you know." He looked around the café. "Give me a minute, and I'll come sit down. I was supposed to take a break an hour ago, but Marcy called in sick last second." He pursed his lips. "No backup." He nodded to the line of stools. "If you sit at the counter, I can hang out with you for a while."

"That'd be nice."

He turned to grab two mugs from the shelf.

"I've been missing our Mickey Dee's tradition. With all the coffee dates, we kind of put those on hold."

His back was to her, so she couldn't see his face, but Xander stopped, his hands tightening on the mugs. After a long moment, he turned back around.

"I've missed them, too."

And this time when he smiled, it went all the way to his eyes.

⌒

Xander, you around?

Just getting off work now. Maladroit Marcy FINALLY appeared.

I'm STARVING. Please tell me you haven't eaten yet.

I haven't eaten yet.

Really . . . ? Or are you just saying that?

Well, I haven't eaten any fast food. I could certainly go for that. ;)

Good! Because I stole the cookies out of the bag, but I'm NOT having dinner with Gary and Mom. No way!

Stealing cookies. What a mad beginning to a life of organized crime. Do tell me more!

Fortune cookies, Xander. And I'm bringing them to share with you (so be nice about it). Gary was absolutely AWFUL when he showed up tonight.

I can't believe your mother dates that imbecile. Truly, Liv. What DOES she see in him?

Safety, I think. :(

I'll swing by your house if you want to make a run for it. I have $20 just waiting to spend on fast food. Burgers! Trans fats! Everything a man's cholesterol-clogged arteries can imagine.

LOL Let me grab the fortune cookies. :D

Fries and fortune . . . The perfect combination.

The night was warm and the parking lot was filled with teens. Some sat on the hoods of cars, others lounged on the concrete-cast tables and chairs by the doors. Liv and Xander sat in his car, though their windows were rolled down to catch the breeze. Xander had his seat half-reclined. His stockinged legs stuck out the window, the silver buckles on his shoes sparkling under the streetlamp. He took another sip of iced tea, the straw rasping as it hit the bottom.

"You ready for your fortune?" Liv asked as she reached for her purse.

Xander shook his cup, rattling the ice. "You don't really believe in that stuff, do you, Liv?"

She shrugged and unwrapped the first cookie. "I do and I don't. I believe in science for the most part, but sometimes . . ." She broke the cookie with her thumb. "I think there's more." She pulled the paper from the broken shell. "I think life gives us little hints."

"Well, let's hear it then."

A shiver rose up Liv's spine as she read: "You will go on an unexpected journey."

"Pfft! That's hardly a real fortune," Xander said, waving away the words. "That could mean anything. Try another."

Liv pulled the second from her bag and opened it. "How about this?" She scanned it, and her lashes flared wide. Tonight *everything* seemed to be talking to her. "Follow the untrodden path," she read. "It leads to greatness."

"Good lord," Xander groaned. "That's even worse than the first one. If this is supposed to convince me of divine intervention, it's not working." He reached out, waggling his fingers. "Here. Give me one this time. Maybe I'll have better luck with the universe's Magic 8 Ball."

She put the third one in his hand.

"You create your stage and your audience is waiting," Xander read in a sarcastic tone. "Good lord, if that's supposed to be a message about Arden, I don't appreciate the universe's sense of humor!"

He rolled the paper into a ball with his thumb and forefinger and flicked it at Liv. The fortune bounced off her forehead and landed in her hair.

"Really, Liv," Xander said. "These are absolutely useless.

They're worn-out clichés everyone uses over and over again. Five dollars says the next one's something along the lines of: All journeys begin with a single step."

"You're being a cynic."

"I *deserve* to be a cynic. I just got dumped." He shook his head. "Fortune cookies are not the secret to destiny."

Liv shrugged. "I dunno. I think there's something to them."

"Something like what? A bored fortune cookie writer?" Xander rolled his eyes. "I don't think he was even trying. I could come up with a better one than that."

Liv pulled the paper ball out of the strands of hair and smoothed it into a strip before dropping it into her purse.

"Here," Liv said. "There's one more."

She unwrapped it, slid her thumb into the groove of the cookie, then stopped. "You do this one," she said, offering it to Xander.

"How about together?"

He put his hand on hers, and Liv closed her eyes, wishing for an answer. For something that made *sense* in a world, which didn't. Xander's fingers were warm around hers. The tingle began. He hadn't moved, and neither had she.

"What are you waiting for?" Xander whispered.

She opened her eyes to find him watching her. His lips were parted, a line of concentration between his brows. He was closer than he needed to be, and he looked concerned (or, she thought, like he was about to kiss her). Liv closed her eyes again.

"Nothing. Just concentrating." She took a shaky breath. "Now."

Their twined fingers pressed down, and the cookie crumbled. The paper dropped to the floor, where it disappeared under the seat. For a heartbeat, Xander didn't release her fingers.

"What does it say?" she asked.

Xander let go of her hand and leaned over to fish the paper out.

"Fortune favors the bold," he read. "Cliché hat trick. You owe me five dollars."

"That is *not* what you said."

"Fine." His gaze dropped to the paper. "At least it's a sentiment I can actually believe in." He looked over at Liv, smirking. "So tell me, dearest, is this the cookie you were looking for?"

"Yes."

"Really?"

"I know what it means!" Liv laughed.

She glanced out the window at the bright moon and the people in T-shirts and jeans lounging in the lot. It had been winter when Liv told Xander her plan to bring Spartan back from the dead. Five months later, she felt the same trepidation to admit what she'd known since the fight with her mother. That she had to take a stand. She had to do this.

"This fortune cookie means something to you," Xander repeated. "Are you absolutely serious?"

"Yes."

He stared at her for a long moment. "Is this a joke? Because I've missed the punch line."

She shook her head. "Not at all. I know that fortune's the one."

"And you know that *how*, exactly?"

"Because I've already made my choice."

Xander frowned. "I don't—"

"I'm coming with you."

"Coming where?"

"To Atlanta," Liv said, grinning. "I'm taking Arden's ticket and coming to Dragon Con."

Part Two

ATLANTA, GEORGIA

10

"DON'T TRY THIS AT HOME!"
(MYTHBUSTERS)

*J*une's arrival brought with it a sense of new opportunities. As impossible as it had felt when Liv had walked through the wide doors of the University of Colorado months earlier, she had survived her freshman year. Now the preparations for the trip to Atlanta, Georgia, where Dragon Con was being held, became her highest priority.

"I need a job," she told Xander. "A good one."

"One job won't cut it," he scoffed. "If you want spending money, you should have been saving all year."

"Well, unless you've invented a time machine," Liv said, swatting his arm, "that really doesn't help me now, does it?"

"Don't yell at me." Xander laughed. "I'm just stating a fact. Dragon Con is fun, but the fun costs a hell of a lot of money, dearest."

Liv scowled. "What's my second option?"

"Get two jobs and hope to hell you have enough."

They blanketed the city with Liv's résumé, calling back to check on progress, and in a week, Liv was working full time as a graphic designer at a downtown photography studio (Gary's competition). During the day, she removed blemishes from people's photographs and created cheesy calendars for Boulder's elderly community. She spent her evenings alongside Xander at Cup O' Joe as a part-time waitress to replace the often-absent Marcy. Liv's meager free time was spent replying to the avalanche of posts for #SpartanSurvived. Though she had a limited amount of time to vid, she was happy to discover Spartan's revival had taken on a life of its own.

Liv scanned the Dragon Con panel list daily. Most of the *Starveil* cast was slated to attend. Mike R. Miles told the press on several occasions that there would be a "big announcement" at the *Starveil* panel, and the Spartan fan forums were burning with speculation as to what that meant. Interest in *Starveil* reached a fever pitch. Liv just wished her father—who'd been a fan every bit as passionate as Liv was—had lived to see the series' resurgence.

Working twelve hours a day, Liv hardly had time to herself. Her occasional afternoons off were spent helping Xander finish his cosplay ensemble. She sewed braid onto the shoulders with meticulous stitches, adding painstaking embroidered details to the finished garment.

"Why did we sew the smoking jacket if you wanted to bring the military coat?" Liv complained, rubbing her pinpricked hands.

Xander preened in front of the mirror. "I wanted both," he said simply.

"Then why the rush? We could have finished this after we got back."

He twirled around. "You don't just bring one costume to Dragon Con." He laughed. "You bring a costume for every day!" He did up the row of mother-of-pearl buttons while Liv tidied the pieces of cloth from the floor. "What are you bringing to wear?"

"Clothes," Liv said, stretching her back.

He came up behind her, resting his hands on her shoulders. "Besides your regular clothes, dearest."

Liv shook her head. "Nothing."

"Are you sure you don't want to?" Xander's hands slid down her arms, and Liv shivered at his touch. "You would be breathtaking. I could help you sew a cos—"

Liv spun around. "No way! No more costumes."

"But you'd be glorious, dearest!" He spread his hands wide. "I can imagine it now! Liv Walden, secret force behind Spartan Survived is feted at the Dragon Con parade."

"Not going to happen." She giggled.

"I'd be happy to accompany you anywhere." He winked. "Even the darkest dens of licentiousness."

"But *not* in costume."

"Cosplay . . . ?"

Laughing, Liv threw a handful of scraps at Xander, who danced out of the way before they could reach him. "No more sewing!"

He grinned and backed away. "It's Dragon Con's loss."

"No, it's my aching back. You don't even know how to sew!"

Liv's nights were spent counting her quickly accumulating money and waiting—*praying!*—for a seat sale. The prayer was answered the last week of July. Dragon Con, for better or for worse, was happening. And with Arden's ticket in hand, Liv suddenly realized what it would mean.

She'd have a chance to meet Spartan . . . *in person.*

"For the love of all that is good and kind, Liv, you have *got* to stop jiggling your leg!" Xander snapped.

"Sorry." Liv forced her knee to stop the rapid bounce that had punctuated the flight from Boulder to Atlanta.

"Just try to relax. Okay?"

"Relax . . . right."

She peered out the window of the plane to where the Hartsfield-Jackson airport loomed. The tarmac was dotted with jets, the sky a blinding blue. Liv's heart felt like it was about to explode, and she rubbed her sweaty palms on her pant legs. Dragon Con wasn't just a dream. It was happening! She stopped breathing as the thought that she was now in the same city as Spartan hit her straight in the chest.

Her leg started vibrating again.

Xander gave an exaggerated sigh. He put a hand on her knee. "Liv, dearest, may I suggest a trip to the powder room?"

"No, I'm fine."

His fingers tightened. "Then could you just *stop*? I swear I'll scream bloody murder otherwise." He pulled his hand back, crossing his arms on his chest. "You are driving me crazy."

The sight of him florid-faced and furious struck her as funny. "Sorry." Liv giggled.

His lids dropped to half-mast. "But you're *still* jiggling."

Liv glanced down, realizing she was. "I . . . I can't seem to stop."

"Try!"

Focusing on one body part at a time, she forced her body to

go completely motionless, but it felt like trying to rescrew the lid on an overflowing bottle of soda. She had so many butterflies her stomach was alive.

"Better," Xander grumbled.

A small laugh escaped Liv's lips, and Xander looked over at her.

"What?"

"The thought of you getting carted off the plane does sound kind of fun," she said.

He glared at her. "We'd miss Dragon Con if I did."

"Might be worth it," Liv teased.

"Are you sure? If you were stuck bailing me out, you'd never get to meet Tom Grander in person, and your mother would have you locked up until you were thirty."

At the mention of Spartan, Liv felt her nerves bounce back into panic mode. "Oh God," she moaned. "This is really happening, isn't it?"

"Yes, dearest," Xander said with dry good humor. "It is."

She turned back to the window, breathing in shallow gasps. The plane was almost at the terminal. She and Spartan were in the same city now. He was seeing the same blue sky. Breathing the same air.

"I still can't believe I'm going to meet Captain Spartan!"

"You're meeting *Tom Grander*, actually," Xander said gently. "Why are you so freaked out about this? Grander is just a person."

"He's not 'just' anything. He's Spartan."

"He *plays* Spartan. There's a difference."

The seat belt sign flicked off, and the plane's occupants surged. Liv looked up to discover Xander pulling their carry-ons from the overhead bin. "How can you hate actors so much when you're studying drama to become one?" she asked.

"I don't hate them. I just don't worship them the way you do."

"But that doesn't make sense."

He handed Liv her bag and pushed his way into the teeming aisle, leaving room for her to follow. "But nothing," Xander said. "In my experience, most actors are self-centered jerks."

"Not all of them." Liv laughed. She dragged her bag up the aisle a step at a time, waiting as people jostled and shoved their way out of the plane.

"Not Tom Grander is what you mean."

"I've watched all his interviews," Liv insisted. "He's so earnest . . . so funny. He really seems like he cares about the audience experience. He wants his fans to be happy."

"He'd be stupid not to," Xander snorted.

"Say what you want. I just don't believe Tom is pulling off some giant lie about who he is. My mom can't stand *Starveil*, but even she likes him. She says he's approachable."

Liv reached the ramp into the airport and began to walk faster. It reminded her of the windowless hallways of a star freighter, and Liv had the odd thought that perhaps that was where they'd filmed those scenes.

"Look," Xander said, pacing her, "an actor is a professional liar. He's a paid busker."

"You're mean, Xander!"

"No, I'm not. I'm honest. Everyone puts them on a pedestal, but we shouldn't. Acting is a service industry, as much as waiting tables. An actor works for us, not the other way around."

"Us?"

"The people in the seats. If we don't come, the actors don't get paid. It's simple economics."

Liv stopped, and the people behind them swirled past like leaves in the wind. "I can't believe you think that lowly of actors when you *are* one."

Xander straightened his stiff upright collar, brushed his hands down his doeskin coat, and smirked. "I'm hardly *just* an actor, dearest." He offered his arm. "Now, shall we disembark, m'lady?"

Liv grinned and slid her fingers into the crook of Xander's arm. At the end of the hallway, the open door beckoned. A wall of people filled the space. When Liv saw them, her stomach flip-flopped, panic making her woozy.

"I feel like I'm going to be sick," she moaned.

"You will." Xander laughed. "But that'll be as a result of nonstop partying and the subsequent con-crud, *not* from meeting Tom Grander." He dragged her into the crowd. "Hold on tight. This ride doesn't slow down for anyone."

And with that, Dragon Con began.

❧

Liv had spent her entire life feeling like a nerd. The social outcast. The freak. In middle school, she'd tried to hide her differentness, keeping her online activities completely anonymous and wandering through fandom as a lurker. But no matter how hard she tried to appear normal, there was some invisible mark that kept her apart from her real-life peers, like they could sense she wasn't one of them. Liv wasn't invited to football parties or asked out on dates. She hovered at the edges of social events, looking in and wishing she could join. By high school, she'd made the jump to visibility—at least online—creating vids, reading fic voraciously, and even wearing the occasional *Starveil* T-shirt to school. But living in Boulder, a city of mountain climbers, sports fans, and activists, she'd always known she was an outsider.

Arriving to drop off their bags at the Marriott, the feeling disappeared.

While Dragon Con took place in a number of downtown Atlanta buildings, the Marriott hotel was the epicenter of the event. The entire atrium floor of the gigantic building swarmed with a melting pot of nerd culture. Stormtroopers chatted amicably with aging television stars while waiting in line at Starbucks. Bewigged anime cosplayers posed alongside pro wrestlers and *Game of Thrones* characters, the lines for panels filled with teenagers and seniors alike. At least ten variations of Captain Matt Spartan had spied Liv's Spartan "Only One Man Calls Me Darlin'" T-shirt and had made a point of shouting out a "Hello, darlin'!" to her. She stared wide-eyed as glass-walled elevators shot up fifty-two floors like pods in a launch tube. Everything—from the glaringly bright carpet swirling with psychedelic lines; to the hotel's open ceiling ringed by story after story of balconies, the distant roof so high it made her head spin; to the people decked out in cosplay—was torn from a science-fiction novel. It seemed Liv had spent the last eighteen years in search of her people, and in one sudden explosion of fate, they'd all been brought together in this place in time. Her eyes filled with tears as a sudden awareness hit her.

They were all nerds.

Xander's friends had a room on the ninth floor. With their bags dropped off in the empty hotel room, Xander and Liv took the elevator down to the atrium. Xander scanned his phone for the Dragon Con itinerary while Liv people-watched. "Badge pickup is over at the Sheraton," he muttered. "We'll need to bring our blue confirmation postcards."

"Confirmation," Liv repeated. A group of young men dressed as Disney princesses flounced past, laughing and smiling.

"You brought the postcard, right?" The sharpness of Xander's tone brought her attention back.

"What?"

"The lost postcard line is the worst," he said. "We'll be stuck there for hours if you don't have it with you."

"I'm sure I've got it here somewhere." Liv dug through her purse and pulled it out. "See? Right here."

"Good. Just don't lose it."

And then they were off into the streets. It was odd to step outside into the bright sunshine after the party atmosphere of the Marriott. It was, Liv realized in surprise, still daytime. People who worked in Atlanta's downtown core were going about their usual lives, but among them surged a tide of convention attendees, rushing through the crosswalks, shouting out greetings to fellow fans, and slowing traffic to a near standstill. Liv and Xander followed the river of convention-bound humanity down the streets.

"You were right," Liv said, grinning.

"About what?" Xander drawled. "You'll have to be more specific."

"This," she said. "It's amazing." The smile on her lips grew by the minute.

With badge pickup in full swing, the Sheraton was shoulder to shoulder with people. A Dragon Con volunteer guided Liv and Xander to the door of a massive ballroom, where they stood in line for what felt like hours. Liv stood on tiptoe, marveling at the switchback line that spread across a space the size of a football field.

"This is just for badges?" she said, awestruck.

Xander grumbled something under his breath.

"I thought that the lines were only for the panels," Liv added.

"Oh, there'll be those lines, too." Xander pulled his pocket watch from the pocket of his waistcoat and peered at the face. "We're supposed to be meeting up with the rest of the crowd at the red couches in the Marriott in half an hour. We're not going to make it." Xander had yet to explain to his two roommates that Liv—a complete stranger to them—had taken Arden's place in their room. "Honestly! I don't have time for this nonsense."

"I can hold our place," Liv offered, hoping she sounded more confident than she felt. "You go ahead and meet up with your friends. I'll find my way back to the Marriott."

"You can't pick up my badge and I can't pick up yours. It's all done with ID." He looked behind them. A sea of faces, many of them in cosplay, stared blindly forward.

Suddenly Xander grabbed Liv's hand. His fingers were warm and sure, and Liv had a moment to think how right it felt before Xander spoke.

"Screw it," he growled, heading back the way they'd come. "This is no time for being sheep."

"But I thought—"

"Just follow my lead."

Xander swung back through the crowd at the entrance. A knot of volunteers were directing people into the queue, which led up to the front of the room, where ten tables had been set up with badges. Others herded attendees who'd lost their receipts for badges into another, equally long line. Once the con-goers reached the desks and had picked up their badges, they exited through the side door, again policed by members of Dragon Con's volunteer community.

"Where are we supposed to—"

"Shh!" Xander hissed. "Just look like you know what you're doing. Have your blue card and ID ready to go."

Liv's hand grew sweaty as she and Xander wove their way to the exit hallway. At the door, a weary-faced man in a Dragon Con T-shirt watched the multitudes pass through the exit, pointing them up the hallway toward the street.

Xander leaned down to Liv, his mouth brushing her ear, and she shivered. "Wait for it . . ."

"For what?" Liv asked, distracted by his closeness.

She felt Xander tense beside her. His fingers tightened.

A young man dressed as a Pikachu came up to volunteer, lifting his badge and asking the man a question. The volunteer turned away from Xander and Liv, pointing to the other end of the hallway. The door was open, the guard distracted.

"This!" Xander jumped forward. "Get inside and get into that crowd. Don't stop!"

Xander was already moving, so Liv had no choice but to keep up. The two of them pushed through, emerging in the chaotic front of the crowd. The line disintegrated at this point;

knots of people milled around desks. Xander sprinted to the first one, leaving Liv to follow. Liv had never broken the law in her life, and she kept expecting the volunteer from the exit to shout at her or an alarm to sound.

Xander gave the table attendant a half bow, his hand resting over his frothy lace tie.

"Alexander Hall," Xander panted, pulling out his driver's license and a blue Dragon Con receipt card. "Esquire."

"Your first name's Alexander?" Liv said. "I never knew—" Xander gave her a sour look, and she swallowed the rest of her words, fighting down a foolish grin.

"You're in the wrong line," the woman at the desk said in an exasperated voice. She pushed her glasses up with an ink-stained finger. "H through M is the fourth line. Over there." She reached out her hand toward Liv, snapping her fingers. "Blue card and license, ma'am."

"Here," Liv said, pushing them into her waiting hand. "L-Liv. Liv Walden. We transferred the card from Ard—"

"Walden," the woman said with a tired sigh. "You're over in the last line, W through Z." She pointed. "Way down there."

Xander gave the woman a warm smile. "You've been most helpful, madame. If there's anything I can do to assist you in the future, please let me—"

The volunteer ignored his thanks, then leaned around him and bellowed: "NEXT!"

Her shout released them. Xander nudged Liv toward the far side of the tables. "I'll meet up with you out in the hallway."

"Hallway. Right."

Before Liv knew it, Xander was off at the H-to-M table, and she was standing at hers, picking up a laminated four-day pass with her name—Liv Walden—across the top. It was done: Her first foray into a life of crime was a success! She looked out the exit door to see Xander lounging against the wall in the hallway. One hand was tucked in the center seam of his waistcoat, the other spinning the pass on the end of a lanyard, a pose of Napoleonic contentment. Liv sprinted to meet him, crossing paths with a seven-foot Wookiee. He roared at her, and Xander stifled a bout of laughter behind a handkerchief.

In the hallway, the crowds of con-goers were twice as bad. Liv stumbled through, finally making it to Xander's side. "I can't believe we just did that!" she panted, her grin so wide it hurt her cheeks.

"Did what?" he said, tucking the silk handkerchief into his pocket. "I stood in line the whole time. Didn't you?"

Laughter bubbled from her throat. "So what now?"

Xander draped the lanyard around his neck and pointed back down the hallway where they'd sneaked inside ten minutes before. "Now we go back to the Marriott to meet our roommates."

A twinge of anxiety filled her chest, but Liv forced her smile to stay.

"And after that?"

"After that we go find the Spartan coven and find out just how Internet famous you really are."

～

A trio of steampunk characters were waiting on the red couches when Xander and Liv arrived back at the Marriott. Two of them were women—one short and young, one tall and middle-aged—fully dressed in corsets, brocade, and elegantly laced footwear. Their companion was a young man wearing a bowler hat, goggles, and a stuffy-looking plaid suit with what appeared to be a jet pack attached to it. A faint trail of smoke from an exhaust tube rose to the balcony above. In avid discussion, the trio unfolded themselves from the couch, standing as Xander and Liv approached. Too many people filled the Marriott, and the room was stuffy with bodies, though Liv swore the temperature dropped a few degrees when they caught sight of her.

Xander gave a bow far more formal than the one he'd given the volunteer at the Sheraton ballroom.

"Greetings, everyone," Xander said. "May I introduce the illustrious Liv Walden, known far and wide as LivOutLoud of the *Starveil* fandom." He swung his arm back to include her. "She's the unexpected guest I texted you about."

"Hi," Liv said, giving the group a nervous wave.

The older woman nodded stiffly. The younger stared at Liv in concern. "But what happened to Arden?"

"Arden and I are no longer an item," Xander said. "Haven't been for some time."

"Oh!'

The man cleared his throat and touched the brim of his hat. "Charmed, m'lady. I'm Mario Torres."

"Mario," Liv repeated.

Xander gestured to his friends. "Liv, this is Emma." The tall, willowy woman inclined her head at the introduction. "And this is *also* Emma." The short young woman gave a shy smile. "Mario is the younger Emma's elder brother, even though I personally think Mario looks a little more like the other

Emma. She's my cousin. The other Emma is staying with friends on the twentieth floor."

Liv's mind swirled to keep up with the introductions. "The other Emma?"

"I'm actually Xander's second cousin," she explained. "But not to worry. We're all friends."

The shorter of the two Emmas stepped forward and offered her hand.

"So is it true?" she asked hesitantly.

"Is what true?" Liv glanced at Xander, but he was busy rearranging the tucks of his shirt. Her gaze returned to the younger of the two women.

"That you're the secret force behind Spartan Survived."

Liv grinned. "You follow *Starveil*, too?"

"It's my first fandom," Emma sighed. "I love it so much!"

And with that, the ice was broken.

Liv had made it to Dragon Con. She had people to stay with and money in her pocket. Now all she needed to do was meet Spartan and she could die happy.

⤙

The Thursday-night party was the biggest event Liv had ever attended. The crowd moved like a choppy ocean, the mass of con-goers rolling over and around the multi-tiered atrium level of the Marriott. People in cosplay were the norm, not the exception, and Liv's "Only One Man Calls Me Darlin'" T-shirt seemed a weak substitute. Liv stared as she passed a full-size TARDIS (with the ninth doctor inside) chatting with a yellow-suited Walter White.

"I can't believe how many people there are," Liv shouted, voice pitched above the pulse of music that filled the room.

"You wait until tomorrow," Xander said. "Thursday is barely the start of the party. Only half are here so far."

"Half?!"

A woman dressed as Tekla—Spartan's kick-ass love interest—strolled past, and Liv's mouth fell open. Her Rebel uniform and boots, the locator on her belt, and headset communicator in her ear were so perfect they looked like they'd been lifted off a movie set. Maybe, Liv thought, they had.

"Where will everyone go if there're twice as many?"

"They go here." Xander chuckled. "It just means less open space." He nodded to the woman in Tekla cosplay. "Told you you should have made a costume. You could have rocked that outfit."

"I never could have pulled it off."

"You'd look amazing," he said. "You'll have to start believing me someday."

"Someday, but not today," Liv said with a nervous laugh.

"Ouch! I only speak the truth, dearest."

Liv sighed. "Fine, fine. I believe you for most things, just not this."

"You *could* pull it off."

"Doubtful, but you're good for my ego. Something that tight just isn't for me."

"Pity," Xander drawled, giving her a slow once-over. "You'd put that woman to shame."

Cheeks burning, Liv turned to watch the woman head into the crowd, giving Xander her profile. "If only I had my own seamstress," Liv sighed. She peeked back at him. "Someone who I could blackmail into making cosplay for me."

Xander stepped nearer as a congo line made of Greek soldiers danced past. "I can't sew, but any time you need an assistant, I'm there."

Liv grinned. "I know. I just like to bug you."

From somewhere above them, she heard a voice shout: "Liv! LIV! Liv out loud!" She looked up, half-expecting it was someone who liked the Émile Zola quote as much as she did. Instead, she caught sight of a group of women of all different ages, many dressed in *Starveil* apparel and fandom T-shirts. They waved to her from the second-floor balcony.

"Liv! I knew that had to be you!" The woman's shining face was its own answer. "Your avatar," she bellowed. "I'm Joanne—JoesWoes! C'mon up and . . ." Joe's face went white. "Holy SHIT! That's Malloy, Liv!" she shrieked. "The actor who plays Major Malloy is standing RIGHT BEHIND YOU!"

Liv turned around to find Xander fading into the crowd. "Xander?"

He looked back over his shoulder. "These are your friends, dearest," he said with a laugh. "Go chill with them. I'm going to scope out the rest of the action."

"But I don't . . ."

He was already too far away to hear, and she didn't feel like yelling that she didn't want to be alone, that crowds like this terrified her. Her chance was gone, Xander already a blur of lacy cuffs and brightly colored coat in the surging crowd.

"Text me!" Liv shouted.

Xander didn't answer.

The coven was nothing like Liv had expected. Joanne was in her late thirties or early forties, with a helmet of wavy auburn hair and the build of a football player gone to fat. She rushed forward the moment Liv neared the crowd of *Starveil* fans.

"Liv!" she screamed. "I told Brian it was you, but he wouldn't believe me!"

Liv found herself trapped in a crushing bear hug.

"Joanne?" Liv laughed as she attempted to extricate herself from the woman's beefy arms. "It's so weird to actually meet you."

JoesWoes let go and grinned. Liv's first impression was shock: the woman was old enough to be her mother. That revelation, followed by the embarrassing thought that Joanne wrote fan-fic in her spare time, left Liv struggling for words. It made sense, of course. Joe had been in the Spartan fandom since *Starveil*'s earliest days, which meant she had to be old enough to write when Liv had only been a child. It just hurt Liv's brain to reconcile the JoesWoes she always thought of as a teen with the matronly woman dressed in a long maxi skirt and faded *Starveil Four* sweatshirt.

"I'm so glad you came along!" Joe said. "I thought you might back out last second, but you made it!" She grabbed Liv's hand and dragged her into the center of a diverse group of people. Their one connecting feature was the *Starveil* clothing and cosplay. "Listen up, everyone," she announced in a schoolmarm's voice. "This here is Liv. You know her as LivOutLoud. I told you she'd come!"

Liv opened her mouth to respond, but Joe didn't give her any leeway to talk.

"Now, this is Kelly," she said, pointing to a dainty young

woman—possibly in her late teens or early twenties—with a wide smile and elfin features. "And this is Brian. StarVeilBrian1981, that is." She gestured to a thin, prematurely balding man, standing awkwardly at the side. He stared down at his feet, ignoring Liv altogether. "And this is Leah, and Denise, and Beth. Over there is Maria, and then Ivy, Jenna, Molly, Alicia, Isabel, Dale, Sherry . . ." The names ran together.

Unlike Xander's standoffish roommates, the *Starveil* fandom was bound together by an intense love of the films and a furious hatred of Spartan's demise. This anger was centered directly on Mike R. Miles, whom the fans held personally responsible for the character's death. Minutes after Liv's arrival, the group was chatting avidly as everyone shared his or her own stories of losing Spartan, and then finding him again through the Spartan Survived hashtag. Liv realized what she'd sensed all along: She'd been right not to take the credit. For one, she hated being in the spotlight, but more important, seeing it unfold before her felt like getting an insider's view into what her small idea had wrought. The fans had hope and anticipation, passion and focus. Spartan, the survivor of the Elysium, wasn't just a character, he had become real to them. A private smile grew on Liv's lips. *She had created that.* Their joy was because of her action. It was her gift to them.

Liv's phone buzzed, and she looked down.

> You look happy, dearest.

She glanced up, peering around the teeming room. There were too many bodies to count, but somehow she found Xander across the open space between the circular balconies. His cravat was loose, his jacket hanging open, like a dissolute aristocrat from *Les Liaisons Dangereuse*. Their eyes met, and he grinned, the distance disappearing. Liv lifted her phone and tapped a reply:

I really am.

11

"INCONCEIVABLE!"
(THE PRINCESS BRIDE)

*L*iv could barely remember how she and Xander made it back to the overcapacity hotel room, but on Friday morning she was in bed alone, the room suffused with morning light. Liv squinted over at the second bed, where Mario and Emma slept, a line of pillows forming a wall between them. She turned the other direction, searching. Where had Xander gone? She looked down at the carpet and grinned. What appeared to be a pile of clothes was actually Xander, asleep in a heap of discarded clothing. He still wore his cosplay, one silver-buckled shoe on, the other dropped near the door, hand outstretched as if caught up in one final court bow. Seeing him, the late-night argument returned. In some strange sense of gallantry, Xander had insisted on giving the entire bed to her.

Liv's smile grew as she remembered the hours of partying. It was ten times what the CU Mixer had been; every person in the Marriott was a fellow nerd, and that fact made all the difference. Even so, Xander swore Thursday's party was nothing compared with Friday and Saturday's. Dragon Con was a celebration on a scale she couldn't imagine. Sleep was optional. Somewhere in the hotel, doors were opening and closing, the shower running in the room above. Liv slid her feet out of bed.

She groaned as the night caught up with her.

Fighting the urge to crawl back under the covers, she staggered to the bathroom, spending half an hour trying to scrub the taste of late-night nachos from her mouth. On any regular day, she'd wear the first thing she found in her closet, but today it mattered. In a few hours, Spartan would be in a large ballroom dubbed the "Walk of Fame." Liv knew there'd be a crowd waiting to see him, and she intended to be one of the first people in line. With shaky hands, Liv applied makeup and dressed in her nicest jeans and a black T-shirt she hoped distracted from her chest. She ran a comb through still-damp hair and winced. She looked plain, boring; the same old Liv as any other day. She sighed.

It would have to do.

Sneaking from the room was easy. No one stirred, though Xander did pull a pink crinoline over his head as she tiptoed past. Liv headed downstairs, fighting the queasy lurch of her stomach as the elevator plummeted nine floors. The Marriott was busy by any normal standard, though it was barely a tenth of the previous night's crowd. Liv grabbed a coffee from Starbucks and on a whim ordered three others, begging the server behind the counter for a bagful of creamers and sugar packets. It was her best decision of the day.

When Liv returned to the room, the coffees became an instant "thank you" for the hospitality. With grateful sighs, Emma and Mario pulled Liv into their conversation, talking about the panels they planned to attend and inviting her to the Steampunk Ball on Saturday night. When the crowd headed off to see a panel on the history of H. G. Wells, Mary Shelley, and Jules Verne, Liv checked her teeth in the bathroom mirror and dabbed her sweaty face. Now that the time had arrived, her stomach was tied in knots. She took slow breaths and wiped the back of her neck with a cold facecloth.

"Liv?" Xander called.

"Yeah."

"You want to go down to the vendor room before we get in line for the *Firefly* panel?"

She tossed the cloth into the bottom of the tub and opened the door. Xander lounged on the bed, one foot balanced on the other knee. He wore a puff of crimson silk at his throat, a tightly fitted waistcoat, and the brocade tailcoat that Liv had helped him sew the winter before. Liv was already sweating in her T-shirt and jeans; she had no idea how Xander wasn't drenched.

"The *Firefly* panel isn't until two, right?" Liv asked.

Xander looked up. "True. But I want to be in line early."

"You go ahead. I'll catch up."

Xander frowned. "You okay?"

"I am," she said with a nervous laugh. "It's just that Spartan—"

"Tom Grander, you mean."

"Right. Tom Grander's down on the Walk of Fame in"— she checked her phone—"an hour." Her stomach did a somersault, and she took a shaky breath. "I—I want to be down there with plenty of time to spare."

"Do you want to grab something to eat before we go?"

"Not a chance," Liv said. "I'll probably throw up if I do."

Xander's face broke into a roguish grin. "Do you promise if you spew, it'll be *on* Tom Grander?"

"Stop it, Xander." She grabbed her Dragon Con pass off the side table and looped the lanyard over her head.

"You look very attractive, by the way," he said. "I do hope Mr. Grander appreciates the effort."

Liv blushed and turned away. "I doubt he'll even notice I exist."

"You sure? I mean, you're part of the reason his popularity's soaring. That has to count for something—even if the person it's helping is Tom Grander." With a catlike stretch, Xander stood from the bed, straightening his clothes and sliding on his shoes. "Now, if you are done with your toilette, we should probably get going. It'll take us a bit to get through the crowds, and if you want to line up early, I'd rather it didn't take us all day to get to the Walk of Fame."

Liv stared at him for several seconds. "But I thought you wanted to line up for *Firefly*," she said. "You'll miss it if you come with me."

Xander gave a one-shoulder shrug, already heading to the door. "I want to hang out with you at Dragon Con. Everything else is just icing on the cake."

～

The line to see Tom Grander moved a foot at a time, taking them toward a table where the actor sat, shaking hands. He was a little shorter than the towering height Liv had expected from his role in *Starveil*, though she'd heard movies did that to people. But average height or not, Tom's face was even more perfect in person. Film did *not* do him justice. He had high cheekbones, a straight nose pert enough to be pretty, a lantern jaw darkened with the perfect amount of morning stubble, and an arching bow of lips, which curled into a toothy grin at the slightest provocation. Liv felt giddy just being near enough to see him with her own eyes, to share the same air as went into his lungs. The woman in front of her sighed, and Liv caught her eyes, the two women grinning in unspoken understanding.

When Liv and Xander had arrived forty minutes before, the line had already stretched out of the ballroom and down the hallway. Spartan was big news this convention. By the time they made it to the final stretch, Liv's heart was beating so fast she felt light-headed. Liv wobbled, and Xander caught her by the elbow, smiling to himself. He let her go, pulling his phone from his pocket. It looked incongruous against the beringed hand and lace cuffs.

"If you throw up on him, I *am* going to record it," he said, tapping through the phone's apps. "Don't think I won't, Liv."

The line moved forward another step, and Liv felt the blood drain from her face. "You're awful, Xander. A real friend would cover for me so I could escape. Recording it would be just plain mean."

Xander put a hand to his heart. "You wound me, dearest. I'm standing in line with you, aren't I?"

She glared at him. "No one *made* you be here. You can leave anytime."

"Ah, but I wouldn't miss this for the world." He chuckled.

Liv couldn't tell if he was joking, but the truth was, she was glad he was here. She had a feeling she might clam up and become mute in Tom's presence. Before she could think about it too much, the line moved again, and then there was only one person between her and Tom Grander.

"Breathe, Liv," Xander said quietly.

She pressed her lids closed, sucking air in through her nose and pushing it out through her mouth like a fish out of water. The room seemed to spin around her, and she caught hold of Xander's arm for support.

"Do you need smelling salts?"

She blinked. The hall reappeared in all its blinding clarity. "You have smelling salts with you?"

"Yes, actually, I do." He pulled a small apothecary's bottle from an inside pocket. "Never attend con without them."

For some reason, this tiny detail—Xander's noticing that she felt sick and having smelling salts to deal with it—suddenly seemed the most endearing thing in the world.

"Thank you, Xander, I—"

But before she could take the bottle, the people at the table moved aside and Liv found herself staring into the very bright, very blue eyes of Tom Grander. He smiled his million-dollar smile. In that moment, Liv's legs stopped functioning. For several long seconds, she just stared.

He was beautiful. Perfect. *Unreal.*

"You're up," Xander said, nudging her forward. "Move."

"Hi there!" Tom boomed. He gave another wide smile. "So glad you could come out to say hi!"

She opened her mouth, but nothing would come out. For a crazy split second, she thought she was going to cry.

"I'm Tom," he said warmly, offering her his hand. She shook it with icy fingers, and he released her hand at once.

"This is Liv's first con," Xander said.

"Well, I'm glad you could make it," Tom said. "It's always great to meet my fans."

His eyes flicked to the person behind her. They were almost done, Liv realized. Almost done and she hadn't said a thing! She took a wheezing breath, and suddenly all the things she'd felt, thought, and dreamed of came tumbling from her mouth.

"Mr. Grander, it's such an incredible honor to meet you."

Tom's gaze returned to Liv, his smile widening. "Thanks!"

"I've been a fan for years. A decade, actually. I saw the first *Starveil* movie with my dad when it first came out, and I've seen every one since then. Your character—Captain Spartan— is more than just a character to me. He's my hero. I've wanted to meet you for years and . . ."

Minutes before, Liv hadn't been able to speak. Now she couldn't stop. It was like a bottle of champagne had been shaken, then uncorked. Every emotion—bottled for the last ten years—released.

"When your character died, I realized I just couldn't let you go. There was no way Spartan could be dead! It was impossible. I couldn't bear the heartbreak."

In the last seconds, Tom's face had taken on the pained expression of a weary parent dealing with a hyperactive child who'd just eaten an entire bag of candy. "That's great," he mumbled. But Liv couldn't stop.

"I started a post about Spartan's death—a challenge to fans everywhere. And before I knew it, people all over the world were making things. They were bringing you back from the dead through videos, stories, manips . . ."

Tom looked up at Xander, the cocky self-assurance switching to anxiety.

"And I'm just so glad you're here at Dragon Con. I'm so glad to meet you," Liv said. "You've been part of my life forever. You're this link to my childhood, to my dad. My hopes and dreams. And I hope you realize everything you mean to me."

Her monologue stopped as quickly as it had started. The bottle was empty, all her words splattered on the table between them. She took a shaky breath, the moment of self-admission leaving her drunk on emotion.

Tom Grander leaned back in his chair. His eyes narrowed. "Are you telling me you're the person behind Spartan Survived?"

"Y-yes! That's me! I came up with it!"

"And you," he said, pointing at Xander. "You're the guy in the video, aren't you?"

"I was just the hired help," Xander said, lifting his hands. "*Starveil*'s not my thing. No offense."

Tom scowled at Xander before turning the same reproach-ful look on Liv. "Well, excuse me if I don't say thank you." His tone was venomous.

"Wh-what?" Liv choked.

Tom's face twisted in disgust. "You caused a hell of a lot of trouble for me," he growled. "More than you probably know. I'm just surprised you had the gall to come up here and rub it in my face."

Liv made a sound—a sudden exhalation—like she'd been punched in the stomach.

Xander's head bobbed. "Pardon me?"

"I—I . . ." Liv's tongue was in knots.

Tom stood up, his chair screeching behind him. "You and your boyfriend should've left well enough alone," he snarled. "I worked for years to get out of that contract, and I finally thought I'd done it, but you had to throw a wrench into the whole goddamned thing!"

"But I thought—"

"No one needed your interfering!"

"But . . . but Spartan died."

"And I wanted him to STAY dead!"

With a muttered curse, Tom stormed away, leaving Liv, and the long line of people behind her, staring after him. Liv swallowed against the stone in her throat. Her eyes burned, her ears rang. Xander stood beside her, whey-faced and silent. He, too, seemed shocked by the tirade.

"Oh my God," the woman behind Liv gasped. "Tom Grander just left!"

"Why?" someone asked.

"I don't know. He started shouting and—"

"About what?"

"Something about Spartan."

"What did she say?!"

"Who is she?"

Liv froze in place, tears blurring the room as the line shattered and disappeared.

Xander leaned in so his words reached Liv's ears, no farther. "Tom Grander's an A-list prick." His hands rose protectively to Liv's shoulders. "You didn't deserve that, dearest. Grander never should have said those things. What you did was—"

But Liv couldn't bear to hear any more. *Tom Grander hated her!* With a cry of pain, she tore away from Xander and sprinted from the room.

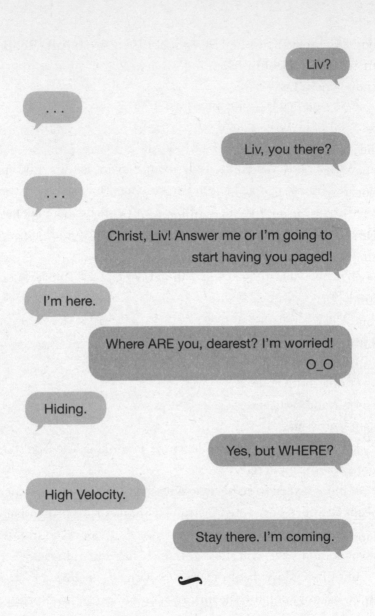

Liv?

...

Liv, you there?

...

Christ, Liv! Answer me or I'm going to start having you paged!

I'm here.

Where ARE you, dearest? I'm worried! O_O

Hiding.

Yes, but WHERE?

High Velocity.

Stay there. I'm coming.

Liv was in the back corner of the High Velocity lounge when Xander found her. She huddled over the table, hoping she'd wiped the worst of her tears away with the napkins a sympathetic waitress had brought her. Xander flounced in like an irritable viscount, clapping his hands and demanding to know where Liv was.

"Over here," she said wearily.

Xander strode past the bar—already busy at one thirty in the afternoon—joining her at the napkin-strewn table. Liv felt a new wave of tears threatening to fall the moment she saw the worry on his face.

"He's a fucker," Xander announced in the same tone he'd use to tell the time of day. "A self-centered little twat with no sense of compassion whatsoever." He slid onto the bench next to Liv, putting his arm around her. "Anyone as narrow-minded as Tom Grander ought to be culled from the herd, if you ask me. A job's a job and an actor has one: entertain. Nothing else." He rubbed circles on her back, and the small gesture left Liv weepy.

"It was my fault."

"Hardly!" Xander snorted. "The man's a pompous little toad! A buffoon unfit for any place except the bowels of a B-rated movie."

Liv sniffled.

"I was *not* impressed by that behavior," Xander added. "And he should *not* have done that to you. Pigeon-livered bastard. Rapscallion!"

"He's not."

"He most certainly *is*," Xander argued. "For God's sake, Liv, you brought the guy back into the hearts of thousands. And if rumors are right, Mike R. Miles is planning to relaunch Grander's career. If anything, he owes you."

Liv shook her head. "Tom Grander wanted Spartan dead."

"But why?"

"I don't know, but he did."

Xander's face set in grim lines. "Look. Tom Grander can say whatever the hell he wants. He's a dick. But the truth is, a movie serves its fans, *not* the actors. If the fans want Spartan alive, they get him alive. Their opinion is the only one that matters."

"I dunno." Liv shook her head, too tired to argue.

"C'mon," Xander said, more gently now. "Grander isn't the only person we came to see." He stood up, offering Liv his arm. "Let's go cheer ourselves up by waiting in a line for an hour."

"You know how to sell it." Liv laughed, though it had a weary sound.

"I promised you the entire Dragon Con experience, and that means more than one run-in with a self-centered actor. This is your first con, Liv. This event was made for people like you." His voice dropped. "For people like me, too."

"All right. I'll go." Liv gathered her badge and left the payment on the table next to her bill. "Thanks for coming to find me."

Xander smiled and pulled her into a tight hug. "It wasn't even a question, dearest."

Liv nodded, wondering why she felt like crying again.

～

Xander insisted that Friday's agenda was "Cheer Liv Up."

"That's stupid," she said. "You should go to the panels you planned. I'll go up to the room."

"Absolutely *not*!" Xander held out his hand, and Liv placed her fingers in his. "You're here for the ambience and experience, dearest. And that's what you're going to get!"

Arm in arm, they did a promenade of the Marriott. Xander shifted into his BBC voice, doing a running commentary on the various specimens of con life. He pointed to a female Han Solo.

"Here we have the delightful Rule sixty-three cosplayer, decrying assigned gender roles and displaying an aptitude for tongue-in-cheek reference."

Liv leaned her head against Xander's shoulder. "I think her Prince Leia partner makes that cosplay."

Xander winked. "Agreed. And if you're ever in the mood, Liv, I'd be happy to play accessory to your cosplay."

His thumb brushed her knuckles distractedly, and she dropped his gaze. "Someday, but not today." But she grinned as she said it.

The next item on the "Cheer Liv Up" agenda was a visit to the Peachtree Mall for a fast-food extravaganza. Liv stared at the teeming lines with openmouthed wonder.

"Maybe I'm not that hungry after all."

"Pfft. Let's go."

Xander put his hand on Liv's back, guiding her forward, and Liv bit the inside of her cheek to keep from grinning. When had *that* become their normal?

"Over there," Xander said. "I see just the place!"

"Where?"

"Keep walking. Tell me when you notice."

Liv laughed aloud as the sign came into view. She spun around and threw her arms over Xander's shoulders, hugging him. "Chinese food!"

"And fortune cookies." He stepped into a line that was at least half a block long. "The wait is quite atrocious, but I can assure you that the food is fresher this week than any other week of the year."

When they sat at the table, Xander held out his cookie for her. "Together?" he asked.

Liv took his hand, but she couldn't focus on a question. All she could think about was how his fingers felt around hers, and what it would feel like if he were to touch her arm, her cheek, her—

"Liv . . . ? Still there, dearest."

Face burning, she opened her eyes to find Xander looking at her, a lopsided grin tugging at the corner of his mouth. For a second, she thought he'd make a joke of it, but he said nothing.

"Sorry. Got distracted."

"I figured."

"I'm ready now," she said. "Let's break this in three . . . two . . . one . . ."

They pressed down on the cookie, and it crumbled between them. Liv snatched up the slip of paper before Xander could reach it.

"If you keep waiting for the perfect moment," Liv read, "you'll never see it arrive."

Xander chuckled. "Don't think you're in any danger of that."

She looked up. "What do you mean?"

He plucked the piece of paper from her fingers and tucked it into his lapel pocket. "You already live in the moment, dearest. I'm the one who needs the reminder."

Liv wanted to ask what he meant, but Xander was already excitedly discussing their next event of the day. They attended two panels: one for *Sherlock*, another for *Supernatural*. With both, the die-hard fans arrived so early the lineups were down the street. Lines, Liv decided, were just part of the Dragon Con package, and she spent her time laughing with Xander while fielding Joanne and Brian's barrage of messages.

@JoesWoes: @LivOutLoud Liv, you're coming to the Starveil panel right?

@LivOutLoud: @JoesWoes Um . . . Maybe. Not sure.

@StarveilBrian1981: @LivOutLoud @JoesWoes YOU HAVE TO COME TO THE PANEL! There's going to be a big announcement. You HAVE to be there!

@LivOutLoud: @StarveilBrian1981 I'll try, Brian.

@JoesWoes: @LivOutLoud I'm gonna let Captain Spartan answer that for me: "Trying is for fools. Rebels just do!" I'll hold your place. Okay, Liv?

@LivOutLoud: @JoesWoes :>S Thanks.

Given Tom's behavior, Liv wasn't sure whether she would go to the *Starveil* panel, but there was still time to decide. The *Starveil* panel, and MRM's much-anticipated announcement, wasn't happening until Saturday.

By the time they left the second panel, Liv's feet were swollen, her clothes creased and sweaty. It had been less than eight hours since she woke, but with the crowds, she already felt like she needed a shower.

"I need something that doesn't smell like other people," Liv said, sniffing her sleeve and wrinkling her nose in disgust. "You mind if we head up to the room for a bit?"

"Not at all . . . I've got another outfit to display."

"You would," she said with a weary laugh.

Xander's costume closet was a Mary Poppins-esque

carpetbag of options. Liv wished she'd brought half as many, if only to deal with the need to change more than once a day. The two of them headed to the elevators, intent on cleaning up before they went out in search of supper. When the elevator doors opened, Liv found herself face-to-face with the *Starveil* crowd on its way to the atrium.

"Liv!" Joanne shouted, pulling her into a hug. "I was hoping I'd run into you. Where have you been hiding, hon?"

"Nowhere. Just busy."

"Isn't that the truth. But you're here now, and I'm not letting you out of my sight," Joanne said. "There's a rib place a few blocks away. Start walking toward the Sheraton; you can't miss it. The *Starveil* crowd's meeting there for dinner. You've got to come!"

"Sounds good," Liv said with a smile. "I'd love to see everyone." She turned. "Do you mind if I ditch you for a bit, Xander?" Joe followed her line of sight, and her eyes widened into saucers.

"Holy SHIT! You're the guy who played Major Malloy in the Spartan Survived fanvids, aren't you!" She grabbed his hand, pumping it energetically. "It's so fantastic to meet a fellow *Starveil* fan!"

Xander pulled his fingers out of her grip and wiped his hands on his silk pocket handkerchief. "I'm no *Starveil* fanboy, madame. I'm just a common man's actor."

Joanne's grin grew ravenous. "Common my foot! You were fantastic in that vid. Liv, did you . . . ?" Impossibly, Joe's eyes seemed to grow even bigger. It seemed for a moment they might pop entirely out of her round face. "Oh my God, Liv— you did it! YOU! You're Spartan Survived, aren't you?!" she

218

screamed. People around them turned in surprise, and Liv felt the blood drain from her cheeks.

"I should have KNOWN!" Joe shrieked. "I told Brian the vidding style was familiar! I *knew* it was that behind-the-scenes footage he'd ripped. It was you all along! I can't believe it, Liv! That was YOU!"

She grabbed Xander's arm and pulled him against the wide curve of her bosom, hugging him with the sticky-fingered stranglehold of a child embracing an unhappy cat. Tug as Xander might, he couldn't get away a second time.

"Bring your friend Malloy along, too!" Joe insisted.

"It's Xander," he hissed as he tried to wriggle free.

"Malloy has to come with us, Liv. He HAS to! I won't take no for an answer. Come! COME!"

Liv caught sight of Xander's tight jaw as he finally extricated himself from Joe's steely grip by peeling her sausage fingers back one by one. He stepped back to inspect the condition of his coat.

"I'll definitely come along," Liv said, grinning. "But Xander might not want to—"

"But everyone's going to want to meet him, too!" Joe crowed. "The group of us are the heart of fandom!" She pointed at Xander, and he retreated another step. "You have to be there, Malloy! Besides, we've got to get ready for tomorrow's *Starveil* panel. Figure out who is going to ask what."

"Joe, I'll come, but I don't think—"

"So it's settled," Joe said, brushing past them. "I'll see the two of you in an hour or so. Just head toward the Sheraton! Like I said: a rib place. You can't miss it."

She disappeared into the crowd. The up elevator had already

left, and a new group of people waited by the doors. Xander checked his reflection in the mirrored panels, the muscle in his jaw twitching like a cat's tail. He smoothed his hands over his coat's lapels and tugged the edge of his cuffs below the sleeves.

"Your friend Joanne is unpleasantly pushy. I thought I was going to have to start screaming for assistance."

Liv laughed. "Now *that* I would've paid to see."

Xander's annoyed expression transformed into an impish grin. "And would you have saved me?"

"Of course I would." She tried to keep a straight face but couldn't keep from giggling. "You're not the only one who can save the day, you know."

He leaned forward, lifting an eyebrow. "And how, pray tell, would you have saved me, dearest?"

"I would have come up with something. But I'd expect you to pay me back for my heroic actions, seeing that I'd saved you from Joe's attentions and all."

Xander smirked. "Oh, I would . . . And it would be delicious, I promise."

Liv laughed and turned away, wondering just how red her face had grown. The bell for the next elevator rang, and both Liv and Xander rushed forward, eager to take their spots. Xander lolled against the glass, indifferent to the crowd, but Liv froze. The entire structure seemed poised to explode, the doors pinching her backside as they closed. She squeaked and pressed closer to Xander, and he slid his arms around her. If not for the thirty other people crammed into a space meant for ten, Liv would've found the embrace exciting. As it was, the intimacy was overshadowed by a growing sense of panic. She pushed her forehead against Xander's neck, refusing to look out the glass wall as the floor fell away beneath them. She felt, rather than saw, Xander brush her hair back behind her ear.

"You all right, Liv?"

"Fine," she muttered. "Just squished."

"Mmm . . . sorry about that."

His fingers loosened on her back, and she immediately regretted her words, but there was no way she was going to explain in an elevator full of strangers that she wanted to be this close to Xander, just not this close to the rest of them.

"I should text Joe and say you're not coming for dinner," Liv said.

"Why wouldn't I come along?"

Liv looked up. "You don't actually want to come with me, do you?"

Xander gave a one-shoulder shrug. "On the spectrum of con experiences, online friends definitely make the cut." He winked. "Besides, your secret's out now, so I might as well meet my die-hard fans. This is my first big role, you know. I've never been famous before, dearest."

Liv shook her head. "You're as bad as Tom Grander."

"Coming from you, that *should* be a compliment."

Liv snorted.

"Believe me. This time, it's not."

12

"WE'RE ALL MAD HERE."
(ALICE'S ADVENTURES IN WONDERLAND)

Getting *down* from the ninth floor was exponentially more difficult than getting up to it. The first elevator that arrived was a wall of costumed fans.

"We can fit," Xander insisted.

"Too full," Liv said, panicked by the thought of a nine-story drop to their death. "Let's grab the next one."

The second elevator arrived five minutes later. If anything, it was more overloaded than the first.

"Oh God, we'll never fit in there," Liv moaned.

"We could have."

The doors closed, leaving them behind.

"Should we take the stairs?"

"Stairs are for cardio, not con." Xander pressed the up button. "DC has a secret everyone knows and no one tells newbies."

"And that is?"

In seconds an elevator going up came rushing toward them. The doors opened, revealing a mostly empty interior.

"Sometimes," he said, "you have to go up to go down."

Liv followed him in, marveling at the scene below them. She could see the full scope of Dragon Con from her bird's-eye vantage, the floor a living mass of bodies. Tiny, toy-size people in cosplay moved in bright splotches of color ten stories down. And it wasn't just *one* section. The atrium level was equally packed, the hallways leading to ballrooms around the hotel teeming with people. With an unsettling rush, the elevator sprang upward, the figures shrinking to specks. Liv's stomach contracted, and she pulled back from the glass. They were incredibly high.

"I knew there'd be a lot of people," she said unsteadily, "but I didn't expect quite this many."

"There are people who come from all across America, from around the world, even. The whole Dragon Con experience brings geek culture together," Xander said fondly. "Sure, the crowds are irritating at times, but con wouldn't be con without them." The door opened, and a crowd of people got on from the floors above.

"You come every year?" Liv asked.

"Every year since I turned sixteen and my mom gave in to my constant whining."

"You, whine?" Liv said wryly. "Never."

Xander rolled his eyes.

"So what's your favorite part?" Liv asked.

"I love everything about it. The whole feeling of being able to be who I want to be." He stared out the glass panels, his smile fading. "There's no judgment here. We're all just friends, fellow geeks. I love that feeling."

Liv wanted to ask him more, but the elevator stopped again, and a group of Marvel characters climbed on, chattering loudly.

She hardly had room to breathe, let alone move. With a groan of connecting cables, the elevator started the sudden drop. Liv looked over at Xander, but he was staring out the window, lost in thought. Floor by floor, the doors opened, one or two people pushing in until every crack and crevice in the already small space was crammed with bodies. Liv had never felt such sympathy for sardines as she did now. As they picked up speed, Liv studiously avoided staring at the half-naked woman cosplaying as Leeloo from *The Fifth Element*. Instead, she read the warnings on the elevator door: 21 PEOPLE OR 4200 LBS. She closed her eyes, fighting the urge to scream.

Sometimes it was better *not* to know.

❧

Dinner was nothing like Liv had expected. After the brief rush of hysteria as everyone realized Liv had been behind Spartan Survived, she found herself at the center of a passionate discussion. Even when she'd answered all the pertinent questions, there was a steady stream of conversation to contend with. Liv struggled to categorize the friends she'd only known in digital format:

@JoesWoes was Joanne, though everyone referred to her as Joe. Loud to the point of unsettling, Joe was one of those people who were easier to connect with online. Joe's tone, Liv decided, was calmer in text, and Liv was glad that she'd gotten to know her via fandom first. Sarah, also known as @VeilMeister, had a different issue. Though Liv struggled with anxiety when talking to strangers or dealing with crowds, Sarah went catatonic. She stared mutely at her half-full plate when Liv asked her how she was finding con. Xander gave Liv a sympathetic look.

A minute later, Liv's phone buzzed.

> Sorry I couldn't answer you, bb. I have a hard time dealing with people up close.

Liv looked over. Sarah was staring down at her phone, thumbs moving back and forth. Liv's phone buzzed again.

> It's not you. It's me. Seriously. I've always been like this. Online works, but face to face? Ugh. Not so much. LOL

Liv tapped in a reply.

> It's okay, hon! I just thought I'd annoyed you somehow. :(

> No! Never. You're AWESOME, Liv! I can't believe YOU were @SpartanSurvived. I adore you!

> So how are you finding con?

> TBH, it's been overwhelming. Too many people. But I really love my Starveil peeps. They make it worth the effort.

> Totally AGREED! And thanks for texting.

> Thanks, Liv. I knew you'd get it.

> Of course, Sarah. (((HUGS)))

> :D X 1000000

Liv glanced up to see Sarah smiling to herself while the young woman at her side laughed and shouted. Vibrant and outgoing, this fangirl was a polar opposite to @VeilMeister's painful shyness. Her name was Kelly, and Liv had known her for years as the fic-writer @SpartanGrrl, who specialized in High School AUs, Baby!fic, and all forms of romantic fluff. Kelly had a surplus of social skills, and she spent much of the conversation hanging on Xander's every word. Liv wasn't sure why that irritated her so much.

A number of lesser-known fandom peeps attended dinner too: Leah and Denise were a lovely couple who spent the evening chatting quietly to each other. Ivy was a published science-fiction writer who had obsessions in the *Starveil*, *Star Trek*, and *Farscape* fandoms. She'd published her own series of books. Beth had flown in from England to attend the con and was as overwhelmed as Liv was. Alicia and Ivy were best friends who'd met in the *X-Files* fandom years before migrating over to *Starveil*. They'd attended the last six Dragon Cons together. Atlanta was their hub, a once-a-year holiday to connect with their "friends family" and escape their regular life.

"Will you guys be coming next year, too?" Ivy asked Liv and Xander. "Alicia and I come every year."

"It's our yearly pilgrimage," Alicia added.

Xander nudged Liv's foot, and she looked up. "See?" he said. "It's not just my fandom that makes the trek."

"I don't know," Liv said. "I hope I'll come back."

Her phone buzzed.

> You HAVE TO come back again! The first DC visit is just the tip of the iceberg!

Liv tapped in a reply.

> I'll definitely think about it.

"Well, I hope you do," Alicia said, then nodded to Xander. "Because Dragon Con friends are like none other. You might not see each other for a year, but when you're back together"— she snapped her fingers—"it's like you never left."

Liv laughed and talked, gravitating toward those like-minded fandom peeps who seemed to share her passions. In minutes, she felt like they were friends she'd known for years. And in digital form, Liv thought, she actually had.

Brian, on the other hand, seemed to have no friends at all, just accomplices. As one of the few men in the group, he had less in common with Liv than any of the women, but his lack of social graces put him further apart than his gender did. A computer programmer by trade, Brian considered himself above the average con-goer whom he described as "the sweating masses." At dinner, he drank whiskey when everyone else ordered soda, and after downing his third shot, his inner dialogue began spilling into muttered obscenities.

When the flustered waiter brought out the wrong type of whiskey, Brian burst into a harangue of angry swearing. Seeing Liv's horrified expression, Joe explained, "Brian is a bit rough around the edges, but he's got his good points, too."

He turned, giving Liv and Joanne an indignant scowl. "I can *hear* you, Joanne." He took another drink. "I'm bad-tempered, not deaf."

She continued, undeterred. "Brian's old school, raised on the West Coast with San Diego Comic-Con. It's got its own brand of crazy."

"What does that mean?" Liv laughed.

"Brian will wait in line for hours and hold your place," Joe said. "He's got standing stamina."

"For how long?"

"All goddamned night, if necessary," Brian grunted. Next to Brian, Xander smothered a laugh behind his gloved hand.

"All night?" Liv said. "That's crazy!"

"Oh honey, you haven't seen anything until you've seen the *Starveil* lineups at Comic-Con. They make Atlanta seem like child's play. That's when you need someone like Brian," Joe said. "He can be an angel when he wants to."

"I've already got plans to hold our places for the *Starveil* panel," Brian announced. "Joe's going to tag me off for bathroom breaks."

"You're coming to that, right, Liv?" Joe chimed.

"I'm, uh . . . not sure," she said, flashing to Tom Grander's face and feeling the familiar pang of guilt.

"But you have to be there!" Ivy gasped.

"You came all the way to Atlanta for this!" Kelly echoed.

Liv's phone buzzed three times in a row, Sarah typing as fast as her thumbs could move.

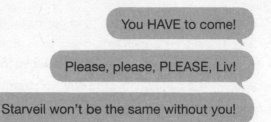

"I'll think about it, guys, I promise," Liv said. "I mean, I *want* to." She winced. "I really do, I just . . . I'm not sure if . . ." She closed her eyes, remembering Tom's seething words. "I just don't know if I can."

The table erupted in chaos.

"But you HAVE to go!"

"Liv, PLEASE!

". . . the whole point of coming!"

Buzz . . . buzz . . . buzz . . . buzz . . .

". . . what you're talking about!"

". . . have to be there!"

"Please, Liv. PLEASE!"

Liv shrank back. She hated conflict, and here she was, caught in the middle of it. "Oh God," she moaned.

Xander stood, and all eyes turned to him. "I'm truly sorry to interrupt, but Liv and I really must go." He pulled out his pocket watch, flicked it open, then closed it with a snap. "Time to go, Liv dearest. The train's leaving the station. Good-bye everyone! Have a wonderful evening."

He gave a brief bow to the group, then tossed down a twenty to cover his share of the meal; Liv did the same. Brian eyed the pile of cash, but the server swooped in and took it away.

"It was delightful meeting you all," Xander said, waving happily. He offered his arm to Liv, and she grabbed hold of it.

"But you can't leave!" someone called. "Stay!"

Liv pushed past the chairs, eager to escape. "Bye!"

Outside she burst into a peal of laughter. "Oh my God, I was scared I'd have to admit what happened with Tom Grander!"

"I could tell."

Liv shook her head. "I don't even want to know how they'd react if they heard what he said to me."

Xander shrugged, heading down the street at a jaunty pace. "I'm sure they'd be fine." He snorted. "Or at least most of them. As to Brian . . . I'm not betting on that horse."

"Thank you for coming along," Liv said. "I'm so sorry you had to go through that."

Xander's pace slowed. "Why?"

"Because . . . I assumed my friends were bothering you."

Xander chuckled. "Not at all, dearest. The stress directed at you concerned me, but the rest?" He waved his hand in the air. "Not so much. People are people, Liv, and at Dragon Con, it takes all sorts."

Liv's footsteps slowed. "So you decided it was time to leave just because *I was upset*?"

Xander winked. "Something like that."

◠

When Liv and Xander came in off the street, the music inside hit them like a wall of sound. Liv stumbled through the crowd, barely avoiding a head-on collision with a group of *Battlestar Galactica* fans dressed in military garb. They laughed and shouted, "So say we all," as they neared. Liv looked past the viper jocks to the vaulted atrium. Busy a few hours before, the Marriott was now bulging at the seams.

Celebrities mingled with their fans. Cosplayers posed with tourists. People danced and drank with Sodom and Gomorrah–like abandon. There wasn't a set dance floor, just knots of people pulled into motion, others joining and then falling away as the urge took them.

"Told you yesterday was a warm-up!" Xander shouted over the cacophony.

Liv tried to answer, but her words disappeared into the roar of the music.

When the Marriott's crowds became too much, they headed to the Hyatt, where a drum circle was being held. A pounding rhythm filled the air of the dimly lit room, dancers—in costume and in street clothes—moving to some primal beat. Liv watched, rapt in the moment.

A smile stole over Xander's face. "You ready to connect to your inner hippie?"

"I—I don't know," Liv said, her eyes widening as a troupe of belly dancers shimmied through the growing crowd. "I think maybe I'll stand at the side and watch."

"You'll do no such thing," Xander said, stepping nearer.

"What?"

He was almost against her, his body starting to bob in time to the rhythm. It should have been a laugh-worthy sight: an aristocrat nodding his head to a primitive beat, but somehow Xander made it sexy.

"C'mon, Liv," he purred. "I've seen you dancing. I *know* that you can move. This is exactly the same."

Liv let out a high-pitched giggle. "But this isn't dancing."

The bouncing moved from his legs to his hips.

"I beg to differ."

Liv glanced over his shoulder to the growing crowd. Everyone else seemed caught up in the movement. "I don't know," she said. "There's no music, just drums. It's . . ."

Xander's fingers slid up her arm to her elbow, resting there. "Try to let go," he whispered. "Feel, don't think."

"I can't."

"You can." He moved a breath closer. "For *me*, dearest."

Liv closed her eyes as his hands drew her up against him. A giggle rose up her throat, but the sound died as Xander's hands circled her waist.

"Let yourself go loose."

"I . . . I don't know how," she gasped.

"You do."

His hands moved her hips back and forth—guiding rather than forcing—until his beat became hers, and suddenly she *was* moving, her body bouncing along to the sound of drums. Liv's lashes fluttered open to find Xander staring down at her. His teeth flashed white in the dim room.

"And now, we start to move . . ." And he pulled her into the dance.

⌣

The second leg of the night was spent in the Centennial ballroom, where they regained their breath at the *Dr. Horrible's Sing-Along Blog* marathon. Liv sat at Xander's side, his arm looped over the back of her chair. He gave a whispered commentary as the vlog series played on the projection screen. Liv grinned and laughed and sang, but her mind was caught on one detail: that having Xander's arm around her felt inexplicably *right* and she wanted more. Dragon Con felt more magical than ever.

When the marathon ended, they returned to the Marriott's main atrium. It was awash with people, and cosplayers outnumbered the nameless fans two to one.

"You were right," Liv said. "I should've brought a costume."

Xander grinned as he led her to a knot of people dancing in the center of the floor. "Admitting it is the first step."

He began to gyrate in time to the pulsing techno beat, and this time Liv took her place at his side with no prompting. "What's the next step?"

"What?!" he shouted.

She threw her arms over his neck, pulling him forward. Xander's eyes widened, his gaze dropping to her mouth and back up.

"I said," Liv shouted, "what's the next step?"

Xander grinned. "The next step will be coming back with me *next* year and bringing a costume for each of the days."

The music changed, and Liv twirled out of his arms. "Maybe," she teased, winking at him over her shoulder. "Haven't decided yet."

He followed her dance movement through the crowd. "Maybe's not good enough," he growled as he caught her hand. "But I'll take it for now. And then I'll work on changing your mind."

Breathless, Liv danced closer. "Good . . ."

Liv and Xander danced endlessly, only stopping when

exhaustion had them wobbling on their feet. They stood at the side of the floor, people-watching. Xander's hair was matted with sweat, cheeks pink. His waistcoat hung unbuttoned, and his shirt was open enough to show a wide swath of muscled chest. When Liv saw it, her stomach tightened, and she looked away before he could see her blatantly staring. For a moment, she saw a familiar glint of blond hair, and her breath caught in her chest. She was certain she recognized the profile as Hank's.

The man turned.

Tom Grander, surrounded by his entourage, stood a stone's throw away from her. Their eyes met and caught. If hatred had a voltage, Liv would have been electrocuted on the spot. As it was, she was trapped in place. Her lungs refused to breathe. Her legs refused to move. Horrified, Liv watched as Tom leaned over to the man nearest him, whispering something in his ear. The other man, too, began to stare.

"Liv? What's . . . ?" Xander's tone shifted. "Oh, that arrogant bastard!"

"I gotta go." Liv forced her legs to comply.

"Go where?" Xander shouted.

"Bathroom break," she said, staggering slightly. "Back in a sec."

She found the hallway leading to the restrooms but accidentally walked into an unlocked storage closet rather than the facilities. It was only then that Liv realized the lineup she'd seen wasn't for a panel, but for the use of the toilets. After waiting in the bathroom line for an interminable time, she hid in the stall for ten full minutes, but there were too many people waiting to stay any longer.

It was time to head back to the atrium.

She headed out of the bathroom, aiming for the elevators.

"Hey!" someone shouted. "Hey, I get that!"

A man grabbed her arm, and Liv jumped.

"What?" she gasped.

A man in Mad Hatter cosplayer grinned down at her ample bosom. "My other ride's a star freighter." He laughed. "Like *Star Wars*, right?"

"*Starveil*," she muttered.

"I want a picture with you, babe."

"No thanks," Liv said, walking away.

"Just a picture."

"No."

She took another step, but the costumed man followed. "Hey!" he shouted. "I said I want a picture!" His tone grew belligerent.

Liv kept walking.

He followed.

"Hey! Don't be such a bitch about it!"

"Sorry!" Liv said, not looking back. "But I'm with someone." Her heart danced against the walls of her chest. The room, packed, made it difficult to get away.

"HEY, YOU!"

She peeked over her shoulder and yelped. The Mad Hatter had almost caught up to her.

"I don't want to fucking MARRY you!" he yelled. "I want a PICTURE!"

Suddenly the crowd parted and Xander appeared. He looked up, catching sight of her expression. "Liv? You okay?"

"Time to go!" she gasped, pushing through the quicksand of the crowd. "Now!"

The Mad Hatter closed in.

"I know what you're like! Fake geek girls who think they can just wear a fandom shirt and pretend they're hot shit!" His voice rose until it was a roar. "I said I wanted a PICTURE! Hey! You listening to me?!"

Liv reached Xander's side, but he didn't go with her, he kept stalking toward the Mad Hatter. Seeing them, Liv realized they were dressed as two sides of a strange nineteenth-century coin.

"Begging your pardon," Xander snarled, "but the lady very clearly said NO!"

The Mad Hatter's attention jumped over to Xander. "This has nothing to do with you, asshole! So fuck off!"

Xander's lips tightened into a white slash of indignation. "If it concerns her, it concerns me. Your behavior is utterly repugnant."

The crowd turned in interest, watching the dispute grow. "And what're you going to do about it?" the Mad Hatter sneered.

As Liv watched, Xander pulled his gloves from his pocket and slapped the Mad Hatter across his face. Despite the hum of the room, a loud pop echoed forward. The action was so bizarre, so out of time, it made no sense. The Mad Hatter jerked back. People broke into applause.

"What the hell!" The Mad Hatter rubbed his cheek. "Did you just slap me with your fucking glove?"

Xander rose to his full height. "I challenge you to a duel, sir!"

"To a duel?"

People around them lifted their phones, recording the action.

"Er . . . something like that."

The Mad Hatter grinned. He cracked his knuckles. "You are so fucked, prissy boy."

Xander took a half step back. "Oh dear."

With a shout of pure rage, the Mad Hatter lunged. The crowd gasped. Xander spun on his heel and sprinted straight toward Liv, his face white with terror.

"RUN!" he shrieked.

Liv didn't know whether to laugh or scream, so she followed Xander. The two of them bolted into the crowd, stopping only when nine floors and a locked door separated them from the crazed con-goer.

Liv slid the bolt into place. "That was just nuts!" she wheezed.

Xander flopped down onto the hotel room's couch. "The demented fan," he panted. "Now *that's* an experience I could have done without."

"Me too." Liv giggled.

And with that, they both fell into an uncontrollable fit of laughter.

⌒

Liv woke in the darkness of the unfamiliar room. Heart pounding, she tried to get her bearings, but nothing made sense. There was a window on her left, but it was on the wrong side for her bedroom. She was warmer than usual, and she could hear the faint sound of laughing and talking coming from far away. She frowned. It wasn't her mother's voice.

Where in the world had she—

"You need more room?" Xander whispered.

She jerked as she realized that the warmth she was feeling wasn't just the coziness of a bed, but of Xander's arms wrapped around her. Flashes of the night returned.

"I'll take the floor, m'lady. It's the gentlemanly thing to do."

"I never asked you to be a gentleman. And there's plenty of room here."

"Are you certain . . . ? I'd be more than happy to provide you ample lodgings."

"Get into bed, Xander! I'm not jumping you. I'm offering you a mattress."

"I acquiesce under duress . . . but only say the word and I shall remove myself at once."

"I'm fine. You're fine. Mario thinks we're nuts. Now go to bed."

"Good night, dearest."

"Night, Xander."

She'd expected *something* after that point—even with the other people in the room—but he'd rolled away from her, and seconds later she'd been asleep.

With the last cobwebs of sleep torn away, the layout of the room returned. A faint glimmer of streetlight filtered in through the windows. On the other bed, Mario and Emma slept on. Liv rolled the other way. In the shadows, Xander's eyes were the glint of two dark coins.

"I can move if you want," he whispered.

"I'm fine," Liv said, hoping the darkness of the room hid the smile on her face. "Sorry for waking you."

A gentle hand brushed her hair. "No worries. I'm a light sleeper."

"Do you want *me* to take a turn on the floor so you can have the bed to yourself?" she asked, hoping against hope that he'd say no. "You know . . . so *you* have more room?"

She felt his laughter rather than heard it. "You must be joking, dearest. There is no place I'd rather be than here."

Liv rolled closer, tucking her head under Xander's chin. She was warm and content, his arms around her.

"Go back to sleep," he said, his voice softer now. "I'm fine."

"I'm better than fine," she sighed.

His fingers brushing over her hair were a comfort, lulling her. Tomorrow she'd consider what exactly was happening with Xander, but tonight she was happy to just *be*.

"Night, Xander," she murmured.

"Night, dearest."

And in minutes, she was wrapped in dreamless sleep.

13

"A SPARK COULD BE ENOUGH TO SET THEM ABLAZE."
(*THE HUNGER GAMES: CATCHING FIRE*)

*L*iv woke to the sound of snoring.

The room was filled with diffuse light, the curtains slightly parted to reveal Atlanta's skyline. She sat up, a tangle of sleep-rumpled hair falling across her face. Liv was cold—inexplicably so—and she turned to discover Xander had rolled to the far side of the bed, his black hair half-hidden by a pile of covers. Disappointment filled her chest.

She'd *hoped* to wake in his arms.

Liv slid from the shared bed, moving carefully to avoid waking Xander. As she crossed around to the other side of the room, she snuck a peek at him. His eyes were closed, a half grin on parted lips. The word *debauched* floated to mind, and Liv felt her cheeks redden, but she closed herself in the bathroom instead of following the thought to fruition. At the time, she'd taken their midnight snuggling in stride, but in the bright glare of morning, she was far less certain about her actions.

What in the world was she doing with Xander? Of more concern, what was *he* doing with her? Liv had known for some time that she had developed a huge crush on Xander. But she wasn't entirely certain he shared the depth of her feelings. He'd come to bed last night, but he hadn't kissed her, and though there was a definite spark to their interactions, Xander *always* flirted with her. Actually, Liv thought, he always had. Even when Arden had been in the picture, the two of them had had a continuous banter. But did it actually mean anything?

Xander flirts with everyone!

With that uneasy thought in mind, Liv showered and dressed as she sifted through past events for some hint of Xander's feelings. Liv wasn't good at just "going with the flow." If overthinking was a skill, she was an expert in the field.

"Coffee will help," she muttered as she headed from the room and down to the Marriott's lobby.

The atrium was already buzzing, and Liv people-watched as she waited in line. Several *Starveil* cosplayers passed by, and Liv felt her anxiety rise. Her hands were sweaty by the time she placed her order. Today was the big *Starveil* panel! And though Liv was desperate to attend, she was nervous about seeing Tom Grander again. It belatedly struck her that while she always thought of the man as Spartan, that was only the character.

By the time she returned, Emma and Mario were awake and dressed. The second Emma had joined them in their room, and Xander was just finishing his shower. She handed him a paper cup as he emerged from the bathroom.

"Coffee," she announced.

Xander brushed her fingers as he took it from her grip. "You know your way to a man's heart," he said with a wink. "This is the second one I owe you, dearest. I'll have to come up with a suitable way to show my thanks."

Too flustered to answer, Liv passed out the other cups to Emma and Mario, and foisted her own drink on the extra Emma in the room. She bit back a smile as Xander took his first sip and sighed: "Perfect. Absolutely perfect." Perhaps caffeine wasn't the *only* way to put her in a good mood.

The first part of the morning was spent at a small independent-film session in the bowels of one of the smaller hotels. Xander played on his phone, apparently "checking his schedule" while Liv scribbled notes about internships and the Hollywood film system as fast as she could. The team that hosted the panel was part of a group of independent filmmakers who had collaborated on several music videos and a short science-fiction film that had made it all the way to Sundance. Leaving the room, Xander offered Liv his arm.

"Feeling like you've found your own kind?" he asked.

Grinning, Liv slid her hand into the crook of his elbow. (When had *this* become the way they walked? she wondered.) "Something like that," she said. "I might try to contact them sometime. I think that's the kind of thing I could do after college."

"Aha—that sounds suspiciously like schoolwork."

"Only a tiny bit." She giggled.

"Then no more for the rest of the day."

"It's a deal."

Lunch took place at the Peachtree Center, where Liv and Xander had to practically fight a group of ninjas to get a table at the food court. Afterward, they took a trip down to the vendor room to purchase fandom items. For the most part, Liv had become acclimatized to the crowds jostling her everywhere she went, but the dealer room felt like arriving in yet another level of compression. Walking room was at a premium. The crowd moved at a plodding pace, and you either kept up with the crowd or were jostled along without your consent. Salesmen hawked television and movie memorabilia at every table. Any geeky accessory you might want, any retro item from your childhood you wished to recapture, any slogan or costume, could be found at small booths that ran in a grid throughout the room. She felt like a child in a candy store, her eyes widening with each step. Liv planned to buy a T-shirt or two, but when a sweaty teen rubbed up against her, Liv's focus became on escape.

She turned to catch Xander's eye: *"Out!"* she mouthed.

With a nod, they began to ford against the stream. It took half again as long, and twice Liv felt like she was going to scream, but they finally made it out the main doors.

"I hate this part of con," Liv said. She rubbed her sweat-slicked arm with the other sleeve and shuddered. "That many sweaty people is just gross." She looked longingly back at the room. "Maybe I'll come back later. There were such cool things in there."

"I hate to tell you, Liv, but it's always like that in the vendor rooms."

Liv hung her head. "Dragnat all!"

"Were you looking for something in particular?"

"The new *Starveil* shirt," she said sheepishly. "The one that says 'There's More Than One Escape Pod on a Ship.'"

"Wonder why," Xander teased.

"I heard from Joe that someone on Etsy actually made a

Malloy T-shirt," Liv added. "People are wearing your face on their chests now."

It was Xander's turn to look longingly at the room. "You wait," he said, "I'm going back in."

He disappeared into the crowd, and Liv was left alone in the hallway. Bored, she flicked through the Dragon Con scheduler on her phone. Tonight was the Steampunk Ball Xander had persuaded her to attend with him and his friends. Trouble was, Liv had nothing to wear. She sighed and flicked backward, scanning alerts. The big *Starveil* panel was this afternoon. At any other con, the *Starveil* panel would be second choice to many others, but after MRM's hints at an announcement, it was anticipated to be one of the biggest of the entire convention. Joe had already texted Liv to say she and Brian were in line; a few *Starveil* fangirls were tagging them out for bathroom breaks throughout the day.

Liv chewed her lower lip. Tom Grander was slated to be at this panel. The idea of seeing Grander again left Liv fighting a mixture of unease and ebullience. She adored the character of Spartan! Tom Grander, however, was another thing. . . . A flurry of movement distracted her and she looked up.

She could see it was Xander, but her brain refused to process the thought. It was him, and yet it *wasn't*. The young man who approached was no longer dressed in a tailcoat and linen shirt. He wore a bright blue T-shirt with "Major Malloy Sent Me" emblazoned across his chest, velvet jacket hanging over his arm. Xander's hair was messed from its regular pompadour and hung in tangles across his forehead. The entire effect was unsettling.

"You're staring," he said drily.

Liv closed her mouth, averting her gaze. "I just like the shirt."

"I'm sure you do, since you're the reason for it." He chuckled. "And here's another thing that'll boost your ego. This one's yours." He pulled a bright green "escape pod" shirt from the bag. "I guessed at your size."

Liv groaned. "I'm not a medium."

"I made sure it was a woman's cut, so it takes account of the curves. I still think it'll fit."

"It won't," Liv argued. "I take a large."

"No, you don't."

"Do too."

Xander sighed. "I spend all my time selecting costumes. Trust me, Liv. You'll fit this medium shirt much better than a large."

Liv crossed her arms, scowling. "Will not."

He stepped closer, his smile turning devilish. "Liv, dearest, I promise you I am well acquainted with your delightful curves. This shirt is perfect."

Liv tried to come up with a retort, but she was tongue-tied by the thought of Xander looking at her. She shook her head, feigning annoyance.

"I will buy you a new one if it's not," Xander said. "But please, Liv. Just try it on before you make me head back into Dante's inferno."

Liv stomped to the nearby washrooms. "It'll never fit!"

"Try!"

But when Liv finally came out of the stall and looked at herself in the mirror, she had to agree. The shirt fit beautifully: loose enough over her breasts but nipping in at the waist. (A waist she rarely noticed she had.) Liv schooled her face into displeasure as she emerged from the bathroom. She'd be damned if she'd tell him that.

When she reached the hallway, Xander was staring into the vendor hall. He looked, Liv realized, as uncomfortable in his new clothes as she did. He turned as she neared, and a wide grin crossed his face.

"I told you it'd fit!"

"Yes, but I'm only wearing it on one condition."

His brows drew together. "Condition?"

"That you wear *your* T-shirt, too."

"Already am."

"Yes," Liv said, her eyes sparkling. "But you have to wear yours to the *Starveil* panel."

❧

The *Starveil* lineup was already down the street when Liv arrived. Brian, Joanne, and most of the Spartan troop were waiting at the front.

"I told you Brian was our secret weapon," Joe said. "He kept you a spot."

"Thanks, Brian." Liv slid into line beside them. "That's nice of you."

"We're going to get great seats," Joe announced. "I'm going to record everything and upload it to YouTube as soon as the panel ends."

"Cool," Liv said. "I'm sure the fans will appreciate that." She looked back down the line, which snaked through the hallway and out the door. "My God, Brian. What time did you arrive? There's got to be three thousand people here."

"Security wouldn't let me line up until three," Brian grumbled. "But I waited out their rounds, then went back again. I was here as soon as lineups began."

"You've been here for three hours. That's crazy!"

Brian gave her a dead-eyed stare. "Hardly. I've been here since three this morning."

Liv's laughter died in her throat. "Well . . . thanks. I owe you one."

Joe peered behind Liv. "So where's your boyfriend, Xander?"

"I . . . um . . ." Liv fumbled with her reply. Should she correct Joe and admit she and Xander weren't officially together, or should she let the misunderstanding go? "He ran to the parade, but he should be here shortly," she said. "There's a group of them going together. Xander texted me to say someone built a working steampunk hovercraft."

"You should have told him to meet up with us," Joe said. "I've been telling everyone about him."

"He'll be here." Liv glanced down the line and frowned. "At least he should be . . ." As she said the words, her phone buzzed.

> The lines are all the way down the street. Where ARE you, Liv?!?

> Up at the very front. Brian was on covert ops. He hid in the hallway and kept us spots.

> Brian needs a hobby.

> He DOES have a hobby. It's Starveil.

LOL True, and he does an admirable job at it. ;)

Hurry up and find us! It's going to start soon.

Just about there. You think we'll have good seats?

The BEST! I bet we'll be able to see MRM's nose hairs. O_O

Good lord. That's a frightening thought. Oh! Hey, I see you there. Mmmmm . . . you look delightful! I knew that shirt would look good on you.

Where are you?

Can't you see me? I'm the fool waving his arms about for no apparent reason.

Nope. I still can't see you. O_o

NOW . . . ? (Come, dearest. This is embarrassing.)

It wasn't until Xander was literally at her side that Liv realized the man approaching was him. Without his nineteenth-century clothing, Xander looked unexpectedly benign, and Liv squeaked when an apparent "stranger" put his arm around her waist.

"Jeez, Xander!" she said with a nervous laugh. "Don't surprise me like that!"

"I didn't try to. I've been trying to get your attention for the last five minutes." He glared down the hallway. "I had some . . . difficulty getting through."

"Difficulty?"

Xander rolled his eyes. "Your clothing selection seems to have tipped people off as to my secret identity."

"Sorry, Batman." She squeezed his arm. "But I'm still glad you made it."

"Me too."

Liv glanced out to the crowd to discover a wall of people staring, openmouthed, at Xander. She expected they'd ignore them after a minute, but he'd caused a sensation. A middle-aged woman came up and asked for a photograph, then a group of teens. After that, Xander hid behind Sarah, who seemed to intrinsically understand his anxiety. Liv joined him where he lurked against the wall, slouching like an angry preteen.

"I hate this," he hissed. "Everyone's staring."

"Yes," Liv snorted. "But that's because they're trying to decide if you're really Major Malloy or just someone who looks a lot like him."

"If this were actual cosplay," Xander said, "wouldn't I be wearing Malloy's captain's jacket?"

Liv bit her lip to keep from smiling. "This is meta cosplay," she said sweetly. "You're you, but not you. Malloy, but not really Malloy."

"Meta, hmm? Why do I have a feeling I'm going to regret this?"

"Oh come on, Xander. It'll be fine." Liv bumped him with her hip. "I came to your panel. Now it's your turn to come to mine." She felt a wave of guilt for asking him to come *without* his steampunk garb. Xander in cosplay was the real Xander, while this version of him looked as anxious as she often felt. Liv smiled up at him. "*Starveil* isn't *that* bad, is it?"

"No, dearest, it's not," he sighed. "But if I get trampled by a mob, I'm holding you personally responsible."

A phone buzzed, and both Xander and Liv checked theirs.

> Introduce me, Liv! COME ON!!! :D

And for the next half hour, Xander, Liv, and Sarah chatted silently, their phones buzzing back and forth as they waited out the last, interminable moments. Liv was leaning against Xander, a smile playing over her lips, as another text—for her alone—came through.

> OMG You two make a cute couple. <3

Liv felt her face begin to burn, and she turned her screen away from Xander as she tapped in a reply.

> THANK YOU!!!!!!! I think so too! :D X 100000

Half an hour of delays later, the door next to Brian opened, and he stumbled backward, falling into the ballroom.

A security officer stared down at him. "Excuse me, sir, but we need to—"

"I'm still in line!" Brian shouted as he clambered to his feet. "I never left the line! I'm the first! The FIRST!"

The guard sighed wearily. "We're going to start letting people in, sir. So if you could lead the line forward. No saving seats, no moving chairs, no running, no shoving . . ." The litany of rules continued long after Brian and the others came through the doors.

The ballroom was the biggest in the Marriott hotel, and it was filled with countless chairs, lined up like ranks of soldiers.

"Hurry up!" Joe said excitedly. "Brian's halfway to the front already!"

Liv caught Xander's hand and tugged him past an empty line of chairs to reach Brian, who had power walked to the front row, directly below the stage. Tom Grander's spot was front and center, a steaming Starbucks paper cup and a water bottle next to the sign that announced him. Twenty more minutes passed as the rest of the long line of waiting fans entered, and the security moved individual people into the remaining spaces in the audience. Finally, the *Starveil* cast appeared.

The entire audience surged to its feet, cheering.

Xander didn't move. He shook his head. "You *Starveil* people don't fool around, do you?"

"Just get up." Liv laughed. "People are staring at you."

Xander climbed to his feet. "I'm up now, dearest. You happy?"

"Very," Liv said, sliding her hand through his elbow and grinning.

"Good. Because I wouldn't come here for anyone else."

Liv felt her cheeks warm. "Thank you."

She brought her attention back to the stage as the crowd settled in for the panel. The first portion involved the making of the *Starveil* movies, complete with video footage. This was followed by MRM's long-winded synopsis of the evolution of *Starveil* from a small-budget indie film into the blockbuster franchise it had become.

Xander played *Candy Crush* on his phone the entire time.

"Xander!" Joe hissed, elbowing him. "You're missing everything."

He put his phone away, sliding as far from Joe as the seat would allow. Liv patted Xander's arm. *"Be nice,"* she mouthed, and he leaned in to whisper in her ear.

"For you, dearest? Anything. But I promise being bad is so much more fun."

Liv could hardly concentrate after the whispered suggestion. Suddenly Xander felt far too close, and the room too hot. She blinked, trying to force her attention back to the stage.

The emcee started with a round of preselected questions that had been e-mailed in by *Starveil* fans around the world. As those ended, a Q & A with the audience began. The first question asked was the one on everyone's mind: "What's happening with the *Starveil* franchise?"

Mike offered to field the question. "I'm not giving spoilers for my own announcement," he said with mock-seriousness, "but Tom and I may have shared a few last night. All in good time." He chuckled. "But not quite yet." He ran his fingers across his mouth, zipping it up, and leaned back in his chair.

The audience broke into a spontaneous round of applause.

Even Liv felt her hands growing clammy in anticipation. What *was* MRM's big announcement?

The next two questions were for Tom. He was in good form, laughing bashfully at his unexpected disappearance from the Walk of Fame by saying he was "still on West Coast time" and then launching into a story about his experiences at Dragon Con. For half a second, Liv was terrified he'd mention something about their run-in, but, according to Tom, Atlanta had been "nothing but accommodating" and he was "definitely coming back next year." Relieved, Liv settled back to listen.

The rest of the questions were the standard fandom queries.

"What was it like to kiss Tom Grander?"

"It was work," the actress who played Tekla answered. "The kind of work you can't believe you actually get paid to do."

The crowd cheered.

"What was your favorite moment in *Starveil Five*?" another fan asked.

"I was standing offscreen when Tom and Brooklyn were filming that last scene, where Spartan sends her into the escape pod. I broke down. Mike had to redo some of the audio because I was crying so hard."

Liv found herself grinning as she was drawn back into the joy of *Starveil*. Years of fandom feelings rushed over her like a flash flood, leaving her blinking back tears as she remembered standing in block-long lineups with her father, wanting, *needing*, to be the first to see the latest film. She loved *Starveil* with a passion. It was a link to her past, and no matter how difficult Tom Grander, actor, might be, the character of Spartan was still one she connected to on a visceral level. Her throat ached, remembering.

Liv wasn't the only one overcome by feelings. A few fans only got as far as a gushing explanation as to why *Starveil* had changed their lives before the emcee took the mic away. "Remember," the emcee said in a patronizing tone. "One-part questions. Save the testimonials for the Walk of Fame." It was a rule only loosely enforced.

As everyone knew, the panel's final act would be the big announcement, which Mike R. Miles had been hinting about for weeks, and the crowd grew restless as the time neared. As the emcee gave his closing comments, a faint chant started at the back of the room. "M R M! . . . M R M! . . . M R M! . . . M R M! . . . M R M! . . ." It grew in volume until the projectors shuddered, and Liv could feel it like a drum in her chest.

She glanced over at Xander. He was back to *Candy Crush*.

The actors onstage joined in the shouting. Finally, Mike R. Miles stood. He took the microphone in hand and sauntered to the front of the stage. Next to him, a giant projection of his face tracked his motions. He smiled and nodded with a show-man's practiced ease, waving away the thunder of the fans.

"Quiet, please," he said, beaming down at the audience. "I've got a little announcement to make."

The screaming grew in intensity. Mike grinned at the camera. His eyes twinkled. It was, Liv realized, a purposeful endeavor to drive up expectation. She chewed the edge of her nail, wishing he'd just make the damned announcement.

After a few more minutes, the din lowered, and Mike nodded. Behind him, the group of actors stood. Tom Grander was smiling, but it looked forced. She frowned in concern.

What was bothering him? Mike looked directly into the camera's lens. His face, half a story high, beamed down from the projection screen.

"It is with great excitement," Mike said, "that I announce that there will be a NEW *Starveil* movie starring Tom Grander!"

Pandemonium ensued. Liv surged to her feet, screaming. Joe caught Liv by her shoulders, hugging her as she squealed into her ear. Kelly burst into tears. Sarah stared openmouthed at the screen while the fangirls fluttered around her like birds. Liv looked back to the stage to discover that Brian—strange, angry Brian—had somehow clambered onto the platform and was shaking the hands of the actors, tears streaming down his face. Mike R. Miles yelled something about "the efforts of the fans" and "crowdsourced plotlines" into the microphone, but no one could hear him over the screaming. Spectators stampeded down the aisles toward the actors and—tracked by the cameras—Brian was led off the stage by security.

The deafening roar of the audience belatedly drew Xander away from his phone. He looked around in confusion, then turned to Liv.

"What in the world just happened?"

"They're bringing *Starveil* back! Spartan's alive again!"

Xander jumped to his feet and grabbed her around the waist, twirling her. "You did it!" he shouted as he set her back down again. "You really, really did it!"

The moment of joy dragged on and on, the roar of the audience slowly dissipating. Liv was grinning as she clung to Xander, so she almost didn't notice the light that came down from above. It was—she would think later—like a sign from the divine. In fact, if she hadn't seen her own image, wrapped in Xander's arms, projected on the giant screen, she might not have noticed at all.

She *did* notice.

"Oh my God!" Liv gasped, jumping out of Xander's arms. "We're on-screen!"

He followed her eyes up to the screen, his expression of joy fading. The crowd's roar had faded to a murmur.

"What in seven hells . . . ?"

"Why, this is a surprise!" the emcee's voice boomed. "We have someone in the audience. It's a character a few of you will recognize."

Xander's blue shirt popped into focus, and the camera zoomed onto his face. He had a deer-caught-in-the-headlights expression. Liv stumbled back, unable to breathe.

"It's Major Malloy!" someone in the audience screamed.

"From Spartan Survived!" another echoed.

The excited roar of the crowd resurged. MRM stood, shading his eyes as he peered offstage.

"Well, I'll be." Mike laughed. "It is! Why don't you come on up and take a bow?" He turned to the audience, reprising his role as ringmaster. "The actor who plays Malloy is in the audience. I think he deserves a round of applause—don't you?!"

The ballroom filled with the thunderous sound of clapping. Blood rushed to Liv's ears. Her stomach tightened until she felt like she might be sick. "Oh God," she groaned. "I'm so sorry, Xander!"

But whatever reaction she expected from him, it wasn't this. Xander's face rippled, the roguish Malloy persona appearing as he swaggered up to the stairs and took the stage. The cast members and Mike R. Miles shook his hand, and Xander picked up a mic.

Malloy's Old Terra brogue boomed through the sound system: "Your determination. Your research. Your proof of Spartan's whereabouts are the only hope we have for Spartan's safe return!"

The audience went wild, and it was several seconds before his amplified voice could be heard again. He grinned and bowed.

"Thank you, thank you," Xander said, his voice returning to normal. "I truly appreciate the applause, but I'm just one part of this phenomenon. The face of Spartan Survived, if you will."

More screaming. Joe bounced up and down like a teen at a rock concert. Alicia pursed her lips and let out a piercing whistle. Liv wanted to disappear.

Xander grinned into the camera. "Now, I don't know if any of you realize this," he said. "But this whole idea really came from one person . . ."

"No!" Liv gasped.

"She's the driving force behind the grassroots movement that brought this franchise back, and her name is Liv Walden . . ."

Liv sank down in her chair, eyes wide with terror. "Please, God, no!"

"She's sitting in the audience right now." Xander stepped toward the stairs and offered his hand. "Come on up, Liv. You deserve this more than I do."

The emcee's voice interrupted. "I, for one, have never had the honor of meeting your friend Liv." He lifted a hand to block the lights as he peered out into the crowd. "Is she here in the audience?"

Joanne jumped to her feet. "Over here!" she bellowed, arms pinwheeling. "Liv's sitting over HERE!"

Liv shrank until she was practically reclined across the seat. "Please don't, Joe!"

But it was too late. The cameras panned back and forth as they searched for the originator of the cry. They found Joanne pointing, an ecstatic grin on her round face.

"Stand up, Liv!" MRM shouted. "Take a bow! We all owe you more than we can say."

Liv's grainy face and torso appeared on the big-screen projector at the moment the entire ballroom exploded with applause. Liv's T-shirt and the "There's More Than One Escape Pod on a Ship" slogan were clearly visible. The audience's cheers grew so loud Liv's ears crackled.

At the front of the room, Tom Grander stood up in front of a roomful of his fans. "Thank you, Liv," he said. "For all you've done for *Starveil*."

The people in the crowd followed Tom's move, rising to their feet around her, giving her a standing ovation. Onstage, the remaining cast stood to join Xander, applauding. If the noise had been loud before, it was three times what it had been.

"Come up, Liv!" Xander shouted. "You deserve this."

She shook her head.

"Please, dearest!"

Liv tried to get away, but Joe and Alicia, and even Sarah, caught hold of her, the central hub of the *Starveil* fandom carrying her toward the stage.

"Please," she gasped. "I can't! I'll die! I swear, I'll die!" (The universe had just proved her wrong; this was, in fact, worse than the moment with Hank had ever been.)

After a half minute of shoving, Liv was at the stairs.

She looked up to discover Xander leaning down to catch her

hand and help her up. Liv's chest was so tight she could hardly breathe, but when Xander grinned at her, it eased. *"Trust me,"* he mouthed, and pulled her up onto the stage.

In the audience, a chant had started, and it took a moment before Liv realized they weren't just saying "live" (as in Spartan); they were actually saying her name. *Hers!* They were chanting for her.

"LIV! . . . LIV! . . . LIV! . . . LIV! . . . LIV! . . ."

She stepped onstage.

14

"THE TRUTH IS OUT THERE."
(THE X-FILES)

*I*t felt like someone had flicked a switch. With Xander's announcement, Liv Walden, computer geek, *Starveil* fangirl, recluse, and perennial wallflower, had been transformed into a celebrity. She was accustomed to being ignored, to having people step in her way, interrupt her mid-conversation, but in the space of ten minutes, the quality of her entire existence changed.

In the wake of the announcement, the audience stampeded through the ballroom. Onstage, the stars stood and were ushered offstage via the talent exit. Xander and Liv received no such offer. They stared, openmouthed, at the screaming mob.

"Xander?"

He grabbed Liv's hand. "Door! Now!"

They went down the stairs only to be met by a sea of people, which rushed forward, catching them in its grip. Liv had never been to a rock concert before, but she had a feeling *this* was what a mosh pit felt like. Hands and elbows pushed and shoved, drawing her farther away from Xander until—with one jerk—his hand was knocked aside.

"LIV!"

"Xander?"

"Liv, WAIT!"

The swirling mass forced itself directly into the bubble of space Liv used to keep her anxiety at bay. People drew nearer, knocking her from side to side.

"I follow you online!" a woman shrieked. "I posted the fic where Spartan had amnesia! Did you read that? Did you?"

"I—I don't—" Liv stammered.

"Loved your videos!" a man interrupted. "They were awesome! You in the film industry?"

"In college, actually," Liv said, searching for an escape. She turned, but a group of young women—age fifteen or so—blocked her path.

"I was heartbroken until the Spartan Survived tag!" one cried. "You kept me going."

"Me too!"

"How can I ever repay you?"

They pressed closer, blocking Liv's exit.

Liv turned back the other way, panic rising. She scanned the room, hoping for a glimpse of Joanne and the rest of the Spartan troop but they'd already moved on, pushed away by the inexorable surge of people. Liv kept moving backward, but the crowd kept coming, and eventually she found herself pressed up against the wall. The mosh pit had been replaced by the zombie apocalypse.

"LIIIIIIIIIIIIV!" they screamed.

"Can you sign my badge?" a young man asked. A pen and card appeared in front of her, but she knocked them aside, struggling to breathe. Her vision began to darken at the edges.

"Liv! LIVVV!!!! I love you!"

"Please," Liv gasped. "I have to go." She took two lurching steps sideways. People moved in, creating a human wall. Liv felt her breathing double in speed, her heart pounding so hard that her chest shuddered.

"If it wasn't for you, there wouldn't be a *Starveil Six*. Thank you!"

"You're my hero! No seriously, you are!"

"—the best thing to happen to *Starveil* since Tom Grander!"

"—can't believe you're actually here!"

"I never thought . . ."

A young woman dressed as Katniss pushed her way to Liv's side. "Come up to the mezzanine," she said breathlessly.

"Mezzanine?" Liv repeated.

"Yes! A group of us are going to play the *Starveil* board game!"

"Sorry, where's the mezzanine?"

"Tenth floor, Marriott," she explained. "We're starting around ten tonight, if you want to come."

"Not sure I can," Liv said, extricating herself from one group, only to find herself surrounded again.

"The mezzanine!" the woman shouted.

"I can't," Liv said. "I'm . . . I'm . . ."

Where was Xander?! She caught sight of him on the far side of the crowd, but the surging waves of *Starveil* fans forced her one direction, him the other. A middle-aged man stepped in her way, blocking Liv's view.

"I love your vids! If you have a second, can I—"

"I need to LEAVE!"

She turned in circles, panic rising, and then suddenly she could hear Xander's voice belting out Malloy's challenge in the loudest in-character voice she'd ever heard. She turned in surprise to see he'd taken the stage. "Attention, comrades. This message is for Rebels across our star system and beyond! As you've no doubt heard, Captain Matt Spartan, commander of the Star Freighter Elysium, has been reported missing in action."

Xander's eyes met Liv's across the crowd. In that split second, she knew what he wanted her to do.

"THAT ASSUMPTION IS INCORRECT!"

The crowd cheered. It was all the distraction Liv was going to get. She sprinted toward the exit and stumbled into the main atrium. Xander had just given her the perfect getaway.

Head down, she crossed the floor, making it to the elevator. She turned toward the wall and pulled out her phone.

> Did you get out, Liv?

I did-THANK YOU.

> No problem. Just need to, er . . . do the same here. Brian's making a bit of a scene with security, but it's not helping quite as much as one might hope.

LOL

> It's fine. ;P I'll be out soon.

I'm at the elevators. Going up to the room.

Gah! I'm still stuck inside. O_O Security just took Brian away! Wait for me!

Can't. Need away from the crowds. :-/

I'm coming! Just. Need. Out. *flails* Heaven's to Pete-I feel sympathy for Grander all of a sudden.

I don't believe you. :) I'm in the room, BTW.

Phew! I've escaped Bedlam. I'm on my way.

Thank you for the distraction.

For you? Anything. <3

⌒

Twenty minutes later, Xander returned. Liv was dozing on the bed, but she jerked awake as he came through the door. Again she had the disconcerting feeling of not recognizing him out of his steampunk garb. His lanky frame, fine features, and jet-black hair carried all the insouciance of a male supermodel, but it didn't look right on him.

"Sorry it took me so long," he said, flopping onto the bed next to her. "I tried to leave twice, only to get sucked back in again." He shuddered. "That was worse than swimming in a tidal pool."

"Back to the ballroom?" Liv yawned. "Wasn't there another panel at some point?"

"There was, but I was pulled aside."

"You were?"

"Yes." Xander glanced down in disgust at the rumpled state of his outfit. "Ugh! I need out of this . . . this . . ."

"Costume?" Liv giggled.

"Exactly!"

He grabbed the neck of the T-shirt and tugged it up over his head, then tossed it into the corner. Liv stared openmouthed at the swath of exposed chest. Darcy emerging from his swim in the lake had *nothing* on Xander Hall sweaty and irritated. While Liv's gaze lingered, Xander leaned over the side of the bed and grabbed a fresh linen shirt from his carry-on. He slid it over his head.

Liv reluctantly closed her eyes as Xander settled back onto the coverlet.

"Lordy," he groaned. "That feels much better."

She opened one eye. "Looks better, too."

A mischievous grin crossed his face. "Aha! So you do admit it!"

"I never said you didn't look better in this." She flicked his collar. "I just said I wanted to see you in the other. But now that I've compared them, I know which one I prefer."

"I like the sound of that." Xander leaned closer. "And am I allowed to request a costume from you, too?"

Liv smothered her laughter in the pillow.

"It might be fun," he said. "Never know till you try."

When Liv finally could control her giggles, she looked back up. "I'll think about it, promise." Xander opened his mouth to argue, but she diverted his attention. "So what were you doing after the ballroom? You said you were pulled aside."

"Yes. I was trying to get away from Miles's assistant."

"Miles . . . as in Mike R. Miles?"

"Exactly, and let me tell you, he was very peeved I wasn't you." He smirked. "You do have a bit of a fan club there, Liv."

"Wh-what did MRM's assistant want?"

"To invite us to a *Starveil* party."

"To *what*?!?"

Xander grinned. "The two of us are going to the *Starveil* cast party tonight."

"But I thought we were going to the Steampunk Ball."

Xander gave a feline stretch. A long swath of rippled stomach appeared, and Liv looked away, suddenly conscious of how close he was to her and how good-looking he was. He hadn't done up his shirt, and it hung open, luring her nearer.

"We could do that, too." Xander yawned. "But I think we should at least pop by and say hello at the *Starveil* Event."

Liv stared at him for a long moment. "But, why? You don't even like *Starveil*."

"But *you* do."

"I—I don't know . . ."

Xander leaned nearer, his smile growing persuasive. "Come along, Liv. Be my date. Please, dearest? For me."

Liv felt her cheeks begin to burn at the word *date*. She needed a cold shower because Xander's gaze, soft and tired, and his body, lithe and oh-so-attractive, were not helping.

"I can't go."

"Why not?"

"Tom Grander hates me. I'll die if I have to talk to him." Liv let out a nervous laugh.

"I'll go with you and be your champion! I'll divert the crowds and clear a path for you." His voice dropped. "This is something you've wanted so badly for so long." He reached out and tugged a strand of Liv's hair. "Why don't you take it?"

He smiled, and Liv's stomach twisted at the sight. She wished he wasn't just talking about the cast party, but everything *else* she wanted to grab hold of.

"But if Tom—"

"Tom Schmom," Xander drawled. "If that bastard says anything to you, I'll eviscerate him."

"With what?" Liv giggled. "You don't even own a sword."

"I don't know, but I'll improvise."

Liv smothered another laugh under her hand.

"There'll be food at the party," Xander said with a wink. "I'm sure I'll find *something* to do the job."

"I'd pay to see you attack Grander with a pickle fork."

"A butter knife sounds better."

Liv giggled, but the sound disappeared as Xander reached out a second time. He drew a line down her arm with the tip of his finger, and Liv shivered. His smile faded until he was looking at her with some emotion she couldn't quite decipher.

"This is your moment, dearest." He leaned closer, and for a half a second, Liv thought he would kiss her. "Enjoy it."

For several seconds, they lay in silence, balanced on some decision. His hand was on her arm, their bodies touching. Liv dropped her eyes, and the moment shifted.

"Maybe I will," she said as lightly as she could. "Who would've thought some crazy idea to bring a character back from the dead would pan out into this? A new film! I can't believe it!" She grinned. "Maybe we should put together one last vid to celebrate the announcement."

"Another?" Xander sighed.

"Oh come on, Xander. It's not going to be *that* bad."

"No, it won't be." He chuckled. "But even if it was, I'd be willing to suffer for my craft."

"Suffer?" Liv snorted.

He raised a brow. "Yes. I picked that up from Tom Grander."

～

Liv and the two Emmas prepared for the Steampunk Ball while Xander showered. Both Emmas had spent months preparing their intricate costumes; and when Liv saw them decked out in a display of finery that would put a young Queen Victoria to shame, feelings of inadequacy overwhelmed her. Liv looked plain, pure, and simple. And she hated it.

"I can't go out like this," she groaned, staring down at her jeans and T-shirt. "I look like a slob."

"You look like any other *Starveil* geek," the first Emma said cheerfully. "You'll fit in perfectly!"

"That's half the problem," Liv said. She scowled at herself in the mirror above the television. "I could barely get out of the *Starveil* ballroom today. People kept trying to talk to me." She sighed. "Maybe I'll just hang out here in the room. You guys go without me."

"Do you have anything other than jeans and tees?" the first Emma asked.

"No."

"You bring any costumes?"

"Sadly, no."

The taller of the two women measured herself next to Liv.

Though she was much shallower through the chest and several inches taller, they wore roughly the same size. "Do you like steampunk at all?"

"Um, sure?"

Both Emmas grinned.

"Then we're in business."

By the time the water in the bathroom shower stopped running, and the blow-dryer started, Liv was garbed in a dress cobbled from the two women's earlier cosplay. The purple skirt from one had been matched with a black silk blouse from another; an embroidered silk under-bust corset whittled her waist down to a whisper of its usual size. Xander's pocket watch (borrowed from the dresser and pinned to her hip) finished the look. But that wasn't all. Liv's normally straight veil of hair had been curled and teased into a bouffant worthy of any Gibson girl. Her lips were rouged, face powdered, and eyes ringed with kohl. In an instant, she was transported back a hundred years.

She stared, wide-eyed, at her reflection in the mirror. She barely recognized the ephemeral, doe-eyed beauty before her. "That's just . . . crazy," Liv said with an uneasy laugh. "I don't even look like *me* anymore."

The first Emma grinned. "Isn't that the point of cosplay?"

"To do what?" Liv asked.

"To be someone you're not," the second Emma replied.

"I suppose . . ."

The transformation was unnerving. Xander's comment about Liv looking like John Singer Sargent's painting of Madame X made sense. Her hourglass figure was exaggerated into something (and someone) she barely recognized. This woman in the mirror was dazzling, but she didn't feel like the real Liv.

The door to the bathroom opened, and a wave of cologne-scented steam rolled into the room. Xander appeared from the fog like a London gentleman. He stood, adjusting the lace cuffs on his shirt for a few seconds, before looking up.

"So are you ladies ready to . . ." His words faded as he caught sight of Liv. "Holy shitballs! You look un-fucking-believable!"

The two Emmas broke into a fit of laughter.

"You have *got* to come up with some better expressions before you start time-traveling, Xander," Liv said. "That really doesn't fit your era at all."

"Era or not, I'm just calling it like I see it." Xander dropped into a low bow. When he stood up, he cleared his throat, his voice dropping half an octave. "I'm in awe, Miss Walden. You are breathtaking. Truly."

"Show him the rest," the first Emma urged, pushing Liv forward.

Everyone cheered as Liv did a quick twirl, the skirt swirling. "I'm wearing sneakers under this," Liv admitted. "There's no way I'm falling and breaking my neck in this getup."

"A lady never reveals her secrets," the second Emma tutted.

Liv took one final glance at herself and then looked back to Xander. He was watching her, but no longer smiling, and a twinge of nervousness rose in her chest. "Does it look all right?"

Xander nodded. "Better than all right," he said. "I'm at a loss for words. Thank you for this." He smiled, and Liv smiled back, and for a moment it felt like they were the only ones in the room. Then Xander held out his hand. "May I do the honor of escorting you to the Steampunk Ball, m'lady?" He tucked Liv's hand into the crook of his arm.

She looked up at him and nodded. The nerves were back, but this time it had nothing to do with being recognized.

"Absolutely."

⁌

The *Starveil* Event, as Xander kept calling it, was a private party at the top of the Marriott. Feet aching, Liv and Xander slumped against the glass walls of the elevator, the floors whooshing by in a rush of vertigo. Liv sighed, remembering the hours of dancing. It was as if every television and movie character from 1960 onward had spontaneously reappeared in a single room. The only people who stuck out were the ones who weren't in costume. And Liv, for the first time in ages, felt completely at ease, because no one had recognized her.

She heard Xander chuckle, and she looked up.

"What?"

"Nothing," he said. "It's just your hair."

Liv patted the teetering updo. "What about it?"

Xander's lips curved in a slow grin. He reached out, tucking a curl behind her ear. "It looks like you've been doing *more* than dancing, dearest."

Liv tossed her chin coquettishly, falling back into the role she'd been playing all night. "Perhaps I have. But it wouldn't be very gentlemanly of you to suggest it." She fluttered her lashes. "Or to ask, Mr. Hall."

Xander stepped closer, fixing the watch that hung from Liv's hip. It had slipped from its hook, and Liv's breath caught as his fingers lingered half a second too long. He looked up, and their eyes met.

"Perhaps I couldn't stop myself," he murmured.

Liv's heart sped up. She could feel Xander's fingers burning through the fabric, and the thoughts that accompanied this were growing more dangerous by the second.

"But a gentleman wouldn't—"

"Even a gentleman can be tempted," Xander said darkly. He crossed his arms on his chest. "My apologies, dearest," he said, tipping his head. "But you are ravishing tonight."

"Th-thank you."

Bosom heaving as she struggled to catch her breath despite the confines of the corset, Liv turned to stare out the window. The subtle dance between her and Xander that had started a few hours ago had grown more entangled with each passing minute. The close quarters on the dance floor—touching by permission—had made the pull stronger. Liv knew she was playing with fire, but right now she didn't care. She felt beautiful and strong, and when Xander looked at her this way, she felt like she could reach out and take whatever she wanted. Now, if she could only keep that niggling inner voice at bay.

Before she could say more, a bell announced their arrival at the penthouse level, and the doors pulled open. The sight that greeted them took Liv's breath away. She had an inkling of what Hollywood parties looked like, but this was far beyond her imagination. *Decadence.* The word appeared in her mind like a bubble. The room was filled with a mixture of people in costume and celebrities. Some Liv recognized from *Starveil*, others she knew from various fandoms: *Buffy, The X-Files*, even an elderly actor from the 1960s' *Star Trek*.

She stepped out of the elevator, and all her confidence evaporated. Tom Grander stood near the couch, a nubile young woman Liv recognized as a Hollywood hopeful hanging on his arm. He caught sight of Liv from across the room, and his smile faded.

Liv grabbed Xander's cuff. "I—I can't—" she gasped. "He h-hates me. I—I—"

"Liv, breathe," Xander whispered. "You can handle this."

"Xander, these people aren't like you or me."

He took her hand. "You can do this. You're not alone." He squeezed her fingers gently. "I'm not going anywhere. All right, dearest?"

Liv nodded.

"Liv! Xander!" someone bellowed. "There you are!"

Liv looked up in shock to see Mike R. Miles crossing the room. Her fingers tightened on Xander's.

"Oh God . . ."

"Liv, sweetheart," Mike said, reaching them. "So very glad you came! I just want to say thank you for all you've done."

"Okay . . . ?"

"Now, if you and Xander here can just follow me, I have a few people I want you to meet . . ."

༄

There was no use trying. Liv couldn't keep anyone's names straight. Beyond Mike R. Miles (whom she'd accidentally referred to as MRM at least twice), she was overwhelmed by a sense of confusion. Men and women, ranging from their late teens to their seventies, jostled for a position at her side, pumping her hand and slapping her on the back.

"Your videos were great!" a nameless exec said.

"Brilliant really!" another added. "Exactly what the fans wanted."

"The concept was absolutely phenomenal. Crowdsourcing. What an idea!"

"Totally inspired the fans!"

"Thanks, but it was nothing," Liv mumbled, searching for an excuse to leave. She could see no way out of the group.

"The support for *Starveil*'s never been higher," one of the producers said. (Liv couldn't remember his name, either, though she was certain he'd done a cameo in one of the *Starveil* movies.) "Unbelievable how this last film took off. You've got the Midas touch!"

"I don't think that's just me," Liv said. "The fans did most of it."

"Not just you," someone else added. "But you were the catalyst. It wouldn't have started without you."

"Um . . ." Liv peered over her shoulder. Xander was only three steps away, but it might as well have been a mile. The woman who played Tekla had him trapped in conversation, touching his arm and giggling time and again. Xander looked up and gave Liv a look of frustration. *"How much longer?"* he mouthed. She shrugged. The *Starveil* Event was proving harder to escape than the cheering fans.

She turned back to find Mike R. Miles and a middle-aged woman in a silk suit waiting patiently for her attention. Mike gestured to the conservatively dressed exec at his side.

"Liv, this is Mr. Grander's agent. She wanted to meet you."

"Good to meet you," Liv said with a cautious smile.

"I can't thank you enough for drumming up the interest for Captain Spartan's character," the woman said. Her voice had a collegiate East Coast clip that matched her patent leather pumps and heavy gold jewelry. "You did what no one else could. I'm in awe."

Liv shook her head. "I wouldn't have done any of it if I'd known Tom wanted out of the franchise."

Mike's smile wobbled, and Liv rushed to explain. "I ran into Mr. Grander on the Walk of Fame. He made it clear he didn't want the character of Spartan to survive. He wanted him dead."

"Ah, yes." Mike laughed. "I suppose that explains why you've been avoiding Tom tonight."

"Is it that obvious?"

Mike grinned. "A little."

The agent joined in his mirth. "Oh, Tom," she sighed. "He has his own agenda. Doesn't he? Quite the bohemian."

Liv frowned in confusion. The two of them were clearly having a moment, and she didn't know why she was part of this.

"Tom's an actor, sweetheart," Mike said. "He's moody. Temperamental."

"That's an understatement," the agent added. She smiled sympathetically at Liv. "But *Starveil Six* came together anyhow. And I want to thank you personally for your efforts. I don't know how you pulled it off, but you did."

Liv felt like she was reading off a script with half the words missing. "But I don't understand."

"*Starveil* is a multimillion-dollar franchise," Mike said. "And because of you . . . and some fancy footwork by Rachel here"—he nodded to the agent—"we've got another movie out of it. If you ever need a place to do an internship, I'm sure I could arrange something."

"You could?"

He laughed. "Seems the least I could do after all you've done for *Starveil*." He waved at a group of people laughing at the side. "Contact my assistant, Sam, if you want details."

Something about Mike's too-wide smile made him look like a shark. Liv looked over at Grander's agent. She, too, had that same hungry grin.

"How did I help exactly?" Liv asked, though her voice had faded.

"Tom's contract with *Starveil* included a rider," the agent said. "That rider was tied into the popularity of the franchise, and the sales from each film. The last time Tom renegotiated his contract, that number was so high—the proceeds so ludicrous—there was no doubt that *Starveil Five* would be the last *Starveil* movie ever made." She waved her bejeweled fingers at Liv. "You see, Tom was in negotiations for a new film: a smaller-budget movie. Much less money. Darker and grittier than *Starveil*. I argued against it from the start, but Sofia Coppola was slated to be the director, and Tom was determined to be part of it. He was desperate to break away from his Spartan character. To set off on his own."

"*Starveil Five* was written with Tom's change of career in mind," Mike said. "I wrote the script for it knowing Tom wouldn't be coming back to do another *Starveil* film." He shrugged. "Captain Spartan's character was killed off in the final act to honor his leaving."

Liv felt the air rush from her lungs. "Oh!"

"But then you and your Spartan Survived group came along and . . ." Mike snapped his fingers. "*Starveil Six* starts filming in November."

"We knew we'd never convince Tom to renege on his contract with Coppola, unless he was tied into a contract," the agent said. "*Starveil* is a proven franchise. It's been everyone's bread and butter for years." The hard glint returned to her eyes. "And now it'll continue indefinitely."

Mike squeezed Liv's shoulder. "You did the work for me," he said cheerfully.

"For both of us," the agent echoed. "Thank you, Liv. Mr. Grander may not appreciate it, but I certainly do."

"You're welcome." The words caught on her tongue. "But I—I have to go."

Liv turned away from the duo. She stumbled through the crowd until she reached Xander's side. The actress was still talking, but Liv grabbed his hand anyway.

"Time to go," she said, pulling him along.

"Oh sweet heavens above," Xander sighed. "I thought you'd *never* arrive!"

"Were you waiting to be saved?"

"No . . ." Xander's mouth twitched. "Maybe?"

Liv had just opened her mouth to answer when a tall figure crossed their paths.

Tom Grander.

Liv swerved sideways, dragging Xander in her wake.

"Hey! Where're we going?" he shouted.

She tugged him past the A-listers and B-listers, dodging toes and knees, as they circled through the party.

"Keep up!" Liv ordered.

"But where are we going, dearest?"

"OUT!"

They wove through the crowd, down hallways and back

again—away from Tom Grander—and finally through the sitting area near the exit. Liv could see Tom Grander following their progress, but she refused to stop. With one final sprint, they pushed past the knot of people by the door and tumbled into the hallway.

"Oh God." She laughed. "That was close."

"Perhaps he wanted to apologize to you."

"Doubtful."

Her gaze flitted down to their joined hands. Xander hadn't let go. He lifted their joined fist and pressed a kiss to her knuckles. Liv's heart was pounding so loudly she felt faint.

"So are you going to tell me where we're going?" he murmured. "Or was this a ploy to get me alone so you could have your way with me?"

Liv moved half a step closer and fluttered her lashes. "Why, Mr. Hall," she purred, "didn't you promise me one last dance?"

His expression rippled in surprise and then happiness.

"Without question, m'lady. The ball awaits."

⁓

Tonight was the party to end all parties, and Liv wanted to dance until she couldn't anymore. Her first Dragon Con was coming to an end, and she intended to build enough memories to last the full year until the next one. Though she'd die before she told Xander he'd already won her over, she was definitely coming back! Liv rocked to the heavy bass beat, swaying in time to the rising tempo. Xander was in his element, his hips rollicking as he slid and spun to the syncopated rhythm. A hundred other dancers moved in time with them, but Xander's attentions were solely reserved for Liv.

The music slowed and then stopped. The next song began. It had a slow, hypnotic beat, and couples began to pair off around them. Liv held Xander's eyes.

"May I have this dance, Mr. Hall?"

Xander gave a low bow. When he rose, he was smiling. "I'd be delighted, Miss Walden."

Xander stood with one hand outstretched, the way Liv remembered learning to waltz in gym class in high school. But the awkward bumblings of sophomore boys were nothing compared with Xander in his element. As she stepped forward, he literally swept her off her feet. The music wrapped the two of them in a haze, Xander's hands tight on her hips as they twirled through the press of bodies. Liv laughed, tipping her head back, as they danced. No question now. Xander definitely felt the same.

He pulled her closer, the faint scent of sandalwood rising as he leaned down to whisper: "You look utterly enchanting, dearest." His mouth brushed against her ear, sending a frisson of electricity down to the base of her spine.

They did another circle on the floor, and Xander spoke again. "You must allow me to tell you how much I admire you."

Liv grinned. "You do?"

"Most ardently."

Heat had begun to build between them, and the layers of fabric were doing nothing to dispel it. Light-headed, Liv's body burned every place Xander's fingers brushed. A waltz had never felt as sexual as this did. She felt like she could live in this one perfect moment forever. She never wanted it to stop or—

The tempo abruptly shifted as the DJ spun one song directly into another, the melodies bouncing back and forth in tandem. Liv stumbled to a stop, panting in Xander's arms. She looked up to discover him watching her.

The other dancers began to move, but Liv and Xander clung together from hip to chest. Tension coiled in the pit of Liv's stomach. Music roared, vibrating their skin. Xander let go of her waist. She expected him to walk away. (He'd done it every time before this.) But tonight, his expression grew warmer and more intent. His hands rose to cup her chin.

"Do it," he whispered. His breath swirled the hair by Liv's face.

Her fingers tightened. "Do what?"

Xander's mouth dropped to hers. "This . . ."

He pulled her in for a kiss, the first they'd shared, and her body burst into flame under his touch. Their lips met in a rush of desire and sensation. Within seconds, Liv's hands were in Xander's hair, her mouth moving under his. The fire spread to every nerve in her body. If Liv had felt a snap of connection to Xander with each brush of his fingers against hers, it was *nothing* compared with the rush of emotion that came with the kiss. Her legs went weak, and Xander's arm tightened around her waist, holding her upright. For a long moment, the only thing in the world that mattered was the taste of him against her tongue, the warm feel of him under her fingertips.

When they finally broke apart, they were gasping for breath. Their eyes met for a long moment. This was the perfect moment the fortune cookie had been talking about, and it was spinning out like something predestined.

I'm in love, Liv realized, *and I'm not even scared.*

15

"ONLY ONE MAN CALLS ME DARLIN'."
(*STARVEIL*)

*L*iv woke first.

As with yesterday, Xander was in bed with her, only this morning, Liv had all the memories of the other things that had accompanied their return to the room. She tiptoed to the shower, blood rushing to her ears as memories from the night reemerged from the fog of her mind. Liv had been kissed before, but she suddenly had a comparison between adequate and amazing. She caught sight of her disheveled hair and kiss-bruised lips and grinned.

Xander was a *good* teacher.

Embarrassed, she climbed into the shower, trying to pull an aura of calm around her. How were you supposed to act after all of that? Liv had nothing to guide her behavior. An unbidden image flashed to mind, and she felt herself redden despite the blasting heat of the water. She had no regrets, but she felt like every emotion she felt must show on her face.

"Coffee," she muttered as she dried herself off. A little distance would help. With this in mind, Liv dressed in jeans and a tee and sneaked out of the room, leaving Xander and the others sleeping.

The main floors of the Marriott were buzzing as the custodial crew tried to repair the damage from the endless partying. Three *Mass Effect* characters slept on the red couches. Other con-goers staggered past in varying degrees of intoxication, evidently still going strong from the night before. Liv let out a sigh of relief as she caught sight of the Starbucks counter. The line was barely twenty people long. *A miracle!*

She joined the line just as an older man, far across the atrium, suddenly changed directions and made a beeline for the Starbucks line. Liv groaned as she saw his *Starveil* shirt.

She turned toward the counter, scanning the options board while wishing, yet again, that she'd brought cosplay to wear. Everyone had seen her at yesterday's *Starveil* panel, and she was in no mood to deal with another fan trying to talk to her. The man joined the line. From her peripheral vision, Liv could see him peering at her, perhaps trying to decide if the girl with wet hair and no makeup was the same person he'd seen yesterday. After a minute, he decided she was.

He cleared his throat.

Liv didn't turn.

"Excuse me," the man said.

Liv took a nervous glance behind her. He was middle-aged, with a long ponytail and a droopy mustache. A hippie gone to seed. He seemed safe enough.

"Yes?"

"Are you Liv?" he asked.

"Uh-huh."

"As in Liv Walden?"

"Yeah . . ." Liv said warily. "Why do you ask?"

He offered his hand. "I'm Sam, Mr. Miles's assistant."

Liv stared at him. "Sam?"

He smiled. "I tried to talk to you yesterday, but you left the cast party before I could catch up to you."

"What's this about?"

"Oh, I thought Mr. Miles mentioned it to you. You're being offered an internship at the studio when *Starveil Six* starts filming."

Liv felt the floor fall away. She was still there, floating, but there was nothing under her. She tried to answer and failed.

"So I take it you're interested?" Sam said.

Liv nodded.

"Good to hear it." He pressed a business card into her hand. "This is my number. Just call me when you're ready to set this all up. I have forms and things to fill out. If you're in a college program, you might be able to claim credit."

"Th-thanks."

Liv shoved the card into her pocket with sweaty hands, watching as MRM's assistant changed directions and walked away. This didn't feel real. Her dream had come true, but in ways far larger than she'd ever imagined.

"Ma'am?" the server at the counter said. "You ready to order?"

She shook her head. "Not right now. I've got a call to make."

Minutes later, she was hidden in the fire stairwell, phone tucked against her ear. While Liv's mother only begrudgingly carried a cell phone and texting was far beyond her expertise, phone calls still worked.

"Could you repeat that again, Liv?" Katherine said.

"I've been offered an internship. It's for the film industry, Mom. And it's a big studio!"

"Did you say with . . . *Starveil*?"

Liv began to giggle. "Not just with *Starveil*, but because of it."

"Oh my God, Liv," her mother gasped, voice breaking. "That's . . . that's fantastic!"

"Yeah, it is! This is it. This is my big break!"

The receiver echoed with the sound of her mother's happy laughter. "Oh, sweetie. I'm so proud of you!"

～

> Xander, you around? I have NEWS!

> . . .

> Answer when you get this. Okay? :D

> . . .

> Heading back up to the room, now. You there?

> . . .

> Xander????

～

Xander wasn't in the hotel room when Liv arrived.

"Not sure where he went," Mario said. "He was gone when I woke up."

Emma frowned. "I thought he was with you."

"No, not with me," Liv said, reaching for her phone.

The screen showed no replies, and the sight of that, more than anything, left her gut in a tight ball. Where was Xander? And why, after the kisses last night, would he be avoiding her?

Fighting nerves, she began to tap in another text, then changed her mind and hit Dial. The phone rang four times before a recording of Xander's voice came through: *"You've reached the cellular telephone of Mr. Xander Hall, Esquire. If this inquiry is in regards to acting services, please leave a message after the beep. If this message is of a personal nature, please leave your calling card on the front hall table at my estate, and I'll respond by mail at my earliest convenience."*

A beep rang through the phone, and Liv hit End before it could record her panicked breathing. Emotions clawed their way up her chest. The embarrassed nervousness she'd been feeling all morning surged. *Why was Xander avoiding her?*

She grabbed her purse, heading for the door.

"Liv," Emma called. "Are you all right?"

She forced a smile. "If Xander comes back, let him know I'm looking for him."

Mario nodded. "We will."

～

Liv took the elevator directly down to the main floor. The crowds finally seemed to have peaked and were waning.

The atrium was a never-ending party, but it was a far cry from what she'd seen the last few nights. Liv found a place on the red couches where she had a view of people coming and going, settling in to wait.

Liv pulled her phone from her pocket. Surely Xander would be back by now. They needed to talk . . . and soon. But when she checked the screen, there were no messages. Concerned, Liv texted the younger of the two Emmas:

Emma, I'm a little worried. I've been texting Xander this morning, but he isn't answering. :(

Really? I just texted him a minute ago.

When was that?

Maybe 10 minutes ago?

Did he seem . . . okay?

No, he didn't. Sorry, Liv. :(

OMG What happened?

Truth? :(

Yes, of course!

He said you had second thoughts.

About what?!?

About HIM.

But I didn't!

Then you should probably tell him that yourself.

I would, but I don't know where he is! D:

I'll text you if I find him.

Thank you.

Any time, hon. :)

Liv took a shuddering breath and slid the phone back into her pocket. Her eyes prickled with unshed tears as the truth hit her. It wasn't that Xander *couldn't* answer his phone. He just didn't want to talk to *her*. She'd spent so long trying to avoid her feelings for Xander that she'd finally convinced *him* she didn't have them.

Liv ran her fingers through her hair, fighting the urge to scream. "I've got to fix this. . . ."

❧

Sunday morning didn't feel like Sunday morning.

It was a party, the same party that had been building all

weekend of the convention. If Friday night had been excitement and Saturday had been for crowds, Sunday had an over-the-top decadence as every con-goer came out one last time to fete their yearly pilgrimage. Costumes were soiled and wrinkled. People hacked as the first signs of the much-reviled "con-crud" took hold in the sinuses and lungs of the sleep-deprived masses.

"Where are you, Xander?" Liv muttered anxiously.

She glanced back toward the elevators, wondering if it was time to give up the search. The atrium was cloying, and she'd been jostled one too many times. The *Starveil* fans who had begun to look to her as their guide were nice, but she didn't have it in her to talk fandom. If she didn't find Xander soon, tomorrow's flight back to Colorado would be unbearably uncomfortable. For a second, the kisses in the hallway and hotel room resurfaced, and she felt her cheeks burn. That hadn't just been her. That had been Xander, too. She needed to let him know how she felt.

Liv checked both directions. She headed into the crowd, dodging elbows and drinks. A woman in a white outfit who looked suspiciously like Flo from the insurance commercial crossed Liv's path, and she barely avoided another head-on collision. Nearing the elevators, she swerved past a group of men dressed in camouflage, belatedly realizing it wasn't the regular green camo, but the same hallucinogenic pattern as the Marriott's carpet. Seconds later, a toddler stumbled into her path, and Liv nearly tripped to avoid stepping on her.

"Fly away!" the gold-wrapped child giggled, her shiny wings bouncing as she sprinted past.

"Who in the world would bring a kid here?" Liv's words disappeared as the child's haggard parents appeared.

Fighting frustration, she moved farther into the crowd, searching for a nineteenth-century man with black hair. For a while, the only thing she could see was costumed partyers and science-fiction action heroes, and then the flash of a camera led her attention to the side.

"Dragnat all anyway," she groaned.

Just when she thought the day couldn't get any worse, Tom Grander appeared. He stood alone, his entourage forming a half-circle human shield around him. On the outside of the C, people snapped pictures with their phones, but no one invaded his space.

He walked to Liv's side, entourage in tow.

"Good to see you, Liv," Tom said gravely.

"Hi." Liv turned the other way, hoping for a glimpse of Xander.

"How've you been?" Tom asked.

"Fine." Liv stood on tiptoe, searching the crowd. "Where are you, Xander?" she muttered under her breath.

"I was hoping to run into you again," Tom continued. "I want to talk."

Liv's attention jerked back to him. "Sorry. Talk about what?"

Tom gestured to the side of the room. "Do you mind if we do this someplace a little more private?"

"I can't," Liv said, looking away. "I'm looking for someone. Tall, with a top hat. Maybe tails."

"I wanted to find you to apologize." Tom's voice was stilted, the words coming out in awkward jerks and starts. "I'm really sorry for what happened the other day."

Liv turned back to him, struggling to catch up to the one-sided conversation. "You mean when you yelled at me?"

"Er . . . yes. And I—I want to apologize to you. I shouldn't have said those things."

"It's fine," she said. "I get what happened. You had—"

Her phone buzzed, and she fumbled to grab it from her pocket.

> He's headed up to the room now!
> GO GO GO!!!

Tom stepped closer. "But I—"

"I don't mean to be rude, Tom, but I have to go," Liv gasped. "Sorry!" She gave him a bashful wave as she darted away. "I've got to find someone!"

And for the first time that Liv could remember, she really *didn't* care that she was walking away from Tom Grander, because she was walking toward Xander.

⁓

Liv found Xander packing.

She stared in horror. "What're you doing?"

"I'm leaving."

"But why?!"

Xander threw another handful of linen shirts into the bag, ignoring her. When he passed by her on the way to the dresser, Liv touched his arm. "Where are you going?" she asked.

He added a pile of cravats to the mix, not bothering to fold them. He slammed the suitcase closed and looked up.

"I've got other friends here," he said stiffly. "I'll leave you with the room. Crash somewhere else tonight."

Liv shook her head. "But these are your friends. Emma and Mario—"

"Will be just fine with one less person in the room," Xander said, cutting off the rest of her words. "I don't want this to be awkward for you." His jaw clenched. "I want you to have a good time."

"But I . . . I was."

He stomped to the bathroom. Liv could hear things being thrown together. The hated tears were on the verge of spilling. She needed to persuade him to stay, but Liv was terrible at declarations. She'd been in love with Xander for almost a year, and even now she struggled to explain it.

When he returned a minute later, she stepped in front of him. "Don't," she whispered.

"Don't what?"

"Don't do this," Liv said. "Don't walk away from us."

Xander's brow wrinkled in pain, and he closed his eyes. When he opened them, the expression was so raw Liv felt something inside her break. She'd caused this.

"I can't stop it," he said haltingly. "I don't want to wreck things, but I—"

"Then why?!" Liv cried.

He smiled sadly. "Because I'm in love with you, Liv Walden. And it's too hard to pretend I'm not." He turned his back to her, plodding across the room to where his clothes lay, half-packed. "I get that you don't have the same feelings for me, and that's okay. But I felt awful when I saw you'd left this morning." His voice broke, and he looked up. "I *will* be okay, but you need to understand I need some space to figure this out."

If Liv had imagined a reunion scene from a romance novel,

she wouldn't have selected the costume-strewn, three-day-old room from the Marriott Marquis at Dragon Con, but that's exactly how it felt. She crossed the carpet, grabbing Xander by the shirt collar and tugging him down. His eyes widened in shock.

"I love you, too!"

"But when you took off this morning, I thought—"

She pulled him closer. "Shut up and kiss me."

"Liv, be reasonable—"

"Kiss me, damnit!"

Xander moved forward at the same moment she moved up, their chins and noses banging painfully together for a half second before their mouths met. This kiss was demanding, desperate, and it hinted at something else to come. In seconds, Liv felt herself danced back against the wall. Their mouths never broke contact, but he pressed into her, his hands growing bold as he reached the edge of her shirt, roving higher. This kiss—standing pressed against the wall—was full-blown spontaneous combustion. Liv was breathless by the time Xander's mouth dropped to her neck.

The door behind them opened with a squeal.

". . . and then she said that he'd have to check on whether they were booking the rooms now or—" Emma's words stopped at the same moment Liv and Xander broke apart.

Mario coughed.

"Hey, guys."

Xander moved in front of Liv, blocking her from their view. "Mario," he said with an uneasy chuckle. "Wasn't expecting you back."

Face on fire, Liv tugged down the bottom of her shirt,

wondering when in the world it had gotten shoved up to her armpits.

"It's no problem," Emma said with a giggle. "We'll get out of your way."

"It's fine," Liv said. "We were just going out for a panel." She turned to Xander. "Right? Our last day at Dragon Con together." She grinned. "Until next year."

He stared at her for a few long seconds. "Are you absolutely sure?"

"Xander, trust me on this. I'm *sure*."

His voice dropped to Malloy's growl. "Then if you're ready, darlin', I'm more than willing."

Liv leaned in, her lips brushing his.

"I think I've been ready for this forever."

Epilogue

"EVERYTHING IS AWESOME!"
(*THE LEGO MOVIE*)

The star freighter's hangar was abandoned. Hanging lights hummed overhead, piles of destroyed engine parts cluttering the otherwise empty room. In one corner, a damaged interstellar transport waited for its repair crew. In the other, a man's figure appeared, his shadow stretching out across the floor as he strode forward. His captain's jacket was tattered, the hem singed by a blaster.

He paused next to the transport and sighed.

"Dragnat all. Where *are* you?!"

A woman appeared from behind the transport. She had a headset hung around her neck and a clipboard in hand. "Over here, Xander!" Liv shouted.

His face contorted in surprise, then joy. "Heavens, Liv, I thought I'd misplaced you again."

"No." She laughed, coming forward and hugging him. "I was still here. Got to get my notes done before they start the next scene."

"Sorry it took me so long to get back. The soundstage is huge! I need a map to locate anything."

"You'll get used to it," she said with a grin. "I did."

Xander's brows knit together, his anxiety visible beneath the stage makeup.

"What's wrong?" she asked.

"Liv . . . I don't know about this."

She put her hands on his shoulders. "Stop it. You're going to be fine. You've done this a million times before."

"But not for real!"

"The vids we created were totally real. They're racking up views even now." Her smile softened. "Relax, Xander. It's only two lines."

He closed his eyes and leaned into her, his arms wrapping her back. "But it's still lines in a *real* film, and if I mess it up—"

"They'll have you do it again. And again . . . and again." Liv laughed. "No big deal. Life is full of second chances."

"That sounds like a fortune cookie."

She shrugged. "Maybe, but it's true."

He put his hand to her cheek, moving in for a kiss. "And I'm glad for every"—he kissed her forehead—"single"—he kissed the tip of her nose—"one."

And with his words, a bittersweet swell of *Starveil* music began, the house lights fading until only the silhouette of the two lovers could be seen, and then, finally, nothing at all.

Acknowledgments

The writing of a book is a lengthy process, but I could not release *All the Feels* without expressing my sincere gratitude to the many people who have shaped it along the way.

Thank you to my husband, my most enthusiastic collaborator, for reading aloud every iteration of this project from beginning to end, so that I could make sure the language sounded "just right." I'm so proud to be part of our personal OTP. Thank you also to my children, for tolerating long periods when I couldn't play, as I wrote, and rewrote, and rewrote again. I owe you one.

A grateful shout-out to my fellow fangirls—far too many to name—who kept me going when my own "Spartan" died. Thanks to Morty Mint, my agent, for his unwavering support and levelheaded advice. And a very enthusiastic thank-you to Holly West, Lauren Scobell, Emily Settle, and the entire Swoon Reads team for their tireless efforts in bringing this project together. *All the Feels* is yours as much as mine!

Finally, a special note of appreciation to Erin, the very *real* woman behind the @CoulsonLives phenomenon, who skipped out of D*C to spend an afternoon with me as we talked about writing, life, the universe, and everything in between. You are one of my dragons.

Turn the page for some

Sw♥♥nworthy

Extras...

Title: **Shadow Soul**

Author: **JoesWoes**

Word Count: **~ 6,000 words**

Primary Characters: **Spartan, Tekla, Malloy**

Pairing: **SparTek**

Rating: **NC-17 for sexuality (NSFW)**

Warning: **Mentions of suicide, death, and war
atrocities**

Tags: **#SpartanSurvived #SparTek #Malloy
#ShadowSoul #Hurt/Comfort #JoesWoesFic**

Summary: **Leaving the memories of the Fight for Io
behind is harder than Spartan had believed. Malloy
helps him come to terms with the horror.**

SHADOW SOUL

The dream begins with a memory: searching for Malloy while the attack
begins. Lost. Terrified.

Spartan jerks awake, Tekla pressed against his side, their hands
tangled together. Beyond the metal walls, the Hyperion's hyperdrive
begins to hum. They're jumping again. (They're *always* jumping these
days.) If they stop, they're dead.

"What is it, love?" Tekla whispers. Her crimson lips are pressed
against the blond curls of Spartan's hair.

Spartan frowns. (He doesn't *want* to remember.) "I had a nightmare."

"About what?"

He doesn't answer.

SwoonReads

Lanky and underfed, Spartan stands at the side of the grassy field, his eyes on his feet. He hates this new elementary school—one in a line of many—but he hates his father even more for leaving them behind. He hates his grandmother's shadowy house that he and his mother now share. Hates the mothball-scented living room and the dusty attic where he sleeps. Today he particularly hates his snot-faced schoolmates, eager to show they're tougher than the new third grader who has joined them. Spartan's already seen the principal once, but he suspects that he'll be there again before the dismissal bell rings.

Hating's easy. (Fighting's even easier.)

A blur of shadow appears in the corner of his eye. Spartan doesn't move, just stares at his newly scabbed knuckles, rolling his hand to release the tension. A scab pops open, and a berry of red blood appears. He lifts it to his mouth, sucking.

The shadow moves again, followed by a voice. "You're that new kid, aren't you? The one that got kicked out a Miss Tran's room."

Spartan looks up to find that one of the boys from his class has appeared at his side. He's small and dark, with eyes that glitter with mischief.

"You figured that all out yourself?" Spartan sneers.

The boy frowns. (Spartan tenses.) And then, oddly, the strange child begins to laugh. "You really are as piss-mean as they say!" The boy grins and offers his hand. "I'm Reginald Chance Malloy."

"You gotta mighty big name for such a puny kid."

"I might be puny, but I could kick your sorry ass," he says, lifting his chin.

Spartan rolls his eyes. There's no prestige in fighting a kid small enough to be in kindergarten. "You and whose army?"

Before the boy can answer, screams from the far side of the field reach them, and both turn. For a few seconds, they watch as a group of students surge around two fighters, scuffling in the dirt. A red-faced teacher heads into the fray, chest wheezing, leaving the boys alone. This is the time for an attack, but Spartan doesn't.

"So what's your name?" the boy asks.

"Spartan."

"Spartan?" He laughs. "What kinda name is that? Sounds like a candy bar or . . . or . . . or a washing detergent."

For a second, Spartan wants to hit him. He's ready, his small hands tightened into rocks, but he's tired of being alone, and this is the first boy who's spoken to him in more than grunts.

He shakes his head. "Spartan's my last name," he admits. "My *real* name's Matt . . . Matthew." His expression grows dark. "But then so's my dad's." His fists release. "And I like Spartan better."

"Your last name . . ." the boy murmurs. His eyes widen, and a gap-toothed smile appears. "You could call me Malloy," he says. "Yeah! Malloy!"

For the first time in days, perhaps weeks, Spartan begins to laugh. "Malloy, huh?"

"Yeah." He shoves Spartan's shoulder. "Malloy's a hell of a lot better than Reginald."

"Better than R. C., too."

The boy grins, like that's the biggest compliment in the world. "Ain't that the truth?"

"So whadya do around here for fun, Malloy?"

"Fight mostly. But I like tag better."

And like that, Spartan gains a best friend.

~~~\o/~~~

Spartan wakes, shaking, body slick with sweat. He rises slowly from his bunk, pulling on clothes with trembling hands and heading into the corridor of the star freighter. He could go to Tekla's quarters, ask her to help him forget. (He has done it many times before.) But he doesn't today. It's too hard to endure her pity. His memory keeps going back *there*, and he doesn't want to.

Instead, he walks to the central command center. They are tracking the Imperial Fleet again, preparing to destroy it. (As they've done every day since Darthku's attack on Io.) Usually, Spartan would at least make a point of arguing for combining forces with some of the other rebel ships—that was the point of the Rebellion, after all—but lately he's been too tired to fight it.

His will died long ago.

With this thought flickering through his mind, he turns another corner and stops stock-still. Tekla is standing in the corridor, waiting for him. He keeps trying to leave her, but she always finds a way back. He doesn't *want* her kindness, but sex is his weakness, and she knows how to exploit it. (There's a reason she's a leader in the Rebellion.)

"You didn't come to my quarters last night," she says, approaching him, hands outstretched. "I was worried about you, Spartan."

He doesn't answer, just stares at her, his mind drawing in details: pale skin and long waves of silver-blond hair. That worried smile. Pain.

She is exactly the same as the day Darthku destroyed the base.

"I need to figure this out on my own," he mutters, then turns and walks away.

<div align="center">~~~\o/~~~</div>

Spartan and Malloy have been drinking for hours, the two of them one-upping the events of their short lives, earning their ranks at the Imperial Academy, when *she* shows up. Curvy, fresh-faced, red-haired: all the things Spartan wants . . . and knows his friend wants, too.

Malloy lets out a slow whistling breath, his gaze dragging up her body. "Well, would you look at that," he murmurs.

"Mmm . . ." Spartan chuckles. "She's quite a sight for sore eyes."

"The kinda girl you don't see too often," Malloy agrees.

"She's a little above *your* game, I think."

"And yours," Malloy snorts in easy good humor. "Jeez, though, look at her legs. Go on forever."

The woman is utterly out of place. She's wearing a black dress with a string of pearls, rather than the fatigues of the standard military clientele the bar tends to attract. Both men watch her as she moves through the room, apparently searching for her friends. When she pauses next to their table, she catches sight of Spartan and Malloy, and a dimpled smile breaks across her face.

"Two for one." She giggles. "The Imperial Academy must have a special on tonight."

Malloy does a quick salute. "Two of the best, ma'am."

Her tinkling laughter hits Spartan right in the chest. With even white teeth, smooth skin, and a freckled nose, she's even prettier up close. He pats the semicircular bench where he and Malloy sit side by side. "There's plenty of room, you know. Take a load off those pretty feet."

"Oh, no. I'm just waiting for the people I'm meeting," she says. "But thank you."

"Waiting goes faster when you're with friends." Spartan chuckles. "And someone as lovely as you deserves more of them." (Malloy rolls his eyes, but the woman doesn't see.)

"Why don't you have a drink with us while you wait?" Malloy suggests.

The woman gives one last look to the teeming bar, before sliding into the bench seat between the two men. "I can't stay long. Just till my friends arrive. Okay?"

"Then we'll try to make it worth your while," Malloy says with a chuckle. "You ready to put up with two military cadets? We can be a little rough around the edges." Spartan smirks and takes note. Malloy's self-deprecation is an art form. Women love it.

"Oh, I don't mind military. My dad's in the fleet. Vice admiral to Darthku." She flashes another dimpled grin. "So what're we having tonight, boys?"

"Whatever you'd like, darlin'," Spartan drawls.

"My name's Selena."

"Selena then." He winks. "Beautiful name for a beautiful girl." She's going home with him tonight. He's already decided. (The fact that he's doing this to compete with Malloy—his best friend and closest competitor in everything—is only an afterthought.)

Malloy is almost as quick, gesturing to the waitress near them. "Your finest whiskey for our lovely companion, Selena."

The server stares at him. "Finest?" she repeats. (They're two dirt-poor cadets. Finest isn't a description they ever use.)

Malloy winks. "The one behind the bar. Gold label with red writing. Glen something-er-other."

Selena gasps. (She apparently recognizes it.)

The waitress shakes her head. "That one can't go on your tab." She puts out her hand, waiting until Malloy drops a wrinkled bill into her palm. "That'll get you one shot," she says, raising a brow. "You sure about that?"

Spartan almost laughs when Malloy's smile wobbles. But Selena moves closer to him, pressing her breasts against his arm. "Thank you so much, honey. You don't have to do that, you know."

"It's nothing. And you deserve the best." He tugs on the front of his hair in an Old Terran gesture of formality. "Please allow me, ma'am."

She giggles, and Spartan shakes his head. Malloy is far better at playing this game than he'll ever give himself credit for. Malloy's dark good looks are a perfect foil for Spartan's blond brightness, and women like one as much as the other. The waitress goes to leave, but Spartan reaches into his pocket and pulls out his own crumpled bill—the last cash he has. (The rest of the night will go on an ever-increasing tab.)

"Let's make that *two* for the lady," Spartan says, then winks. "Finest, of course."

"Oh, but you don't have to." Selena laughs. "One is plenty. Really. I hardly ever drink."

Spartan winks at Malloy over her shoulder, then turns his attention back to her. "Don't have to, but I want to."

Malloy grins. He's on his game, too.

The drinks arrive, and the three make a toast. Selena coughs when she takes a sip, the fumes hitting Spartan's nose seconds later. Ten minutes after that, she has an arm over each of the men's shoulders. (The best whiskey in the bar is a heady concoction.) And when her friends belatedly arrive, they join the trio, though none of them break Spartan's concentration. When he competes, he competes to win.

Trouble is, Malloy does, too.

The next few hours pass in a haze. The gold-label drinks are replaced by increasingly rot-gut whiskey, and by the time they stumble out onto the street and into the darkness of the alley, Spartan knows he'll be getting lucky. Selena's hands are moving over all the places Spartan has imagined tonight. The only problem is, she's sharing those affections with Malloy, too, and Spartan still hasn't figured out how to tell his friend to piss off.

She kisses Spartan—tasting of whiskey—but the second his hands move to her breasts, she turns to embrace Malloy. Before he knows what is happening, Selena's undoing Malloy's belt, sliding it down his narrow hips. Malloy groans as Selena's mouth moves down his muscled body—from Malloy's lips to his neck, chest, stomach, lower. . . . Her red hair darkens to auburn in the shadows of the alley while she crouches before him.

Malloy gasps and drops his head against the brick wall of the alley, a near-pained look of ecstasy on his face. "Oh god. Don't stop."

Spartan scowls. He's lost this game as well as his petty cash; the thought is a bitter pill to swallow.

"Later then, you two," he says, turning away. Spartan hunches his shoulders in annoyance. He has to walk home. There's no fare in his pocket. It irks him. "Gimme a shout tomorrow, Malloy."

He's almost to the end of the alley when Selena's voice stops him.

"Leaving so soon, Spartan?" she purrs. "I thought the three of us could go back to my place. You know . . . and play."

Spartan doesn't turn back at once. Everything has changed in the last seconds. He can hear Malloy panting, can see the oily reflection of streetlights in the alley's puddles, can smell the faint musk of Selena's perfume clinging to his clothes.

But he's my best friend, a voice inside him argues.

Your only friend, another voice adds.

Spartan slowly turns. Malloy is looking at him with something like pain. He's breathing like he's been running. Selena's hands are around his neck, and her eyes seem far less innocent than they did in the bar. She bites her lower lip as he stands, undecided.

"What do you say, Spartan?" Malloy asks in a shaky voice. "You up for something new?"

"I don't know if . . ." Spartan's heart tightens, all his arguments disappearing. "Do you, Malloy?"

Malloy slides his arm around Selena's waist, walking forward. His jacket is askew, buttons open, pants slung low on his hips. There's an expression on his friend's face that Spartan doesn't quite understand.

"I'm willing if you are."

And when they reach Spartan's side, *Malloy's* the one who leans in and kisses him.

~~~\o/~~~

Tekla's waiting for Spartan when he emerges from the showers. She's draped in a towel, her body teasing him with hints of curves and hollows and promises of damp flesh. (She's chosen her weapons of war well.)

"Hello, darlin'." He chuckles, walking nearer, letting her see the effect she has on him. "You're lookin' mighty fine."

She doesn't smile.

Instead, she slides her hands up his arms, staring at him with that pained concern that makes him want to scream.

"You had the dream again last night, Spartan," she says quietly. "It's getting worse, not better."

The blood drains from his face. "I did?" Suddenly the shower room is too muggy. He can't breathe for all the steam.

"You did," she says. "And I couldn't wake you up this time."

~~~\o/~~~

Malloy catches Spartan in the hangar minutes before he escapes. The Imperial shuttle stands open, packed with stolen supplies and ammunition, the start of a new life. The cubby in the bunk room the two friends share is now empty except for Spartan's Imperial uniform, one he'll never wear again.

"So this is it?" Malloy sneers. "You've turned coat, leaving me behind?"

Spartan tenses, but doesn't stop packing. "Walk away," he growls. "Pretend you didn't see me."

Malloy crosses the floor. "You know I can't do that."

"Then turn me in." Spartan throws his blaster onto the empty copilot seat. "Go ahead. I don't care." His lips twist angrily. "It's what a good little soldier would do."

Malloy grabs his shoulder, spinning him around. "Stop it!" he hisses. "You know what they do to suspected rebels."

Spartan holds his eyes. "Yes, I do."

"Then why are you leaving?"

Spartan shrugs off Malloy's hand. "I'm doing the right thing. The honest thing." His eyes narrow. "You should, too."

"It's not that easy, and you know it."

"It never is."

Distant footsteps echo from the open door of the empty hangar, and both men fall silent. The skeleton crew of the Imperial ship has given Spartan the chance to escape, but if he's caught, he'll be dead before the shift changes. (Or worse.)

"Come back to the bunk room. Let's figure this out. I'll pull some strings so you can get a paid leave—a transfer even. You could go back to Terra. Maybe find Tekla, talk to her."

Spartan doesn't even answer. He climbs into the shuttle, begins programming in his coordinates, blocking Darthku's tracking devices one by one. He already knows the code for the hangar door. (That cost him a month's wages, the jump coordinates twice that.) But Malloy needs to be off the flight deck before he goes, or they'll suspect him of assisting. The truth doesn't matter to the Imperial Fleet, just the semblance of justice.

"You need to leave," Spartan says, reaching for the hatch.

Malloy grabs the door before it closes. "You're going to die out there!" he shouts. "You'll never be able to stop running!"

Their eyes meet. There are too many things to say. Too little time. They catch on Spartan's tongue, choking him. Malloy is more than his best friend. He's his brother, competitor, fiercest ally, and sometimes lover. If there's ever been a shadow side to Spartan's soul, it's Major R. C. Malloy, and it feels like he's tearing himself in half as he leaves his best friend behind.

Malloy lets go, and the door begins to close.

"You could always come with me," Spartan offers, last second.

Malloy turns on his heels and walks away.

~~~\o/~~~

Spartan wanders the corridors of the Hyperion, lost and untethered. He knows it's only a matter of time before the fighting starts again—Tekla will find the Imperial Fleet eventually—but the delay feels like a lifetime. It was so easy before. He knew why he fought. He knew who.

But since Io . . .

Spartan shoves the thought away and heads to the star freighter's gymnasium. Here he wraps his fists and attacks the punching bag, pummeling the canvas until his hands throb and the voices in his mind go silent. If he can't forget through sex, pain will be his anesthesia.

He's sweat-slicked and shaking when the horn echoes through the ship. An announcement follows seconds later: *"Captain Matt Spartan, report to the central command center,"* a robotic voice intones. *"Captain Matt Spartan, report to command immediately."*

Spartan keeps punching.

~~~\o/~~~

They're under attack and fighting for their lives when Spartan sees Malloy again. It's the first time since the long-ago night he left, turning coat and joining the Rebellion. The shock of it—seeing his oldest friend among the ranks of nameless Imperial soldiers—slows him. He turns, pausing, as his eyes catch Malloy's.

"No, you . . . not now," Spartan whispers.

That's all the opening the nearby soldier needs.

Spartan wakes, face pressed against the cold concrete of a cell, a man's hand on his arm. He's been tortured before, and it's not an experience he wants to enjoy again. His hands come up in fists before he even realizes who it is.

Malloy puts a hand to Spartan's lips. His friend's fingers are warm and gentle. And so much like the times before when Spartan has reacted before he's realized what he's done, he turns his head and bites the heel of the hand across his lips. Malloy hisses and leans down, replacing his hand with his mouth.

For ten long seconds, the kiss drags on—desperate with need—and then Malloy lets go of him and stands. It's over before it's begun. Spartan wonders if his memory has betrayed him. They shared everything, once. Clothes, friends, lovers. Now all he has is Malloy's back as he stares the other way.

"Get up," he whispers. "It's time to go."

Spartan sits up slowly, wincing as the muscles over his ribs shout in protest. His head throbs in time to his heart, and flashes of the final moments of hand-to-hand combat appear: *seeing Malloy in the crowd, pausing in shock, an attack from the side, darkness.*

"Where to?" Spartan croaks, but Malloy silences him with an angry look. Malloy tiptoes to the door, peering out.

Spartan crawls to his feet and glances around the small rectangular space. No windows, no cot, just a door and a drain. He stumbles when he tries to walk, but Malloy catches him. For a second, it's all too much. If Darthku's troops are going to break his will, they've sent exactly the right man to destroy him. Malloy is Spartan's Achilles's heel, and he knows it. His wounds are nothing compared with the ache in his chest.

"No . . . I can't," Spartan gasps. "I can't do this. Not with you."

He wishes he'd died in the fight.

"Hold on," Malloy whispers. "I've got you." His arms, warm and strong, wrap Spartan's chest. For a moment, it's all Spartan can do to stay upright. Sobs hitch his breath, and he presses his face to Malloy's neck, breathing in gasps. His friend's cologne washes over him, drowning him in memories of the two of them as young men, sleeping, curled one behind the other, in a single bunk. Everything's gone wrong in the time since then, the whole world gone to pieces. Spartan himself a broken man. The bugs destroying everything. The Rebellion hasn't soothed his wounds, just made his well of pain deeper.

"I'm so sorry, Malloy," he gasps. "I shouldn't have gone. I—"

Malloy grabs Spartan's shirt, dragging him so close their mouths are almost touching. "Stop it!" he hisses. "They'll hear you and kill us both."

The vehemence shocks Spartan into silence.

"Who?" he mouths.

Malloy's face ripples with pain. "My men, of course. They're coming to kill you."

Twenty minutes later, Spartan's off-world and flying toward the Rebel stronghold. Malloy, back in command, is planning the funerals for the three soldiers—his own men—who died as they tried to stop Captain Matt Spartan from escaping. No one knows it was Malloy himself who held the blaster that killed them.

No one, that is, except Spartan . . .

~~~\o/~~~

Tekla is standing outside Spartan's quarters, looking angry and worried, when he comes back from the gym. She has a communicator in her hand and tucks it away as he appears. Spartan's limbs are rubbery and loose, his body so tired each step takes conscious effort.

"You didn't respond to my page," she says grimly. "I was worried."

"Didn't hear."

"Were you sleeping?" she asks in a quiet voice. She's asking something *else*, too, but he won't think about that.

"Nope. In the gym. Had the music up."

Lies. All lies. Spartan doesn't care. He tries to push past her. (There's no point in punishing his body if she's going to bring the pain all back again.) But today Tekla doesn't move. She catches his wrist, holding tight. He closes his eyes and breathes slowly, fighting the urge to shove her away.

"I'm tired," he says in an icy voice. "Let me go."

"I think we should talk."

He looks up, catching the look of pity before she can properly hide it.

"There's nothing to talk about."

"There is. If you'll just—"

He rips his wrist free, pushing through the door and slamming it behind him. He hears the handle turn, but he's locked it.

"Spartan? Spartan, open the door. Let me in," her voice echoes from the other side. "C'mon, Matt. Please, baby. Open up for me . . ."

He rests his head against the cold metal of the door. Malloy's laughing face flickers in his mind and he winces.

Tekla means well, but he doesn't want to be saved.

SwoonReads

Major R. C. Malloy stands across from Tekla, his face anguished as she rages, Spartan watching in growing concern. Malloy is his longtime friend. His once confidant and blood brother. He may be a turncoat, but if Malloy is, then they are, too.

Tekla's convinced he's a spy. (And maybe, Spartan muses, he actually is.)

"Why'd you show up now?!" she shouts at him. "Why not six months ago when the Rebellion began? Why not sometime after that?"

"I had to wait until it was safe," Malloy explains.

"Until it was convenient." She sneers.

Malloy pins her down with his stare, contemptuously ignoring the shackles on his wrists and feet. "If I'd declared at once, I've no doubt Darthku would have killed me."

Tekla smirks. "Might still happen."

Malloy's eyes narrow as he stares daggers at her. "Then you'll never get the intel I brought. You want to know Darthku's plan or not?"

"Oh, there are other ways to get answers," Tekla growls. "Care to test me?"

Most men would cower at the threat of torture, but Malloy's chin rises. He could be standing at a podium, not as a prisoner.

"Not particularly," he drawls. "I'd suggest checking Darthku's intel first. It'll save *me* a world of pain and *you* a world of embarrassment."

"I don't embarrass easy," she scoffs, "and there are other ways to fact-check." Tekla steps closer and pulls a folding blade from her pocket. "You see?"

"Tekla," Spartan warns quietly. She doesn't hear him (or doesn't listen).

"You can either start talking . . . or I start helping you." She opens the knife, dancing it over her fingertips, an angry smile on her curving lips. "It's all up to you."

Tekla and her damned blade, Spartan thinks. She likes the fear it brings. Malloy's eyes widen as she brings the razor-sharp edge to his chest.

"There are men and women who *died* because of you," she murmurs, dragging the tip of the knife along the front of his shirt. A thin tear appears where the fabric is tight. A line of muscle jumps in Malloy's jaw, but he otherwise seems calm. "I'm sure they'd like to make sure I get the truth."

"You can play your little game," Malloy says in a haughty voice, "but it isn't going to change the—" Tekla digs the blade deeper and a red flower appears under its tip. "Facts," Malloy finishes.

"I'll know the truth when I hear it. Keep talking."

The knife slides up Malloy's neck, pausing on top of his pulse point. The skin puckers. Malloy is leaning as far back in his chair as he can, his neck corded with muscle.

"Tekla." Spartan's voice is louder this time.

"You led the attacks on the Ceres shipyards," she hisses, her face only inches from Malloy's. "Tell me why you'd do that if you actually intended to rebel." The blade wobbles, tip disappearing for a split second.

"Tekla!"

"You led that attack, Malloy," she says, voice rising. "You were Darthku's hand. You brought his justice!" The knife goes higher, a dotted line appearing as it notches the smooth skin of Malloy's jaw and cheek. "That attack killed friends of mine. Men, women, children."

"I was following orders," Malloy says, his eyes dark with rage and pain. "Everybody follows them in the fleet. Everybody—"

He gasps as she reaches the hollow under his right eye.

"So what do you say?" Tekla snarls. "Eye for an eye?" The blade leans in, closer . . . closer . . . "Seems fair to me." The knife dips in and Malloy's gaze jumps to Spartan, pleading.

"Tekla, for the love of god, *stop*! I'll vouch for him, all right?!"

The knife clatters to the floor, and she spins to face Spartan. She's breathing hard—looking much as she does after sex—cheeks flushed, eyes wild. Beautiful in her anger, but no longer in control.

"You'll do *what*?!"

"I'll vouch for him." He steps up and puts a shaking hand on Malloy's shoulder. "I trust Major Malloy. He's my friend. And if he says he's honest, he is."

Tekla's eyes turn to ice.

"Th-thank you," Malloy says hoarsely. "I-I owe you one, Spartan."

~~~\o/~~~

Spartan sighs as the image fades. It's a memory, of course. Malloy's not actually there. (He's had a hundred such thoughts in the weeks since they parted ways.) On the other side of the command center, Tekla looks up and frowns. "Do you need something, Spartan?" Her words are more gentle than he deserves. They have a war to fight, after all.

"I . . . I was thinking about Io again."

Tekla nods to her second-in-command, gesturing Spartan to follow her into the hallways that spread like a spiderweb through the star freighter.

"What about Io?" she asks sympathetically.

"The people who joined us there. The refugees."

She frowns and waits for the rest.

"There were people on the surface when we escaped," Spartan says. "People left to die. They won't . . . *can't* . . . survive a winter on their own they'll—"

"Yes, there were Rebels left behind," Tekla says firmly. "But their deaths let us live." She shakes her head. "You can't save everyone, Spartan. This bloody war has certainly shown us that."

"But, but . . . they can't live like that!" he argues, voice rising. "What happens when winter comes? They'll kill themselves before they let

SwoonReads

themselves be taken by Darthku's troops. You have to go back for them, Tekla. To leave them to starvation, it's . . . it's inhumane . . ."

"I'm sorry," she whispers, voice catching. "But I can't."

It's an endless argument. One that's been raging since Darthku destroyed the base and they escaped to fight another day. Spartan puts his head down, his gaze on the grated flooring, so she's almost upon him before he catches sight of her boots. Seeing them, his eyes rise in panic.

She knows his weaknesses.

Tekla's got her arms on her hips, her lips pursed in that look of obstinacy that months of living with her taught Spartan to both love and hate. He doesn't say anything to her, just stands there. Watching *her* watching *him*. Without conscious effort, a memory floats to mind. Tekla standing in the watery light of the windows in the apartment they shared.

It is the morning of the end.

Tekla's words interrupt before the cancerous memory can take hold.

"If I thought it would do anyone any good, I'd go back to Io," she says gently. "But it won't, Spartan. You know that as well as I do."

"It *will*. There are people there. Our people!"

Her expression changes. He sees the emotion at once—sympathy—and he hates her for it.

"Returning won't change what happened," she says. "It won't bring him back to you."

He's too angry to respond. *Of course he knows that!*

"I love you, Spartan," Tekla says, "but I—"

Spartan turns on his heels and storms away.

~~~\o/~~~

The dream begins with a memory.

It's early morning on Io, and Spartan's moving over the top of Tekla, his hands tangled in her silver hair. His tongue plunders her mouth while she runs her fingers over his skin, tracing the striations of muscles.

Tekla's body is soft and pliant in his arms, leaving no sense of where she begins and he ends, the feel of her a drug.

Suddenly the door bangs open, the two of them jerking apart in an instant.

Malloy stands in the doorway, a jaunty grin on his lips. "Didn't mean to interrupt the happy little reunion," he drawls, "but we're all about to die." He tosses a blaster on the bed. "Grab a gun, you two. We've got company."

Tekla's the first one out of bed, yanking on clothes before Spartan has even processed what his friend is saying.

A sonic boom rattles the windows, and the three of them turn as one. Framed by the shuddering panels is Tekla. Behind her is the bulk of the Star Freighter Hyperion roaring toward the base.

"Hyperion just broke atmosphere," she says in a hollow voice.

"Hurry up!" Malloy shouts. "There's not much time!"

~~~\o/~~~

Spartan wakes in the star freighter, bile rising in his throat. He takes a sobbing breath, his body shaking like palsy.

"It was the dream again, wasn't it?" Tekla says from the darkness at his side. "The last day on Io."

He doesn't answer. Can't.

A faint light wraps around her when she climbs from bed, her body leaner than it was six months ago. She's wearing the loose tee and gray pants that were her uniform in the Rebel quarters on Io. (Six pairs of the same folded neatly in the dresser of the bedroom they once shared.) She stands watching him in silence, her head tipped to the side.

"Spartan? Answer me."

He pulls on his clothes in jerky movements. He can't push the dream away anymore. Can't make the memory disappear. He sees it everywhere, the words of that long-ago day taunting him at random moments. Memories of the dead abruptly too real.

All the death, the death, the death . . . his mind screams.

Tekla's shoulders slump, her voice breaking. "You've got to talk about this. It's not healthy to pretend it didn't happen."

He grabs her shoulders, shaking her as a dog shakes a rabbit. "Why?!" he screams. "Why should I remember?!" He lets go, and she stumbles and falls.

Tears fill Tekla's eyes. "Because he did it for you."

~~~\o/~~~

The windows are shuddering, screams rising around the Rebel base. Two more booms follow the Hyperion's appearance, Imperial ships in quick pursuit.

"What the hell?!?" Spartan growls.

"Darthku's found the base!" Malloy shouts. "We've got to *go!*"

Tekla grabs the blaster from the bed, dragging on a shirt as she darts from the room. She meets Spartan's eyes in the doorway. "Meet me in the hangar!" she orders, then disappears. (She says nothing to Malloy at all.)

"Dragnat all!" Spartan mutters, grabbing clothes thrown willy-nilly across the floor. Malloy turns to leave. "Wait for me!" Spartan bellows. Everything's moving too fast.

Malloy pauses and smiles. (Spartan will remember that afterward.) "I've got to delay Darthku's troops," he says. "You catch up with me later, all right?"

Spartan tugs on a pair of pants, slides bare feet into his boots. "Fighting side by side," he says. "Just like old times."

Malloy's smile fades. "Yeah . . . Old times."

In seconds, he's out the door, leaving Spartan to follow. When Spartan reaches the courtyard, the world is falling to pieces. *Io burning.*

There are raised voices in the compound. Spartan presses himself against the lee of the wall until they pass, then jogs down to the hangar deck where the interstellar transports await. *Hurry . . . hurry . . .* an inner voice warns. Every second of delay is too much.

Malloy's not there.

But where's he gone? Spartan needs to find him! His friend and comrade in arms is the last of the Imperial Guard to turn coat, and Darthku will never let him stand trial if he's caught. The major will be an example. A martyr. Stripped and tortured until agony itself destroys the person he is. (Spartan's seen it happen before.) With Io under attack, there will be no reprieve.

Spartan's mind darts cat and mouse through the places Malloy might have gone: the hangar, command, ammunitions room. Panic rising, he finally reaches the barracks.

"Malloy!" Spartan cries, listening with half an ear to the fighting going on outside the walls. "Where are you?!"

There's no answer.

Spartan heads to the washhouse at the same time a single report of gunfire echoes. This time it is nearer.

"Malloy!" Spartan shouts. "Where *are* you, dragnat all?!" He pulls open the door to the showers, stepping inside the darkened bathroom without turning on the light.

Two things strike him at once. First, that the door won't open all the way; something is blocking it. Second, that it smells like copper.

In that moment, Spartan's foot slips. His legs go out from under him and he falls forward, landing, with a thud, against Malloy's still-warm body. The young man's eyes are wide and blank, black hair matted with blood. His mouth hangs open, silently screaming, a blaster clasped in limp fingers.

"No!" Spartan shrieks. "No, you can't! Please, God, *no!*"

But even saying it, Spartan knows it's true. He considers staying, waiting until Darthku's Imperial Guard takes the holdout and dying at his friend's side, but he knows Malloy would want him to live. He also

Swoon Reads

knows Malloy's death has given him one last gift: the cover Spartan needs to escape.

<center>~~~\o/~~~</center>

Spartan wakes in Tekla's quarters. She has her arms wrapped around his chest, and she's rocking him like a child.

"Shh . . ." she croons. "Just a dream . . . just a dream . . ."

Spartan takes a sobbing breath and buries his face against her chest. *It was never just a dream.*

"I—I keep dreaming of that day," he gasps. "I keep dreaming of Io!"

"What about it?"

"About Malloy."

Tekla pushes him back onto the bed, kissing Spartan until his sobs fade, then moving down his body. "Relax," she whispers against his skin. "Let me help you forget. . . ."

He closes his eyes as she tastes him, his hands tangling in her silver hair. Flashes of the past rise in time to the sensations: Spartan and Malloy standing outside the elementary school side by side. The same friends, years later, sitting in an academy dive, a redheaded woman with her arms around them. Malloy arguing with Spartan on the deck of their last post. Spartan flying away, not looking back. Two friends in a war with no end. Spartan hanging onto Malloy's neck in an Imperial jail cell. Malloy in a chair, Tekla's blade to his neck, the blade glittering red. Malloy's eyes wide and empty, a sheet of blood spreading in a pool beneath his still body.

Malloy . . . Malloy . . . Malloy . . .

And finally, after weeks of denial, the dam breaks. Spartan rolls to the side, catching Tekla in his arms and sobbing against her chest.

"Why?!" he roars. "Why did he have to die?"

"I don't know."

"I tried to find him that day! I wanted to save him!"

"Shh . . . I know," she whispers as she strokes his hair. "It's all right."

"He's gone, and I never—" His voice hitches with sobs. "Never told him the truth."

"I know."

"I loved him, and he still died."

Her hand on his head pauses for a long moment before she resumes her petting. "I know, my love. I know," her voice breaks. "But Malloy *knew*."

And for some reason, at that moment, that's exactly what Spartan needs to hear.

<div align="center">~~~\o/~~~</div>

A Coffee Date

with author Danika Stone and her editor, Holly West

"About the Author"

HW: I'm going to start with my favorite question. If you were a superhero, what would your superpower be?

DS: I'm going to tell you that I *am* a superhero, and my time-stealing ability is actually my superpower! Of course this is kind of a joke, but my husband always accuses me of that, and all I can say is that I write lists, and I do things off my list constantly. Like, if I have two minutes, then I try to do a paragraph of editing or something like that. And I swear that's the only way I get anything done. So, yes, that's my superpower. I would steal time from other people so I can efficiently get things done.

HW: That is a fabulous superpower! I'd never have thought of that. *All the Feels* features a lot of cosplaying and a trip to Dragon Con, which I know you regularly attend. What do you like to cosplay as when you go?

DS: Well, I have a big list of things I've cosplayed. Usually it's a character I've seen on television and just obsessed over. It doesn't just have to be TV, either; it could be a movie. Like once I went as Marie Antoinette with these giant skirts. I have yet to go as Agent Carter, but I would *really* love to. Once I went as Six from *Battlestar Galactica* because I'm super tall.

It's always just a neat way of representing this character who's interesting. Not necessarily that you *like*, because I certainly don't *like* Cersei Lannister—I have also cosplayed as her—but she is interesting, and it's a fun way to represent yourself and what your interests are.

"The Swoon Reads Experience"

HW: What was your experience like on the Swoon Reads site?
DS: I had not had any experience with crowdsourcing before, so I had no idea how supportive the community would be. I posted *All the Feels*, and the very next day, there was someone saying, "I'm reading it and I really like these characters!" It was a weird feeling! In fact, it was a feeling I hadn't had since writing for fandom years before. Because usually you write in this little tiny bubble and no one touches it. Then you send it out and two years go by and someone says, "Well, we can either do something with it or not." But this was so different! It was this amazing, positive experience. These comments just would keep coming in, and I was able to interact with readers. It kind of bridged two worlds I loved.

HW: You used to write for fandom? What did you write?
DS: Oh, that vault is locked!

HW: I'm a huge fan of fanfic and fanfiction writers. It's a great way of learning how to write.
DS: Exactly! I totally agree. And it's interesting. There are a lot of amazing writers that are active in fandom. People who write as a career, and as you get to know them as a person, you're like, "Whoa! I had no idea." Yes, it's like this secret place that's just so perfect.

Swoon Reads

HW: Back to you and Swoon Reads, once your book was chosen, we swore you to secrecy. What was that like?

DS: I feel like I need a GIF to express my emotions here. Because of course it's something you work *so hard* for—and I had written for many, many years—and this was HUGE. So it was really exciting. I just wanted to scream at everyone. Like, I would go into my regular job—which is a teacher—and I just wanted to shout to everybody. But of course I couldn't tell anyone! Not even my mom, because I love my mom, but she can't keep a secret for the life of her.

"The Writing Life"

HW: When did you first realize that you wanted to be a writer?

DS: Second year of university, I took a creative-writing class, kind of on a whim. Because while I really loved painting, I'd done some writing in high school—like fandom stuff—and I really enjoyed it, but I didn't almost think of it as real. Like I felt like I was just playing in someone else's sandbox. When I took that course, I had this amazing instructor, and I realized that I could actually write. It was this massive leap. Like it isn't just playing anymore. You have someone to help shape it.

So I think that was the big step. And then the second step happened when I was writing this crazy master's thesis, and I needed something to keep me sane. I couldn't just write about research. It was making me crazy. So I would say to myself, "You have to write a thousand words about metadata," but at the end of it, I was allowed to just play. I could write about whatever. I could write fanfic, I could write characters, I could write poetry—

it didn't matter. That would be my carrot. And it was amazing. So as I plotted my way through this master's thesis, my other writing just grew and grew and grew, because it was the thing that I loved, and I was using it to keep me going.

HW: Do you have any rituals or anything you do to get yourself in the mood? Like, do you get writer's block and then have to do something to switch yourself out of it?

DS: I have a couple things I do that are just kind of my things. Usually when I'm writing a story, I gather a box of items that I call my memory box. When I was writing *All the Feels*, I had a pocket watch in there. Just little things that I can draw on. I also create a cover and put it on a book and set it beside my bed so I have this little fake cover that I'm always looking at as I'm going to bed like, "You have to finish this book and make it real." But my biggest ritual is just that I have to write every day. Even though it might be terrible, I have to write something.

HW: Where did you get the original idea for *All the Feels*? What sparked Liv and Xander?

DS: The two big sparks were: (1) I had a brother-in-law who, if he is not at work, is in cosplay. He is an amazing person, and I *love* that! Because of course I do cosplay whenever I'm at Dragon Con or a convention, but to cosplay as a way of life is a very different thing. And (2) I happen to be close personal friends with @CoulsonLives. She was the driving force that brought Agent Coulson back to life. When she saw *Marvel's The Avengers* where he gets killed off, she was like, "THAT IS NOT HAPPENING." And she started this Internet movement to bring him back from

Swoon Reads

the dead, where everything was hashtagged #CoulsonLives. And I saw her changing the world in a way and thought, *Wow, that is a really cool idea! I would love to write about that.* Not about her, of course, because she's a private person, but what if you decided that canon is not going to be canon? *You're* going to change it. So those two ideas together sort of bloomed into this beautiful little story that I loved writing.

HW: What is the best writing advice you've ever heard?
DS: At first, I gathered all these quotes, thinking I should use this one or that one, but for me, the best writing advice actually came from my dad, who is a hiker, and he would get us kids to go long distances with him. He would say, "Oh, it's just over that hill," and we'd be like, "Where?!" "Oh, just over that little turn there in the trail." And we would go on these crazy-long torture hikes. But we would never really notice how long they were, because he was constantly lying to us and making us break it into little segments.

So when I was starting to write my thesis, I remember talking to my father and I was panicking, "Whoa, it's a book! You have to write a book!" And I remember him saying, "Well, you just break it into little parts. You write sentences and you make them into paragraphs, and then you put them into chapters, and you do a few chapters and you've got your thesis."

Although my father passed away before I really started doing novels, I really have always stuck to that approach. I just tell myself, "I'm going to write a thousand words today." I never, never worry about where I'm going next; I just keep going forward. And I think that's the best writing advice. You just have to keep going.

Swoon Reads

All the Feels
Discussion Questions

1. Have you ever been devastated by the death of a fictional character? Who and why?

2. Liv takes her fortune cookie fortunes very seriously. Do you have any superstitions?

3. Liv is so upset by the end of the last *Starveil* movie that she takes it upon herself to start an online movement to change it. If you could change the ending of any book, TV show, or movie that you were disappointed by, which would it be and how would you change it?

4. Xander is very into steampunk cosplay. If you could pick any era's fashions to dress in, which would you choose?

5. Liv and her fandom friends are so passionate about their fandom that they create their own fan content. Have you ever written fanfiction or made fanvids, photo manips, or other fandom-related creations? If so, what were they? And if not, what book, TV show, or movie would you like to create things for?

6. Most of Liv's friendships are conducted online, but Xander worries that she doesn't socialize enough in real life. In your opinion, are online friendships any more or less beneficial than offline ones?

7. After Liv's fandom life takes off online, her mother becomes increasingly worried that it will negatively affect Liv's schoolwork and ultimately forbids her from participating. Do you agree with Liv's mother's actions? Why or why not?

8. When Liv first arrives at Dragon Con, she feels like she's finally found "her people." Have you ever had that experience? When and where?

9. At Dragon Con, Liv finally meets Thomas Grander, who plays Matt Spartan, but he is not at all what she expects. Have you ever met a celebrity, and if so, were you surprised by what they were like in real life?

10. If you were going to Dragon Con, who or what would you cosplay as? Why?

Swoon Reads

What's a little harmless kissing between friends?

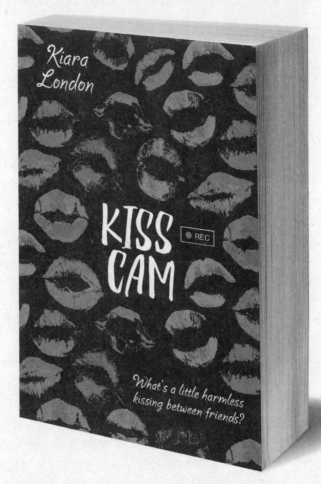

A trio of vloggers push the boundaries of their friendship by giving in to fan requests for a "Kiss Cam" segment.

AVAILABLE OCTOBER 2016.

Maybe We've Had Better Ideas

It's not until Friday afternoon that the idea of a "kiss cam" is taken seriously. I promptly dismissed the idea upon its initial suggestion, knowing that things could get out of hand if left up for discussion. The case was closed after that—or so I thought.

Things are starting to go haywire at our chosen lunch table. Lenny brings up the comments from our last vlog and begins coming up with an argument as to why we should do it. Jasper leans over the table to see the evidence himself and quickly tries to rope me into the idea.

"Juniper, it's the absolute worst idea," Allison remarks when it looks as though I'm going to give in.

I know it's a bad idea—a funny and unpredictable idea, but a bad one, nonetheless. I know what she's worried about, but there is no way anything between Jasper and me could develop now. We're *just friends* for a reason. Why ruin a good thing with complications? I figured that out freshman year when he started dating Bree. I had a crush on him and I thought maybe he liked me back, but then he went and dated her instead. I decided then and there not to let him get to my head. Everything with him was just friendly, and feelings were never allowed. No complications meant no feelings could get hurt.

And kissing without the complication of feelings? What could be so bad about that?

I had previously thought I would never give my kisses away so easily, but after sifting through the comments, I have to admit our viewers' reactions are worth it. There's something thrilling about having people so invested in you. It's like being persuaded onto a roller coaster you'd never dare to ride otherwise and ending up drowning in your own giggles as you swoop down a near-ninety-degree drop.

Plus, it's fun reading about the excitement people get from a segment where their ship is smashed together by the lips. I'm a crowd-pleaser, to say the least, and it's not even like Jasper and I are doing anything *bad*. Our viewers know that there's nothing actually going on between us—they only *wish* there was. We're being teases, and that's what makes it exciting.

But Allison dropping her two cents into the piggy bank of opinions makes a good dose of reality shoot back into my system, and my excitement deflates like a balloon. She's seen things go terribly wrong between Jasper and me before. Maybe she's right and I can't justify the idea the way I thought I could.

Sighing, I lean away from the computer screen. "She's right. This *is* ridiculous."

"We *all* know kissing between friends never goes well," Allison tacks on.

"We're *not* normal friends," Jasper reminds her. "We live on the Internet, and this kind of thing happens on the Internet all the time."

Cirrus Stone

DANIKA STONE is an author, artist, and educator who discovered a passion for writing fiction while in the throes of her master's thesis. A self-declared bibliophile, Danika now writes novels for both adults (*Edge of Wild*, *The Intaglio Series* and *Ctrl Z*) and teens (*All the Feels*). When not writing, Danika can be found hiking in the Rockies, planning grand adventures, and spending far too much time online. She lives with her husband, three sons, and a houseful of imaginary characters in a windy corner of Alberta, Canada. danikastone.com